Praise for *Capturing Hope*

"*Capturing Hope* is a beautifully written, poignant story of two souls who use the bitterness of their circumstances to serve others during the war. A captivating romance blended with page turning suspense makes this novel the perfect completion to the Heroines of WWII series."
– Candice Sue Patterson, author of *Saving Mrs. Roosevelt* and *The Keys to Gramercy Park*

"Angela Couch delivers a fast-paced, harrowing WWII drama set in war-torn Poland in *Capturing Hope*, part of the eclectic Heroines of WWII series. Nadia, a heroine used to a world of wealth and glamor, must escape the Nazi invasion with a street-savvy American photographer. Their flight is soon joined by a rag-tag group of refugees, mostly children. With unexpected twists, the author delivers a satisfying read that takes readers deep into the jarring history of a country's people abandoned to annihilation, exposing small pockets where rescue, love, and hope might survive."
– Naomi Musch, author of more than a dozen novels, is an ACFW Carol Award finalist, FHLCW Reader's Choice finalist, Selah Award finalist, and Book-of-the-Year finalist. Her recent titles include *Season of My Enemy*, *Lumberjacks & Ladies*, and The Voyageurs duology.

HEROINES OF WWII

CAPTURING *Hope*

ANGELA K. COUCH

BARBOUR
PUBLISHING

Capturing Hope ©2023 by Angela K. Couch

Print ISBN 978-1-63609-691-9
Adobe Digital Edition (.epub) 978-1-63609-692-6

All scripture quotations, unless otherwise noted, are taken from the King James Version of the Bible.

This book is a work of fiction. Names, characters, places, and incidents are either products of the author's imagination or used fictitiously. Any similarity to actual people, organizations, and/or events is purely coincidental.

Cover Photo: © Natasza Fiedotjew / Trevillion Images

Published by Barbour Publishing, Inc., 1810 Barbour Drive, Uhrichsville, Ohio 44683, www.barbourbooks.com

Our mission is to inspire the world with the life-changing message of the Bible.

 Member of the
Evangelical Christian
Publishers Association

Printed in the United States of America.

DEDICATION

To Jonathan.
I see you. I need you. I love you.

ACKNOWLEDGMENTS

I have been blessed with a wonderful family and community who have made this book possible. A huge thanks to my husband, whose support is invaluable. To my kids, who put up with me when I'm on a deadline. To my mother-in-law and others, who take the time to read through my rough work so readers don't have to. To Amy, for a wonderful first edit and great advice. To the Cardston Scribblers, for talking shop and offering encouragement and advice. To my editors at Barbour, who believed in me and helped bring this story to life. To God, who fills in where I lack and gave me the story to write.

❚ CHAPTER I ❚

Poland
August 31, 1939

Hiding away with *any* novel would be preferable to this, but Nadia Roenne forced her mouth into a demure smile and tipped her head to one side, ignoring the thirty-four pins scraping her scalp. The pretense of happiness was a finely developed skill. Talk of *pleasant* weather—which in reality remained unbearably hot for a dinner party and caused beads of sweat to form along Nadia's spine—did little to improve her mood.

All of that, she had been trained to disregard. But she could not overlook *him*. Nadia glanced across the drawing room at the brown tweed suit that had no business at this party, never mind in this house.

"How delightful that your father invited an American," Manina spoke from beside her, no doubt having followed Nadia's gaze. Two years younger and a close neighbor—if you counted the thirteen miles to the nearest estate of any size and wealth as *close*. "And handsome."

Nadia withheld the urge to roll her eyes, already hearing her *matka*'s lecture on such a rude display. But really, with the possibility of war on their doorstep, could they not discuss Hitler's threats and slander against Poland or the movements of his troops to the shared borders? Characters like Manina were exactly why Nadia avoided romance novels.

A sigh of resignation escaped Nadia's lips, and she glanced across the room at the American speaking with her father—probably about

Germany and war. Handsome? The man's dark hair was in need of a trim, and his nose was a little too large, though she supposed it suited the shape of his face. The slight shadowing on his jaw suggested he had not taken the time to shave that day. "*Rustic* might be more apt."

Manina's ruby lips stretched upward. "Is not everything about America rustic? What an adventure it would be to travel there." She flipped a dark curl over her bare shoulder. Nadia almost regretted her own choice of a gown with cap sleeves, but only because of the heat. She had no desire to attract any of the men present tonight. She had yet to meet one who offered any incentive to rearrange her life.

"*Przykro mi*," she apologized, "I again must disagree. With all of Europe at our fingertips, America has nothing to draw my interest." Especially if the photographer her father had taken such fascination with was anything to judge by. But then *Tata* was always collecting new projects and pets—why should she be surprised by this one?

No, surprise was not what she felt. But she knew better than to acknowledge the darker feelings.

"You would not mind, would you?" Manina's plea pulled Nadia's attention back to the conversation at hand.

"Mind what?"

The younger woman's eyes widened. "You were distracted by the American. Now you owe me an introduction."

Nadia gritted her teeth, trying to maintain a neutral expression.

"*Proszę*. While he is still speaking with your father."

The problem was, he never left her father's side. . . Or was it Tata never leaving his side? Years of deportment lessons forbade the groan that ached to be released, but resisting would be like throwing peas against a wall. "Very well, but I have no intention of remaining for any conversation." Despite that being what she longed for. She squared her shoulders and started across the floor, knowing better than to hope for her father to speak of anything of worth in her presence.

The American noticed them first and drew up a little taller, though he did not look her in the eye. "Miss Roenne."

Her father had the audacity to look amused.

Nadia ignored the first, who apparently had a very short memory. They had been introduced that afternoon, and the man could not remember how to address her already? "*Ojciec*," she addressed her father, choosing to speak in Polish. "Miss Manina is unable to contain her fascination and requests an introduction to. . ." She bit back what she wanted to say, knowing it would only earn her a reprimand. "To the American."

"Of course." His graying mustache rose with his smile as he switched to English for the introductions.

Nadia glanced around the room at the other guests in their fine clothing, many sporting fashions from Paris. Her gown hailed from Germany—one of her mother's insistences that caused more friction between her parents this past year. How could she exit gracefully? Perhaps into the gardens where a handful of local musicians began the first strains of music. When the possibility of dancing this evening had been mentioned by Matka, Nadia had suggested the phonograph would be sufficient. But Baroness Roenne never did anything in small measure.

Except perhaps show affection.

Nadia tucked the unkind thought away, but with a party of less than twenty souls, why dance at all?

"Either of these young ladies would gladly walk you through the steps."

Tata's statement jerked Nadia back to the conversation.

"I enjoy watching," the American said with apology tinging his voice. "I would hate to bruise the toes of these charming ladies."

Relief washed through Nadia. It would not be the first time her father compelled her to entertain one of his "projects." And she had no desire to be trod upon.

"I will make certain they play a waltz to start. Surely the waltz is a common enough dance even in America?"

The American opened his mouth, but Tata was already moving toward the wide french doors opening into the gardens. The American looked between the two women, a hint of red in his cheeks strangely satisfying to Nadia. Still, he never met her gaze. She was about to suggest he lead Manina onto the patio when one of her father's acquaintances from the Jagiellonian University of Krakow stepped into their circle and invited her friend to accompany him into the gardens. The man was no more than thirty and not unattractive, but Manina glanced back, disappointment visible, while allowing herself to be led away.

"I hate to disappoint Baron Roenne," the American said after a moment of silence, "but I'm not a dancer. Even the more modern dances—"

"Do not tell me you would prefer a swing or, what do you call it, the jitterbug? Sounds like a strange insect." She would not admit to her own preference of the livelier dances. Matka always refused Nadia's suggestions anyway—easier to stop making them.

"I'm surprised you've heard of that one." The American chuckled and glanced at the thick Persian rug under his shoes. At least his shoes looked clean, though not polished. "I can pull off a swing, but I try to avoid anything faster. Perhaps your father is right about the waltz."

Nadia afforded him a tight smile. Unfortunately, she would do anything for her father. Thunder rumbled in the distance, and Nadia glanced at the open doors with sudden hope of rain. A good downpour would save her from stepping outside with the American.

The first stanza of one of Strauss' waltzes prodded her to action. No indecision. Tata hated indecision. "Thankfully, I am an excellent dancer." She met the American's gaze.

He offered a quick nod and extended his hand, but she refused to accept it. Not until she absolutely had to. She turned and led the way through the doors where the soft breeze carried a hint of summer roses. A large stone patio formed a wide circle in the heart of the gardens. The musicians sat on the edge on the stonework under the glow of electric lights strung high to illuminate the area. Several couples had already begun their sweeping loops, but pathways beyond tempted Nadia with thoughts of escape. Instead, she turned and allowed the American to catch up. "Shall we?"

One side of his mouth turned up, but his eyes had darkened as he stepped to her, waiting until she raised her arms into position before following suit. It seemed her slight had wounded his poor feelings. She refused to feel guilt. She had condescended to dance—was that not enough? Nadia bit the inside of her mouth against the ache of emotion swelling in the back of her throat. No, *she* would never be enough.

"Your English is very impressive," the American said as they followed the current of dancers. "Better than my Polish by far."

Perhaps conversation would save her from the downward spiral of her thoughts.

"Thank you," she replied shortly. "English is not my favorite language, but it is sometimes useful."

A dark brow rose. "That's fair. I always figured if I hadn't been raised with it, I'd never stand a chance learning it."

"Humble of you to admit." Nadia bit her tongue. Father would be livid if he heard her unkind comments.

The American seemed unaffected. Instead, his lip turned up on the left side. "The one thing I can be truly proud of."

It was her turn to arch a brow. "Learning English or your great humility?"

"Both, now that you mention it." His eyes twinkled with the smile he withheld.

"Are you allowed to be proud of humility? Would not one annul the other?"

"In most cases it would, but I'm very talented." His shoe bumped against hers with a misstep but thankfully not with enough force to cause discomfort.

"It is unfortunate your talents do not extend to other areas." She pasted on a tolerant smile.

"That'd make it more difficult to maintain my humility, wouldn't it?" He stumbled with another misstep. "At least you can't refute my honesty. I never claimed to be good at dancing."

A laugh escaped Nadia before she could force her smile back into submission. "I suppose."

"Yet you are undoubtedly very proficient in a many great things," he said easily, seeming to relax into their banter. "Languages. Dancing. Your father says you are a prolific reader and a gifted artist with your watercolors."

Nadia's heart thumped. She wished she could inquire exactly what her father had said, but instead she soaked in the morsel of praise. Perhaps she would paint something special for Tata.

She instantly corrected the idea. The American had probably misunderstood, or Tata had only been trying to make her sound better than she was for his own sake. Why embarrass herself?

"So perhaps it's the humility you lack." The man said it lightly, but his brown eyes held a challenge.

She raised her chin. "I have not had much need for humility."

"I suppose not."

A moment passed before she pressed a change in topics. "I must inquire, what keeps you here?"

"Better manners than to leave my dance partner in the middle of a song."

Her lips pressed thin. "I mean in Poland. If you have spent any time in my father's company, I imagine you well informed of the latest intelligence out of Germany." Jealousy curled hot fingers around her heart.

"He does seem very informed about the goings-on in Germany. I admit I was surprised he insisted on hosting a dinner like this right now."

"Are they that close?"

His foot slammed into hers with enough force to bruise, and she bit back a yelp.

He came to a halt in the middle of the patio while the other couples continued around them. A curse slipped between his teeth before a muttered apology.

"Just dance." Matka would shun her for days if she caused a spectacle— Nadia had quickly given that up as an effective way of gaining her parents' attention. But since it was obvious the American could not manage to talk and dance at the same time, she would gladly sacrifice the former. She turned her attention to a movement near the doors. One of her father's friends hurried to him. They disappeared together into the house.

What a relief when the music paused and Nadia could step away. This time she politely accepted the American's arm and allowed him to accompany her toward the doors. It felt as though every gaze followed them, no doubt wondering why she would lower herself to become part of the entertainment. She spared a glance at the man beside her, a full head taller and broad through the shoulders but sporting that stupid tweed jacket that made him stand out like a fish taking flight. Did he realize he was an amusement, a spectacle? Tata should have at least provided him proper attire if so intent on bringing him here. Even cars were polished and stamps placed in a gilded frame.

Tata shoved back inside the drawing room, causing the door to slap open against the wall. Everyone looked up, some standing from where they visited, others moving to see from the gardens. The music died with the squawk of a violin.

"I apologize, my friends. I had hoped for one last evening of revelry, but I have reason to believe German troops will be upon us by morning."

⋛ CHAPTER 2 ⋛

September 1, 1939

Chaos erupted, a flurry of activity as the room started to clear. David slipped back against a wall near one of the large windows to take stock of what was happening. He blended in more with the servants than guests anyway. He shook his head at the thought. The servants were better dressed than him in their dark livery. But the baron had not been very specific in his invitation to dinner. For the same reason, David was stranded here well past midnight with no transportation back to Kraków.

With the room suddenly clear, he maneuvered toward the baron's study, where the man had insisted David leave his camera so he could more fully "enjoy" himself. The thought made him groan. He found much more pleasure in capturing the world around him and pausing it in time than any of the activities this evening had held. Except perhaps sparring with Lady Nadezhda, or *Nadia* as her father called her. He had somewhat enjoyed that.

By the time David found his camera and the soft leather satchel that held his gear, the house seemed deserted. Even of servants. Lights continued to gleam off the gilded picture frames that plastered the grand walls of the halls, generations of Roenne ancestors who had held claim on this area despite wars and unrest. A foreign idea to David whose family was used to being a first or second generation in everything they did. But much in this land was foreign to him.

"Reid!"

"Sir?" David slung his satchel over his shoulder and pivoted to Baron Roenne whose bow tie hung loose and top button had been freed. Even his hair was messed. All composure displayed earlier in the evening was absent.

"The Germans will not stop until they wipe Poland off the map. I believe that was Hitler's wording earlier this year." The baron's accent grew heavier with each word. "It is time you returned home."

David opened his mouth, but no argument came. The baron had shared what he had learned not only of the Germans' preparations for an invasion, with months of anti-Polish propaganda bandied throughout Germany, but of the more sinister actions of the Nazis toward political enemies and Jews in general over the past couple of years. While David was not religiously Jewish, knowledge of his mother's lineage made remaining unwise. Really, if Poland was about to become a battlefield, no one would be safe.

He waved David back into his study. "I will help you."

The offer took David by surprise. He had assumed the baron was simply hastening him on his way.

"If you will accompany my family, ensure they arrive safely in London." The pieces slid together. "What about you?"

Baron Roenne shook his head and moved around his desk. "I will remain here for now." He sank into his large leather chair and unlocked a drawer. "But my wife and daughter must leave for Warsaw tonight. I have already telephoned a friend there who is making arrangements."

"I understand, sir, but—"

A revolver clunked against the top of the desk where the baron deposited it. He reached back into the drawer. "This contains everything you need." A thick envelope appeared, and the baron thrust it into David's hands. The baron's gaze burrowed into David as though to read his soul. "Swear to me you will keep them safe."

"Keep him safe, David."

David averted his gaze as flashes of memory snatched his breath from him, leaving his head light and his chest hurting.

"Keep him safe."

Something heavy pounded in another room, against the front door.

The baron lurched to his feet, but his gaze quickly returned to David. "Swear it."

David forced a nod. Perhaps this was his chance for redemption. And if not that, the opportunity to prove to himself that he could be trusted.

A crash not so far away was followed by an eruption of shouting in a foreign language. Not Polish this time.

"Speak it," the baron demanded.

"I swear I will do everything in my power to see them safely to England." But even as David said it, dread weakened his arms. If he failed again? How many more lives would he wear on his conscience?

The baron shoved the envelope into David's hands and rushed past, only pausing a moment at the door of the study. "Stay here."

The door slammed.

Stay here for how long? Would the baron send his daughter and wife to the study, and would they leave right away? Was there time for anything else? The voices had grown quieter, though he could still hear a rumble. He cracked the door open, hoping to make out words for the little good it would do. He spoke little Polish and less German. All he might have success in interpreting was the tones. Anger. An argument. The baron and baroness' voices he recognized. The German's was an older voice—well, at least middle-aged. At twenty-six, even forty seemed ancient. And yet David suddenly questioned if he would live even that long.

The envelope grew heavy in David's hand, and he slid it into his satchel alongside his camera. He glanced around the study. Had he forgotten anything?

The five-shot snub nose revolver stared up at him from the desk. The voices in the front hall again climbed to a crescendo. David stepped across the room and checked the chambers. Loaded. He hadn't used a gun for a couple of years, and only once had he fired a revolver. But he knew rifles. He'd hunted as a youth and knew how to kill. Just not another person.

Would that be required to fulfill his promise?

———— ≈ ————

"Nadezhda, go to your rooms and pack your things quickly."

Nadia looked from her mother, who gave the order, to her father, who stood with reddened face, toe to toe with the German officer who had invaded their house. An old acquaintance of her mother's, apparently, but there was something in the man's crystal-blue gaze that made her question if there had been something deeper between them at one time.

Father's growl centered her thoughts. "Neither of you will leave with this man."

"You care so little for your wife and daughter." The German spoke his own language, which they all knew well enough. It was the smirk he wore that gnawed at Nadia's patience. "Your country will be overrun. Within hours our armies will be across your borders, attacking from every side."

"*My* wife and daughter are none of your concern."

Instead of answering, the German turned to Matka, his expression growing frustrated and almost panicked. "Save yourself, Giesela. Come with me now. I will see you safely back to your father's home."

She gave a shaky nod and hurried toward the stairs, snatching Nadia's hand as she passed. "You will come."

"But. . ." Nadia glanced back at the men, at Tata. She had been to her grandparents' estate in Germany in the past. Would this be so different? Just until the tensions between the two countries resolved?

Father's voice rose above the rush of their feet and the distance growing between them. "I will see to their safety. Leave my house!"

"I will not," the German spat in reply. "You may not care for her, but I do."

A growl. The thud of boots. Curses in both languages.

Nadia yanked away from her mother and spun back to see her father and the German gripping at each other's coats while trying to strike. A fist caught Tata's chin, and he stumbled back against a wall and large mirror reflecting the whole of the foyer. He gripped at his chest, at his heart. Nadia started toward him.

A shot echoed off the high ceilings.

Nadia's step faltered. *"Nie."*

Scarlet appeared as her father staggered away from the wall. His chest trembled as he sucked a breath. He collapsed, his body crumbling forward onto the marbled floor.

"Tata!" Nadia tried to run to him, but someone grabbed her from behind.

"What have you done?" Matka's voice crackled. It took a moment for Nadia to realize she was not the one accused.

The German officer turned, eyes wide, his hands empty—unlike one of his soldiers waiting near the door, who returned a revolver to his side holster while mumbling something about Tata reaching for a weapon.

Nadia jerked free yet again and raced to Tata's side. No breath. Why was there no breath? She gripped his shoulders, rolling him toward her. Blood soaked his linen shirt and evening jacket. His chest remained too still.

Breathe. Oh, please, breathe.

"This changes nothing," the German officer stated.

Nadia tightened her grip on her tata. How did this not change *everything*?

"We must leave." The German's voice grew more forceful. "Giesela, hurry with your belongings and anything of value. We have little time. I suggest a servant be sent for your daughter's things. My men will escort her to the car to wait for you."

Leave? They wanted her to leave her father like this? They expected her to go with them after what they had done? Nadia forced her eyes upward to find her mother, who was already on the stairs, hastening toward her rooms.

"Komm!" Hands gripped Nadia's arms, dragging her to her feet. A moment of struggling brought a second soldier to her side, his hold as sure as shackles. No way to fight them. The more she tried, the firmer their grasp.

She clamped her eyes closed and willed her mind to think past the shock and pain pulsating through her center—as though she had been the one to take the bullet.

Focus!

Tomorrow. There would be time to cry and wail tomorrow. But she refused to allow these men to force her away from her home. She refused to turn to her father's enemy—her enemy.

"Release me. I will come on my own." She willed her voice not to tremble and kept her gaze upward, away from the scene at her feet that would crumble her again. She rotated to the German officer. "But if I am to leave, I will pack my own belongings."

He gave a short nod, and the vices on her arms eased. "You have five minutes. My men will accompany you."

She walked past him without reply, though very aware of the looming shadows trailing her. It was not until she reached her chamber door that she noticed the blood staining her hands. Her stomach lurched while her heart throbbed. She stiffened her resolve. "You will wait here for me." She spoke in German, a language once as dear to her as Polish but now tainted with a growing hatred for those who spoke it. She slipped through the door and locked it before they could respond. She sank against the solid wood, though centuries old, and managed a trembling breath. But there was no time for even that much luxury. She had to clear her mind, think of some way to escape her guards. Germany was now her enemy. Her loyalties were to her father.

She raised her hands to look at them and the reminder of the reality that was impossible to escape. After washing, she searched her wardrobe for something more practical than the long evening gown she wore. A midcalf skirt she'd bought for her time studying at the university and a simple blouse. The late summer heat felt oppressive, but she grabbed a cardigan as well and then emptied her jewelry boxes into her largest handbag.

What else, what else, what else?

She glanced around the room, but her brain was buried in too much fog to focus on anything more than the passing minutes and her lack of escape. The door rattled as someone tried to open it.

"I need more time to dress," she called out. "If you wish to be useful, send for my maid."

Voices mumbled in the hallway.

Nadia grabbed a pair of walking shoes and ran to her private drawing room with a balcony. She pushed the glass door open and stepped into the cooling air for the little good it did. Given the height of the second story and hard flagstones below, she was still trapped.

A fist thundered against her door.

"Psst!"

She startled and swiveled to her right, where a dark shadow stood on her father's balcony. "Who—"

The reply came in English. "You're going with them?"

Relief emptied her lungs. "Not if I can help it."

"Toss me your things, then."

She nodded and hurried to comply, grateful as he snatched the bag from the air despite her wayward throw. She slipped on her shoes. "What now?"

"The ridge. Can you make it across?"

Nadia looked down, noticing for the first time that a heavy beam protruded from the wall and ran between the two balconies. Maybe a foot deep, if that. And an almost twenty-foot drop if she fell. She shook her head. "Nie. I cannot make it."

The banging on her door turned to shouts for the servants to bring a key.

"Lean into the wall and take off your shoes. Your bare feet will grip better." He seemed far too confident in her ability, but it fed her own confidence. It was that or be forced back to Germany with the men who had murdered Tata.

She yanked her shoes and stockings from her feet and tossed them at the American, feeling oddly satisfied when one of the shoes almost clipped his chin.

He's not your enemy, she reminded herself. At the moment, he seemed her only ally. She slid over the iron banister, clinging to it and trying not to picture the textured flagstones below. Or the very thorny rosebushes against the wall.

"Steady," he whispered.

A shout of success boomed from the hall outside her door, followed by the clicking of a lock. Both of her feet touched the beam, and she pressed her cheek against the cool stone of the wall. Footsteps thundered through her room in every direction, including toward the balcony. Heavy boots. Impatient German bantered back and forth through the room. But to rush could kill her.

"Here!"

At the frantic whisper, she dared a glance at the American and his waiting hand only inches away.

"How could she have gotten past us?" one of the German's demanded next to the glass door that would lead them to her.

She threw her hand into the American's, and he gripped it with two of his own to drag her over the rail. In the same motion, his arms wrapped her and pulled her into the darkened room.

"*Nichts!*" The voice came from her balcony.

She closed her eyes and allowed her lungs to fill, though the arms around her had not relaxed their hold. She wiggled from his grasp but did not dare a glance back. They could not leave without detection, but these rooms might also be searched.

A tug on her arm indicated it was time to move again. Into the private sitting room adjacent to her father's bedroom. The room smelled of wood polish and cigars, and an ache pulsated through her chest. She was led to the bedroom, where the American searched the room with his eyes, probably looking for a place to hide. Footsteps shuffled down the hall in their direction. He moved toward the bed, but she pulled away and darted toward the closet. Nadia had never hidden in her father's room, but the corner bedrooms on this floor all had similar closets built into the eaves. The front was full height, but they sloped toward the back.

She swung one of the doors open and pushed past her father's array of suits. Her fingers brushed the false wall. The nook held no light, and she dropped to her knees to slide her hands across the board. The door to the sitting room shook with someone's attempt to gain entrance. Thankfully, Father always locked his door.

"*Schlüssel! Schnell!*"

Nadia hurried as well. Sweat moistened her face. Her finger slipped into a small hole, and she tugged. The board slid toward her. "Come." She did not look back but slid into the true depth of the closet, trying to make room for the American to follow. He did and pulled the door and then the board back into its place as the key clicked in the latch of the sitting room door. More footsteps. Frustrated voices. She strained to understand what was said past the heavy breathing beside her and the pounding in her own chest.

"We have no time for this!" the German officer barked.

She heard her mother reply but could only make out the words "choice" and "idiot girl," followed by slamming of drawers, rustling, and clanking. Nadia's stomach roiled at the thought of her father's possessions being rummaged through, probably in a search for anything of value. *Vultures.*

Finally, the footsteps retreated, and Nadia dared to shift her cramping legs. She hugged her knees to her chest and pressed her face against them. Images of her father assailed her, and suddenly she was grateful for the absolute darkness. The man whose arm pressed against hers, whose breathing warmed her neck, would be unable to witness her breaking heart.

≣ CHAPTER 3 ≣

Instead of breathing easier now that the Germans had withdrawn, David's chest tightened, every sense now attuned to the woman beside him in the blackness. She smelled of lavender and roses with the slightest hint of mint. Her breathing had turned jagged, though she seemed to be fighting for control of her emotions. A tremble moved through her.

David pressed his eyes closed against the memory of her father's body. He hadn't gotten a clear view with the house suddenly streaming with Germans, but he saw enough to know the man was dead. He suppressed the urge to offer comfort, though an arm around her shoulder seemed natural in these close quarters. No, she had made her distaste abundantly clear not even an hour ago. He knew very well that even a change in circumstances didn't alter feelings and prejudices. He would keep his distance—while making sure she reached safety.

The roar of an engine outside shifted his focus to the spin of tires and spit of rock. He eased away from Nadia and pressed against the board. It popped free and leaned against the hanging clothes. Men's clothes. As he climbed from their hiding spot, not only could he guess whose bedroom this was, but apparently it had been ransacked for anything of value, sentimental or otherwise.

Though his acquaintanceship with the lady of the house had been brief, he guessed sentiment had little to do with it. Neither of the Roenne women seemed to care for much other than their fine clothes and house.

A sniffle from beside David reminded him not to be so quick to judge. He stood back as Nadia looked through the room, gently closing drawers, shaking her head while her shoulders tensed. After a few moments, she started for the door, purpose in her stride.

He followed, knowing immediately that she was headed back to her father's side. Thankfully, by the time they arrived, someone had draped a thick tablecloth over the baron's body, though traces of crimson had stained the white. A group of servants stood nearby, talking tensely. Probably trying to make plans if the German army really was crossing their borders. There didn't seem much reason to doubt that now.

David reached for Nadia's arm, but she immediately jerked away. Instead of looking at him, she addressed the servants while motioning to her father's body. They looked at each other, then three men, a younger and two older, moved to comply. In the same motion, Nadia turned away and started deeper into the house. Toward her father's study.

David followed, trying to formulate the right words. "Lady Nadia, your father asked me to see you safely from Poland."

She spun, her eyes wide. Her head shook—or more trembled. "He would not have me abandon our country for our enemy." Fire leapt in her eyes. "They murdered him."

"Not to Germany. To England, to Poland's allies. He had friends there and made arrangements for you and—" He stopped himself from mentioning her mother.

Instead of acquiescing, she planted her hands on her hips. "And when did he make these grand plans? When was there time?" An accusation if he'd ever heard one.

"If you'd spent any time in his company the past few weeks, you would know he was very aware of what has been happening on the other side of the German borders. The anti-Polish propaganda. The movement of their armies. Hitler's threats."

Her glare seared through him. "Unfortunately, he was too busy in your company. But I have been paying attention. I know the British and French warned Poland to keep our armies away from the borders so as not to show aggression." She spat the last words, fully demonstrating aggression. Time to regroup.

"Your father wants you safe. He made plans for you and your mother."

"I do not have a mother," she snapped. "Not anymore."

David blew out a breath and started past her into the study where he had stashed his things. The revolver remained tucked in the back of his belt.

Thankfully, Nadia followed. "You said he made plans for me. What of himself? Had he intended to stay?"

David hooked his satchel over his neck. "As far as I know, yes. For now, anyway."

When he glanced back, her arms were folded across her chest. "I will not leave either then." She shook her head, her eyes hazing. "I must see to my father's burial. And there is the estate."

"That isn't what he wanted for you. The very last thing he made sure of before his death was your future. He wanted you to have one."

"The Polish army will buy us time."

David shook his head, frustration surging. "What Polish army? They aren't ready to take on the Germans—who have already walked through Austria and Czechoslovakia without protest against them."

Her chin tipped. "We have allies. Britain and France will come."

"Then they would have been here already. Instead, like you pointed out, they've kept Poland from protecting herself. Listen, Your Highness—"

Her eyes flashed and then narrowed.

"I know you're angry right now because of what happened to your father. And I know you don't want to abandon everything he spent his life building and protecting. But I don't believe any of this means anything compared to how much he loves you. Honor his last wishes and leave Poland."

Her eyes glistened with tears he had yet to see fall. "What is in it for you?"

"I'll be leaving Poland with you. Other than that. . ." David glanced to the door. He wasn't about to bare his soul to her, but he could offer her something. "A favor for a friend."

"A friend." She seemed to contemplate the word, something between a grimace and a smirk pulling at her lips. With a shake of her head, she walked past him to her father's desk and took a book in hand. She ran a finger over the thick cover. "Very well, prepare the car. I will need to give the steward instructions and pack a few things." She turned on her heel, taking the book with her. David rolled the tension from his shoulders. They had already outwitted the Nazis. A few hours would see them to

Warsaw and then on an airplane to England where he would gladly part ways with the woman.

———————≈———————

Do not think. Do not feel. Nadia repeated the mantra over in her head as she walked away from her father's room where his body rested on the bed as though he only slept.

What am I doing? How can I leave? Not tonight.

Too much had already happened. She needed time to consider her options. Time to say goodbye. Time. She needed time.

Yet a few minutes later, she stood in the humid summer night—or was it early morning now?—the engine of her father's beloved Packard humming. She had made every arrangement she could despite the earliness of the hour, but it felt as though she were abandoning him just as her mother had. Nadia forced her feet down the wide marble stairs. *This is what he wanted.* At least according to the American. As much as she disliked him, she did trust him. With how disingenuous so many of her acquaintances were, the earnestness he exuded was almost startling.

The man stood at the back of the car, hefting in a square metal gas can. Father's driver came with a second. "Do you think those will be necessary?"

The driver, Piotr, glanced from her to the American, and she could guess whose idea it was.

"Better safe than sorry," he mumbled while taking her two suitcases and dropping the back hatch on the car. "Let's go, Your Highness."

She glared at him. "Do not call me that."

A half smile, a smirk really, was his only reply as he stepped around her and swung open the back door for her. Instead of moving to the driver's seat, Piotr took a step away and nodded, as though in farewell. Nadia twisted to the American. "You are driving?"

"It's easy enough."

"How will the car be brought back here to be kept safe?" The Packard sedan was a rarity in this part of Europe and a beautiful car. Tata loved the machine.

"Your father left instructions to leave it with a *Pan* Wojcik in Warsaw. I'm guessing he figured it would be safer there for now."

She allowed a stiff nod and climbed into the car. A shout stopped the door from closing. Her father's valet, Jakub Rabinowicz, jogged toward them, the whites of his eyes large even in the dim light. Sweat rolled from his brow. He stepped past the American and gripped the door. His breath burst in gusts from his chest.

"Proszę, take my wife and children with you. I have listened with your father and know too much of what they say is happening in Germany—what the Nazis have done to Jews."

Nadia shook her head. She had heard the whispers and even some reports. Businesses and licenses confiscated, and families rumored to have been taken away in trucks. Who could say what was real? She still clung to hope that the whole of the German army would not make it this far.

"What is he asking?" the American questioned, an edge to his voice. "I didn't catch it all."

"He wants us to take his family. They are Jewish, and he fears—"

"Of course." The American cut her off and gripped Jakub's shoulder. "Tell him to hurry and bring them. We must leave immediately."

The man trembled and spun back to the house, beckoning to a woman with a baby. Three children scampered from the side of the steps where they had been waiting. They hurried around the car, the father sweeping up the youngest of the children, a girl around four. He took the front seat, squeezing one more child, a girl on the verge of womanhood, between him and the American. The mother pressed the middle child against her side, leaving a full foot between them and Nadia, but the odor of sour milk and vinegar knew no boundaries. The child, this one a boy of seven or eight, stared up at her with large eyes.

"*Dziękuję*," Jakub said as the car rolled forward. "Thank you."

Nadia almost replied, but the words clogged in her throat. He did not address her but the American, his gaze intense on the man steering the car away from the manor.

"You speak English?"

"*Tak*, some."

"Good," the American replied with a nod.

Nadia settled into the thick leather seats, wishing they would swallow her. She did not want to be here anyway and was obviously no longer required for translations. Part of her wanted to protest that the American had no right to make any decisions without her. This was her father's car—hers by extension. Everyone else was inferior to her position—a project, a valet, servants. . .

She got the feeling that the American did not care and saw them all as equals. Maybe he was right to. She had lost both of her parents and her home in one evening. Soon, if she followed through with her father's wishes, she would be in a foreign country. Bitterness seeped through her. It seemed she was also to lose her identity this night.

⚏ CHAPTER 4 ⚏

David stared at what little of the road was illuminated by the headlamps. Shadows beside the road flicked by. Little else could be seen other than the blackness surrounding them. . .little to distract his mind from sleep. . .

The car swerved.

He blinked hard and forced his brain to clear. Stretched his neck and stifled a yawn that made his eyes water. The moisture offered much-needed relief from the dry burn as he fought to keep them open a while longer.

"A little farther," he whispered to himself, barely over the soft din of snores and heavy breathing surrounding him. He wasn't sure how much farther but probably a couple more hours. They had passed through Katowice about two hours ago by his estimate, leaving another two or so hours until they reached Warsaw in the wee hours of the morning. Would anyone even be awake when they arrived? Or was it just as wise to pause and rest here?

He glanced beside him at the sleeping children leaning heavily against their father. The car's motion seemed to lull them to sleep despite the discomfort of their positions. He had enough siblings to know the dangers of overtired young'uns.

His chest ached as he released a sigh. As a middle child, he'd grown up close to all his siblings. Two older brothers and a sister, and two younger brothers and a sister—in that order too. He tried to picture where each of them was last he'd heard. Most stayed in Idaho. Only Luke, the brother three years older than him, had moved out of state. Not that Montana was so very distant. No one had wandered quite as far as David. Most had settled within a few years of high school, married, and had kids of their own. Safe back in the States.

The girl beside him shifted, her head slipping lower on her father's arm and sister's legs. The younger girl kicked her legs, waking the older one just enough to cuddle back into her father's shoulder. Within a minute, both had settled again. Their father had no such luck. He turned a yawn toward the window and then glanced back at his sleeping wife, baby tucked against her chest.

David offered a tight smile and a whisper. "Get much sleep?"

A nod. "Przykro mi."

David acknowledged the apology with a nod. Thankfully, he knew some Polish and understood enough of it to usually piece together what was being said. Just not enough to carry on a decent conversation. Easier to stick with English. "Might as well rest while you can. What are your plans once we get to Warsaw?" If the Germans wanted the country and Poland's allies didn't hurry to their aid, relocating to the capital wouldn't buy much time.

Jakub had probably considered the same. He shook his head. "I not know." His accent hung to every word along with a sense of impending doom. Is that what awaited Jews in Poland?

For all they knew, that's what awaited everyone. Hitler's threats had become progressively intense through the summer, according to Baron Roenne. It was all the man had wanted to discuss when not asking questions and telling what he knew of America.

"You might as well come with us to meet Mr. Wojcik. Baron Roenne has arranged for a plane out of Poland. Maybe there will be enough room." Though even as he said it, doubts arose. How big could the plane be?

Jakub nodded, but David caught the tightening of his grip around his daughters. Love and responsibility. Other's lives depending on you. David focused on the dark road. Maybe that was why he hadn't allowed himself to find a wife and start a family like the rest of his brothers. Why he kept running.

He glanced in the small rearview mirror. Nadia met his gaze in the dark. He startled, thinking she'd been asleep like everyone else. He glanced back again and caught her glower.

"Did you get any sleep?"

"I am fine." Yet the edge of her tone suggested quite the opposite. "Perhaps you need sleep, and I should drive."

"You know how?"

"Of course." Her voice weakened, and David wondered if she was remembering something of her father. He wasn't sure he'd be holding himself together as well as she if something like that happened to his dad. Yet he couldn't believe she didn't care just as much or more for her father.

Maybe she was simply stronger than him.

"Are you awake enough to continue?" she questioned.

Now he was. Even if she was an excellent driver, he hesitated to stop the car and risk disturbing everyone else. "I'm fine for now," he said with a stifled yawn. He didn't have to look back to clearly imagine the roll of her eyes and jutted chin. The thought almost made him smile.

A flash of light and a boom jolted him, and he swung his gaze toward the north. More lights, like golden flares in the night. More pounding. Bombers? Only a few miles north of them.

David slammed his palm against the dashboard, hunting for the headlights switch as he slowed to the side of the road. The lamps went dark.

"What are you doing?" Nadia questioned.

A baby released a wail from beside her, and children whimpered. Soon all eyes had been drawn out the windows.

"What's over there?" David asked. Why would the Germans bomb the middle of nowhere over twenty miles from the border?

Jakub looked back at Nadia, and a few words passed between them. Names of towns or other locations.

"Wielun. A small town," Nadia finally supplied.

"How small?"

"No more than fifteen or sixteen thousand people live there."

"What else is there?" Why would the Germans target a small town?

"Nothing. Not of importance."

"Military, bridges, warehouses?" What was the logic?

Jakub glanced at Nadia and back to David before speaking. "It is just a town. Just people."

A show of lights and thundering continued its horrifying display across the night sky. David dug out his watch, needing to know. He could barely make out the thin hands in the moonlight. Half past four in the morning. Most folks would still be in their beds.

Even as the baby quieted against his mother's breast, a sob rose from the back seat.

"My wife's family. . .their home is Wielun," Jakub whispered, apology in his voice.

The flashes of light fell into the background of a flickering glow in the north. The whole town seemed as though on fire. David's grip tightened on the steering wheel until his fingers began to feel numb. If only the same could spread to his chest and the ache growing there. If his own family was in danger, he wouldn't be able to stand by and watch. He'd risk anything. . . .

Jakub reached a hand back and took his wife's, speaking to her in Polish. Something about the children. The dangers. Nothing could be done. Something about prayer.

Helplessness was not a new sensation, but the one he hated more than any other. Even prayer couldn't bring loved ones back from the dead.

"You are right," Jakub said from beside him. "Even Warsaw will not be safe soon."

David forced his hand to release its grip and grab the gearshift instead. He stared into darkness, not willing to risk alerting the Germans to the lone car. He had to focus on his promise, and the new one he made to himself—to do everything possible to get this family out of Poland as well.

———≈———

Nadia's stomach roiled, whether from thoughts of Wielun's fate or from the sway of the car as it sped around curves through the rolling hills dressed in dark greens. Reaching Warsaw by dawn was the goal, and already the sun breached the eastern horizon. The inhabitants of the city would soon awake. How many knew that their country was under invasion, that they were again at war?

War. She mouthed the word, not daring to fully voice it. Her chest hurt. They had only known real independence and freedom for fewer years than she had been alive. Would it be stolen so quickly? If only Tata would have shared more with her. He had known it was coming.

The child beside her whimpered, asking for breakfast despite the earliness of the hour, only to be hushed by his mother.

"We will be there soon," the American said from the front. He had a map spread on his lap and appeared to trace it with his finger while steering the car down a narrow road on the outskirts of Warsaw. A few minutes later, the car jerked to a stop near a large iron gate. A tall hedge hid the estate from the road. He pushed the papers aside. "Let me make sure I am at the right place." He glanced at her in the mirror. "You may as well wait here."

"I think not." She did not wait for him to open her door, climbing out of the car and stepping down to the cobbled drive. A few steps opened her view of a redbrick manor. Three stories of elegance and wealth. And flickers of memory. She had been here before with her parents. Years ago. "This is the place. Bring the car."

The American nodded and climbed back inside. She stayed to the side of the cobbled drive, needing a moment to stretch her legs and clear the fog from her thoughts. She breathed deeply of the cool morning air, but even that could not ease the numbness in her center. Her head ached almost as much as her heart, and she felt little better by the time she reached the steps where the American waited, watching, until she raised her gaze to his. Then he quickly looked away. He jogged up the granite steps to the mahogany door and rang the bell. The door opened almost immediately by an older man with gray at the temples and deep lines creasing his face.

"Pan Wojcik?"

The man's blue eyes widened. "You are the American, tak? Reid?"

A nod. "Baron Roenne told me to come to you." He stepped aside and motioned to Nadia as she stepped up to join them. "This is his daughter."

"Tak, I know Lady Nadezhda." The corners of his eyes wrinkled with a smile that never touched his mouth. "Your father telephoned last night telling me to expect you." He pulled the door closed behind him and led them down the steps. "All is prepared, but we must hurry. The Germans have crossed multiple borders and have filled the skies with bombers. We do not have long before they will reach Warsaw."

Pan Wojcik opened the front door of the Packard before startling. "Who are these?"

"Jakub Rabinowicz was my father's valet, and this is his family. They also have hopes to leave Poland if there is a way."

Pan Wojcik shook his head. "There is only room for three besides the pilot."

"My mother chose not to come, so there will be one extra seat." Nadia swallowed a surge of bitterness. "Perhaps Pani Rabinowicz would wish for it with her baby in her arms. What of the children? Would there be room for any of them?"

Something between a groan and a sigh came from Pan Wojcik. "Bring them, and we shall see. But hurry." He climbed into the front seat while the children scrambled back onto their father's lap. It left little room for the American behind the wheel. Thankfully, the drive to the airfield was short. A man waited next to a small yellow plane that was already on the runway.

"Finally, you are here!" the pilot shouted and hurried toward the waiting vessel. So small.

"Is that plane big enough to fly us to England?"

"Not England," Pan Wojcik supplied. "To Lithuania first. Then a boat to England."

She nodded understanding but felt only slightly better.

"Come, come," Pan Wojcik beckoned.

With no option, Nadia hurried to the back of the car, lifting the heavy lid of the trunk and clicking it into open position so she could pull out her suitcases.

"Will we go in the airplane?" a worried voice asked Jakub.

"I want to!" the boy said almost giddily.

"I don't know," came the quieter answer. "Hush and wait."

Nadia stared at her belongings. Changes of clothes, jewelry, a handful of beloved books. . . all suddenly losing their significance. She let the trunk fall back into place with a bang.

She glanced at the American who stood near the plane, taking note of the space—or lack thereof. Jakub had gathered his family beside the car and spoke with his wife in hushed tones. Pani Rabinowicz's lips pinched tight as she shook her head at her husband's words, but she also wore a look of resignation.

Nadia walked to the plane with only her purse. This was Tata's wish. She had no choice but to leave Poland.

"Jakub." The American didn't look at her as he hurried past. "There is room enough for your wife and baby." There was something different about his voice, a resoluteness in his gravely tones. "And two children. If they sit together, they will fit on my seat."

Jakub's mouth opened, and he looked at Nadia as though to confirm what he thought he heard. She shrugged. The American could do as he wished.

The morning air did little to cool the heat rushing through Nadia as she waited for Jakub to lead his wife, baby, and two children out onto the runway. The American came alongside her. "No luggage?"

"The plane has enough to carry."

He shook his head as though he thought her words lacking. Did he think she would prefer the children to remain behind—that she would be so heartless as to begrudge them space? What did it even matter what the American thought? She would never see him again. "And if the invasion is successful and Poland is overrun?" she asked. "You are willing to risk remaining behind?"

"If the Nazis are coming, and if there is any truth to the rumors of what is happening to Jewish families in Germany, then it's better this way. My exit from Poland was not a requirement." His mouth turned up at the corner, though he still did not meet her gaze. "As long as you are on that plane, I have kept my word to your father."

"Lady Nadezhda!" Pan Wojcik bellowed from where he stood ready to close the small door on the side. Jakub stood beside him, his boy just behind. Inside the plane, his wife and daughters waited, their faces wet with tears. Soon they would also be separated from their father and brother. But were the rumors true? Would Jakub and his son be at more risk than any other Pole?

The pilot turned over the engine, and the plane roared to life.

"You must leave now," Pan Wojcik ordered, waving her forward.

Again a hand warmed her arm, and she looked into the brown gaze of the American. "*Nie mogę.*" She barely heard her own voice.

"What?"

She pulled away and rushed to Jakub's side. "Your family needs you. Your children. Take your son and go."

His eyes widened, and he shook his head. "I can't. Your father did this for *you*—for you to be safe."

"There is no time to argue. Get on the plane." She tried for a confident smile but was pretty sure it fell short. "I will be fine."

He looked from his son to the rest of his family waiting for him on the plane. He met Nadia's eyes with a look of pure gratitude, and warmth rushed through her like nothing she had ever experienced before. Then he was gone, his son in his arms, as he climbed aboard the plane.

"No!" The American gripped her arm. "You can't stay here. I promised your father."

"We will find another way. There is time."

"You don't know that." He looked torn but jerked away to help close the small door. They stood back while the small plane circled and raced down the runway, lifting off and taking to the clouds. A family together. Soon to be safe far away from any fear of war and loss. She closed her eyes and soaked in the feeling of rightness, pushing aside the nudge of fear. . .and hurt. Unlike every member of that family, there was no one who would miss her.

≣ CHAPTER 5 ≣

David sat in the driver's seat of the empty car, teeth aching. He tried to relax his clenched jaw, but even the radio seemed static to his sleep-deprived brain. All he could think about was when Nadia announced that she would not leave. The moment replayed over and over in his mind, tightening the muscles in his jaw.

He jerked as the door opened behind him, and the lady herself slid onto the seat. Her reflection in the small mirror showed raised chin and piercing blue eyes as they again met his. For once he was fine holding her gaze, letting her see the anger there.

"Pan Wojcik has offered a place to stay until other arrangements are made," she said stiffly.

"And how long does he figure that will be"—David tried to keep his tone even—"before other arrangements can be made?" The last few words had to be pushed between his teeth.

Her jaw dropped a little. "You are angry." She almost looked smug at the notion. "What have I done?"

"You didn't get on the blasted plane." He wanted to throw his hands up but kept his grip on the steering wheel despite the fact they weren't going anywhere in this car. Nope, they would be right here for the foreseeable future—except there was nothing foreseeable about the future unless they accepted Wielun's fate as their own.

"That was my choice to make." Her accent thickened as her words sharpened.

"Your father wanted you on that plane. He arranged *all* of this to get you out of here."

"Do not speak of my father. You do not know him or how he loved Poland. My choices are *nic* of your concern."

"None? They are now," David mumbled and seized the door latch. He needed to walk, to clear his head. She opened her mouth to say more, but he pushed out of the car, grabbing his satchel as he went, and slapped the door closed behind him. He started across the wide yard away from the grand house, hanging the bag over his shoulder and fumbling with the clip.

A small bridge led over a creek. The grove beyond showed hints of autumn color, perfect to refocus his brain. He pulled out his camera and peered through the lens, moving until he had focused on a single tree. Then a single leaf. Yellow merged with green, with thin veins spread throughout. His breathing deepened as he steadied the camera. He wouldn't waste his limited film on the scene, but this is what he needed to refocus his thoughts. As much as he'd love to drown them in a numbing drink, that wouldn't help him figure out the next step.

A soft humming started in the northwest and slowly grew. His heart kicked in his chest. He knew that sound. From a few hours ago.

From Wielun.

Get her out of the car.

David shoved the camera into the bag as he ran, sprinting back the way he had come, the hum becoming a roar overhead. He grabbed the hood to pivot to the other side, cracking his shin on the chrome bumper. He threw open the passenger door and gripped Nadia's wrist.

"Co?" The word died as the rumbling grew, and her eyes flew heavenward. He yanked her forward, back toward the creek and the trees. The ground trembled under them as brick and mortar burst into the air, the boom of the explosion deafening.

The world around them erupted with an opus of explosions.

David dragged Nadia the last several yards into the grove before pulling her to the ground. She curled into a ball, and David instinctively wrapped his arm over her. If she didn't survive this, at least he wouldn't have to live with that knowledge.

Even as the bombers passed and the volley eased, David could not pull away, listening for more to come. The bombardment had moved to the center of the city, and the sound echoed in his head. Yet gradually he became more aware of the heavy breathing of the woman under him. The scent of roses seemed so foreign to what had just happened—what continued over Warsaw.

Nadia shifted, and he pulled away a little. She turned her head to look at him, her eyes wide and searching. And innocent. Fearful. This crazy woman who had just given up her chance of escape so a family could stay together. His anger of minutes earlier fled, replaced with a fledgling of respect.

He sat up, and she followed suit. For long moments, they remained in place, listening. Waiting. Though he wasn't sure for what. Another bombardment? For the skies to quiet? For reality to sink in?

"We can't stay here," David finally managed, finding his feet. He secured his camera bag across his body.

Nadia gave a shaky nod but made no move to stand until David offered his hand—which she released just as quickly as she gained her feet.

"We should leave Warsaw. The countryside will probably be safer."

"Until it is overrun by German soldiers and tanks." She started back the way they had come. "I have friends in the city. Even Pan Wojcik may still. . ." Her voice faltered as she stepped from the trees and viewed the once stately house. Half the structure had caved in on itself, rubble spread for hundreds of yards. A fire roared near the center, threatening what remained.

"I think he has enough problems of his own." But at least the man was alive, standing a ways away, hair powdered with ash or dust as he faced what remained of his home, a woman at his side along with several others. Did any remain inside? How many had been killed today throughout the city, if not right here within view?

A gasp preceded a sob, and David followed Nadia's view to what remained of the Packard. A large portion of the stone wall had crushed the car, shattering every pane of glass, and demolishing the cab where they had sat.

"Nie." Her shoulders trembled.

David fought down frustration. "It's just a car. We'll find something else."

Her head wagged, and she glanced back at him. "My father. That car was his love. All things *American*." She spat the last word. "He had it imported from the great United States of America. With such pride." She turned away. "Now it is nothing."

He is nothing.

She didn't have to say the words for David to hear them clearly. He stood back while she sank to her knees, arms wrapping herself. Still no tears. Not that he didn't understand pain so deep that there was nothing he could do but *feel* it. Agony and desolation that hung over him with enough weight to crush bone. . .and yet no one else would ever see the extent of the damage done.

David suppressed the urge to offer comfort. It was not his to give, and she probably had no desire for it—at least not from him. Instead, he pulled his camera from its cocoon and took a close look at the quickly changing world. It was safer on this side of the lens.

⫚ CHAPTER 6 ⫚

"Why?" Nadia whispered the word as they walked through the streets of Warsaw. The skies finally quieted, and she suggested they make their way toward the district of the city she was most familiar with and the homes of extended family and friends. She could only hope the upper-class region of the city had fared better than where they currently traveled. Several tall apartments had been hit in the bombardment, collapsing brick walls and leaving heaps of rubble on the streets. Several fires also raged out of control while buckets passed from hand to hand in an attempt to curb the destruction.

"*Dlaczego?*" she whispered again.

Why the callous destruction of civilian life and property? Even if the Germans wanted control of Poland, should not their targets be military and government? Not families. Not the innocent.

Nadia averted her eyes from a display of bodies pulled from the rubble, laid out on the sidewalks, some hidden under sheets and blankets, others in plain view. Mangled limbs. Crushed bones—even skulls. She glanced back at a small hand that looked as though it reached out from under a flowered quilt. Nadia struggled against the urge to step over and release the child from under the covers, but logic fought stronger. Death had won again. Such destruction was no respecter of persons.

At least Jakub's children were safe from this. They had almost an hour's advance toward the northeast before the attack came.

Pain spiked through her toes, and she stumbled forward. Her arms flailed as her eyes flew open. Stronger arms wrapped around her, jerking her to a stop and pulling her upright.

"Maybe we should stop to rest." Warm air swept past her ear with the American's words. "You look to be falling asleep on your feet."

Nadia pulled away as soon as her feet were under her. "I am fine." Yet even as she said the words, she recognized the lie. Her feet hurt—especially the toes she had just slammed into a brick—her legs ached from the miles they had probably walked, her head throbbed, and her eyes just wanted to close in sleep. Not that sleep would come if she tried. Not after all this. She started walking again, wanting more distance between her and the child under the flowered quilt.

He picked up the suitcase they had rescued from the car and followed. "You're not fine. You haven't slept more than a couple hours in almost as many days, and your father's dinner party was the last food you've eaten."

"I have no appetite. What food or sleep have you had?"

He gave her a pointed look before shifting his gaze. "I never claimed to be fine." The corner of his mouth twisted. "Though perhaps that is just your obvious struggle with English, and you can't *fully* express to me how utterly exhausted you really are. I do understand Polish passably well if that's easier."

She rolled her eyes at his ridiculousness. "I speak better English than you."

He chuckled—a sound that shouldn't seem so strange, so foreign. But to this place and time, where people wept or worked in silence, it was. "I can't argue that," he said as though pleased with himself.

She quickened her pace only to be halted again by his hand on her arm. "I'm serious. We need rest and food."

She glanced back, for the first time truly looking at the man, the red of his eyes and the dark stubble shadowing his jaw. "I suppose." She tipped her head to give one of her most assessing looks. "For your sake."

He seemed surprised; then a smile made a brief appearance. "You're so kind."

"*Taaa, wiem wiem.*" She decided a translation might be in order. "I know." She glanced about and immediately became very aware of where they were. She needed a clean bed and real food. Not something she was comfortable asking for in this community. The rumble of wheels on the street ahead sped her feet, and she hurried toward a wagon pulled by two large horses. It maneuvered to the side and pulled to a stop, the driver—a middle-aged man in worn slacks, canvas jacket, and a cap frequently worn by Jews—about to climb down.

She greeted him and asked if he would be willing to deliver them to their destination across the city.

"Nie mogę." His boots landed with a heavy thud on the ground.

"I will give you this." Nadia pulled a pearl earring free and held it out to him. "It is real and worth a small fortune."

He turned the pearl over between calloused fingers and finally nodded. "Very well, but I have little time."

Nadia spun around to her American and motioned to their not-so-fine carriage. All right, little more than a wagon for hauling who-knew-what. A far cry from thick leather seats and rubber tires, but it was better than walking. She allowed herself to be handed up into the back of the wagon, and her American climbed up beside her, settling at the front and leaning back. She sat beside him, shifting a sack out of the way. The American took greater interest in the folds of burlap and dug out a long, thin carrot. A grin spread across his face. "I'm impressed. You found us both transportation and lunch."

"You will eat that?" Dirt still hid in the ridges. And it was uncooked.

"If you'd be so kind as to ask for permission."

She did so and gained a grunt and a nod from the seat above. The American needed no extra encouragement before gnawing away like a barbarian. "It tastes great. You should have one." He pulled a second carrot free and dangled it in front of her face as though he expected her to bite for it like an eager pony. She pushed his arm away and reclined as best she could. She would wait for something that did not still smell like a field.

Nadia closed her eyes and allowed herself to relax. The rattle of the wagon and squeak of the axle could not keep sleep at bay—instead, the rocking motion tugged on her heavy eyelids. Her head lulled to the side, only for her to pull herself back upright. She slipped lower. Her head steadied against something firm but comfortable. Consciousness fell away.

———— ≈ ————

David chewed slower, trying to quiet his bites while Nadia's head settled against his shoulder. He slipped his arm behind her back to provide more support. After the two carrots had satisfied the intensity of his hunger, he allowed his own eyes to close, though he tried to open them every now and again to make sure the wagon continued down the road. Not that he knew Warsaw well enough to recognize anything they passed. He'd been in the country for only the summer, visiting the village his grandparents had lived in and the university in Kraków where his grandfather had been a professor before he had immigrated with his family to the States. An old acquaintance of his grandfather's had introduced David to Baron Roenne—a patron to the university. The baron was well-known for his fondness of all things American. He had eagerly welcomed David, wanting to practice his English and talk politics. The baron had also taken an interest in David's photographs and promised to share his appreciation with others of his acquaintance—people who could promote David's career in Europe.

None of that seemed to matter anymore. He should have heeded the calls from American authorities suggesting US civilians leave the country, but David hadn't felt ready.

He opened his eyes and took a hard look at the city. The destruction was not widespread, but it left a scar. One that would only fester and deepen. He had seen the Polish planes take to the skies to defend their city. He had even seen a Nazi bomber streak downward with a plume of black smoke. But how long would the Poles be able to hold their enemy at bay? How long before the Germans arrived with their tanks and armies?

He glanced at the woman against his shoulder, careful not to disrupt her rest. How different she appeared from twenty-eight hours ago when he had arrived at her family's estate. Silk replaced with a simple, though expensive blouse and skirt now covered with dust. Her hair had begun to fall from its pins despite her frequent attempts to put her locks to rights. But, just like with the city, what he saw was nothing compared to the damage within.

The wagon jerked to a halt, and Nadia started from his shoulder, glancing sideways at him as she pulled away. The driver said something about their location, and Nadia thanked him. David was increasingly grateful for his grandmother's stilted English and peppering of Polish words throughout their conversations.

David didn't pay much attention to the area until he'd helped Nadia from the wagon. It was hard not to watch her graceful movements, and the subtle touch of her hand to her hair and the straightening of her skirt, as though they were making a social call. She started across the street, and he looked up for the first time at the grand house she was headed toward.

Perhaps he should be more conscious of his own appearance. "Who lives here?"

She didn't pause until she reached the tall doorway and tapped the knocker. "My cousin—well, my father's cousin."

The door opened to a butler, judging from his crisp apparel. Had no one informed the man that a war had started?

Nadia spoke first, a request if someone in particular was home. David didn't try to remember the lengthy name and title. They spoke back and forth for a moment, Nadia introducing herself and then glancing to him. And hesitating. There was something about the searching look in her eye, like she had forgotten something. She repeated her name to the servant but made a dismissive hand gesture toward David by way of introduction.

David wasn't sure whether to laugh or be insulted. He settled for a bit of both. "You don't remember my name, do you?" He'd never once heard her speak it despite the time they'd spent together traveling across the country and trying to stay alive. He'd saved her life, and she still didn't care enough to remember his name.

She opened her mouth, and he saw the apology forming in her expression, but just as quickly she lifted her chin. "It was inconsequential at the time we were introduced. You were no more than a—" Her jaw tightened.

Her suitcase set aside, David crossed his arms over his chest while trying to keep his expression amused. "Go ahead and finish."

Her shoulders pulled back. "Speaking straight from the bridge, you were no more than a project of my father's. Always, an artist of some variety that he must throw his money and attention toward. But you, an *American*. How could he resist but to bring you home and show you off to all of his friends like something new and shiny?"

Pain kicked under his ribs, but he'd had plenty of practice hiding hurt. "Kind of like his car?"

Some of the fight slipped from her, and she turned away. Footsteps on the marble stairs suggested their conversation was over. David stepped behind her and lowered his voice. "My name is David Reid."

"I cannot guarantee I will remember," she whispered back, her voice still far too smug. Though he sensed a hint of teasing as well. Or was that merely hopeful thinking on his part?

"I will happily remind you anytime."

She glanced at him, brows arched, and something awoke within his chest. He mentally gave himself a shake. She was the daughter of a Polish baron and hadn't even bothered to remember his name. The last thing he needed was to actually care.

⩫ CHAPTER 7 ⩫

September 2, 1939

Nadia sank deeper into the porcelain tub and allowed the warmth to surround her while she tried to lose herself in *The Doll*, though it was almost too much of a romance novel for her tastes. Any distraction was welcome, she reminded herself. She sipped tea. Sweeter than her preference, but she hesitated to complain or request for a new cup to be made as she would have at home. After the past forty-eight hours, just holding a cup of tea felt a luxury. Along with clean hair, free from the dust and lingering odor of smoke. After a day of rest and hot soaks, she almost felt human again. The comfort made her eyes grow heavy, and she set her book and tea aside for the sake of finishing her bath so she might collapse for the night—even if it was barely five or six in the afternoon. Sleep had not come easily last night despite down pillows.

Not with thoughts of Tata and the invasion and what would come next.

She groaned. Even the thought of tomorrow brought a hundred questions. Not just how they would travel to England—even with the German advance, it couldn't be so difficult—but what would life be like once she arrived? No doubt Tata had also arranged a living for her there. Probably with a friend of one of his many distant cousins. Europe's ruling class—whether ruling or not—was a rather tight-knit group as they tried to marry among their class. Probably the main reason she had yet to marry. The only other option was to marry wealth as her father had done. She had witnessed firsthand how well that had worked out for her parents.

A low hum hardly breached her thoughts as she replayed the final minutes between her father and mother and that horrible moment that froze time.

The hum grew, along with a distant popping sound. The water surrounding her rippled, and the lights flickered. A siren's wail pierced through the thick walls.

Nadia leaped out of the bath, splashing water across the tiled floor. Her feet almost slipped out from under her as she grabbed for a velvet robe and yanked it on. Her clothes sat only feet away, but the roar overhead drove her into the dim hallway, lit only by a small window at the end. She took the stairs downward, two at a time, hoping to find someone, while dreading the same.

"There you are!" The American sprinted up the stairs toward her, meeting her on the first landing. He grabbed her arm, pulling her along. Somehow through the wail of the warning sirens, a boom rocked the earth. One, then another and another.

Down more stairs, the cold air brushing across her bare legs. Into blackness.

A light appeared ahead, waving, bobbing with someone's movements. A man appeared in the light of the electric torch, motioning them toward a doorway. Within, people held several other torches and even antiquated oil lamps that lit the cellar and those hiding within.

Walls of bottled and canned goods left few good places to sit, but the American—or *David*, for she had no intention of having to ask his name again—led her to a crate and pulled her down beside him. The room fell quiet, lord and servant alike listening for what was happening above them. How would they know if the house was hit? Would they be able to escape this place, or would it only serve as their tomb?

Quick, shortened breaths made her brain buzz, and her vision began to waver. Would it be better to be crushed or to suffocate in the dark? What would it feel like to be only partly crushed—just as some of the wounded on the street? Bleeding. Crying out in pain.

The floor trembled under her bare feet. Bottles jingled against each other on the shelves.

If the walls fell but only trapped them in here in the dark, would someone find them in time? Already her lungs burned with need.

An abrupt shake stole her attention. "Breathe," David ordered, his grip rough. "Slowly. Fill your lungs."

She stared at the man kneeling in front of her, concern in his dark eyes. And forced her lungs to expand.

"That's it. Deeply." He breathed with her, slow and steady. In through his nose and a hiss between his lips on the way out. "We're all right." David probably didn't intend it, but she could almost hear the "for now" in his tone.

"I hate this feeling—being trapped." She hugged the thick robe to her chest, cool air of the cellar seeping through to her damp skin. The cold tile under her feet seemed to creep upward with a shiver.

"The door is right there." David motioned behind him, and she focused on the hallway. "Just beyond that is the kitchen with easy access to the street." A pause. "Though you don't look like you're ready to take a stroll."

She jerked her gaze to him and the subtle curve of his mouth. "Then let us hope we can stay here until this passes." She scooted back until she could lean against the cold, hard wall. Her feet came off the stone floor but remained hanging and frigid. If only the robe reached past her knees, allowing her to cover her toes. Her wet hair dripped water, and the air seemed to reach every last inch of her damp skin, growing colder with each moment despite how warm it had been upstairs.

"Here." David stood to remove his tweed jacket and laid it over her legs. Now, free from sight, her feet were free to be pulled up on the crate and tucked close. Matka would not be able to chastise her. "Can't have you freezing."

She tried to offer a smile of gratitude, but she couldn't find the strength. She closed her eyes and focused on not falling apart. Would this ever end? She wanted to sleep in a comfortable bed with no dreams and no thoughts. Not to huddle in fear and wait for the pounding to stop—both in her head and throughout the city.

David settled beside her, his ever-present camera bag tucked close on his other side. "You're exhausted. Try to sleep." His own eyes were red with exhaustion. He dropped his hat on the camera bag, and she wished she had the strength even to chuckle. His hair stood at all angles, still moist from a recent wash. He must have caught the amusement in her eyes, for he quickly combed his fingers through his almost black locks and then leaned his head against the hard wall.

"How can anyone sleep in such a place?" She had been dreaming about sinking into the bed upstairs again. Satin sheets. Clean and smelling of fresh lavender. Her eyes rolled back as she pressed her lids closed. Oh, how they burned!

"I've slept in worse conditions, and I wasn't near as tired."

She could not help but look up at the man, though he sat far too close. "Really? Worse than a chilly cellar smelling of onions?"

"And garlic. Pretty sure I smell garlic." He gave a thoughtful look. "And is that vinegar?"

"You digress. Where have you slept that was worse than this?"

"Winter camps in Idaho with the Explorer Scouts. Freezing cold. A canvas tent and a few quilts between you and hills of snow. Rocks digging into your spine. Your brother's stinky socks drying out over your head."

A slight laugh escaped, though she was not sure where it had come from. "I am sure you exaggerate. Why would any free soul put themselves through such torture as you suggest?"

His shoulder raised with a shrug while his eyes remained closed. "To prove one's manhood."

"And did it work? Were you sufficiently a man?" She did not know why she pursued the conversation with him, other than the distraction it provided. Though the bombing seemed more distant now, there was so much she did not want to think about.

"Of course," he said with exaggerated flair before his voice softened to a whisper in her ear. "Would you expect me to admit otherwise?" His head ducked, and he almost looked humble for a moment. Or sad. "Even earned my Ranger award. Not that anyone cared."

"I may, but I have no idea what that even means."

His shoulder lifted, brushing his arm against hers. "Just a bunch of camping and leadership training. Nothing too impressive."

She shook her head, again letting her eyes close. The image he painted was so hard to visualize, so foreign. "What is camping like?"

He shifted beside her. "Canvas tents, cooking over a fire."

"Rocks digging into your spine."

He chuckled. "My bedroll never stayed together too well."

Nadia would settle for a single blanket right now. "Idaho? I believe that is quite a way to the west, is it not?"

"Yes. Thereabouts."

She let the quiet settle between them and listened in on some of the nearest conversations. Concern for family and friends elsewhere. Hope that the Polish fighters and antiaircraft cannons were meeting the Germans with force enough to discourage future attacks. A woman weeping in a far corner, those surrounding her unsuccessful in attempts to calm her. How interesting that station suddenly seemed to matter so little when everyone was simply hoping to survive whatever came next.

Conversation with the American was a much better distraction. "Tell me about your life in Idaho. What was it like?"

His voice rumbled lazily. "Not sure how to explain it. We made do. Busy. Lots of hard work. Lots of family."

"Brothers and sisters?" Jealousy tickled her insides with its sharp fingernails.

"Four brothers and two sisters."

"Seven of you!" She could not imagine. "Your poor mother."

"I would agree if it were seven of *me*, but the other kids helped ease her burden."

Nadia shook her head at his attempt at humor, though she couldn't help but be grateful for it.

"Especially my sisters. She probably could have used more girls and fewer boys."

"But she *made do?*"

"She's a pretty remarkable woman."

"I have no doubt. Seeing she allowed you to reach adulthood." It was hard not to tease in return.

His laugh resonated in the space between them. A pleasant sound that somehow helped ease the tension in her own chest.

"I wonder what that would have been like," she mused. To have a mother who loved her and a houseful of siblings. To not be so. . .alone.

"What?"

She opened her mouth to change the direction of the conversation, but his hand on her arm stopped her tongue. With the silence came the whistle of a curious wind.

BOOM.

The building shook as the air ripped with a deafening roar.

Strong arms pulled her off the crate, wrapping over her as they hit the floor together. For the second time, he had placed himself between her and whatever danger there was. An image of him flashed in her mind, the panic in his eyes as he had raced up the stairs to find her. He had run toward danger. For her.

The grand house might crumble down on them, but she had never felt so protected.

Too soon he pulled away, finding his feet. Aside from the woman sobbing, everyone in the room seemed to be listening to the world above them. David grabbed his hat and shoved it on his head. He shrugged off the camera bag and shoved it onto her lap. "Hold on to this. Someone needs to make sure nothing is on fire. They seem to like incendiary bombs."

"What?"

No answer came as he jogged from the room, several other men joining him. Nadia climbed back onto the crate and wrapped his jacket around her. She wanted to follow but instead held her robe tighter and pulled the tweed as far as it would go to tuck underneath her toes. A shiver shook her, but she wasn't sure if it was from the chill or fright. She tried not to think of where they would go from here or what they would do while she counted the minutes, waiting for David's return.

Something uncomfortable settled into the pit of her stomach.

Relief flooded her as soon as David reappeared with one of the other men who had gone with him. He came directly to her, and her breath came easier. "The house is fine."

"What was hit?"

"It wasn't a bomb."

"Not a bomb?"

"A German plane was shot down. It crashed into the house next door."

Another shiver. She wanted to ask if anyone, other than the German pilot, had been. . . But how could she? Of course people were killed. Hurt. Frightened.

Oh, how she hated the Germans.

She hated the pilot who caused such terror. She hated her mother who had turned her back on her own husband and daughter. She hated her grandparents in Germany who had seemed to side with the Nazi Party when they had taken power. She hated the half of herself that shared blood with such people.

"You're freezing." David's words did little to penetrate her anger. Of course she was cold sitting in a pantry with wet hair and a moist robe. "I'll get your clothes."

She did not register his words until he was almost to the door again. She stared for a moment, then forced herself to her feet. She had to stop him from risking his life for her. The sirens still blared. Bombers still swarmed the city. Just because the last had missed the house did not mean their luck would continue.

☰ CHAPTER 8 ☰

David sprinted up the stairs. There seemed to be a break in the air traffic over this part of the city, but who could say how long it would last—how long the Polish Air Force would hold them off? He needed to find Nadia's clothes or at least a blanket to warm her up and get back downstairs. While the rest of the house felt overly warm, the cellar had been made to hold the cold, moist air. They had enough to worry about without her falling ill.

David huffed a breath as he reached the second floor. Okay, maybe he didn't like seeing her uncomfortable.

Well, not too uncomfortable. Part of him wouldn't mind making her squirm. How was it possible to forget his name after being introduced and involved in other introductions? Maybe if he had a strange *American* name, but David was pretty traditional throughout the Judeo-Christian world. Or Reid. If she could remember half of the Polish names he couldn't, she shouldn't have a problem with *Reid*.

He shook his head at himself. He shouldn't let her get under his skin like this. Better to focus on the task at hand. David had made sure he'd seen Nadia's bedroom when they'd first arrived in case of another attack, but locating it in the dark in a house this large was another matter altogether. Footsteps pounded up the steps after him, and he jerked around. Nadia. His jacket over her robe, camera bag over her shoulder. Damp hair loose and heavy hanging over her shoulders.

An unexpected fear kicked his gut. "What are you doing here? It's not safe."

"Exactly. It is dangerous." Her accent was thicker than usual as she tried to gain her breath. "Only a fool would take such risk."

"I'm not arguing. I would just feel better if you weren't an equal fool."

Her glare narrowed. "How dare you?"

"Can you really argue that?" He took a step closer. He really needed to finish his mission, but not until she headed back downstairs. "Staying when you should leave. Following me instead of staying safe."

Her mouth opened, then snapped closed.

He took the victory. "Head back to the cellar."

"Nie."

"Why are you fighting me on this?" He spoke through gritted teeth. "I'm trying to protect you."

Her voice rose. "I never asked that of you."

"But your father did. I promised him."

She flinched, then stepped forward and jabbed his chest with a finger. "You promised him you would fetch me my clothing in the middle of a bombing? How does that keep me safe?"

He opened his mouth. Then thought better of answering that question or letting his mind wander down that path.

Thunder rolled and the house heaved. Plaster crumbled down on them. David grabbed Nadia and felt her tremble in his grasp. She was right about him being a fool. He should have stayed put with her until it was safe and not risked either of their lives.

His recklessness was what got people killed.

How hadn't he learned that yet?

David pulled her down the stairs, making it back to the main floor before Nadia jerked to a stop. "*Słuchać.*"

That chastisement he knew well enough from his grandmother. Probably because he'd never been great at listening. "What?"

Nadia wasn't looking at him. She remained silent.

But he couldn't hear anything. No sirens blaring a warning. No planes overhead. No more pounding. Just quiet.

Nadia gave a fleeting smile. Not one of happiness but one of *we survived*. He offered the same. For now they had survived. But the Germans would be back. Whether by land or air, it was only a matter of days or weeks before they reached Warsaw.

≡ CHAPTER 9 ≡

September 3, 1939

David awoke to darkness and a throbbing head. Exhaustion hung from his limbs, but he forced himself into a sitting position while trying to remember where he was and why. A thin mattress on a floor. Quilts adding some warmth. A cot several feet away held Nadia, pale hair fanned across her pillow, face at rest except for a pucker between her eyes. What nightmares had followed her into her sleep?

After the air raid, and with so much uncertainty, most of the household had dragged mattresses and bedding to the cellar of the grand home, sleeping on the floor or small cots instead of the comfort and privacy of the bedrooms. Who knew when the Germans would strike again?

Who knew how much time they had left to flee Poland?

David slipped from the blankets and pulled on his shoes. With so much company, he hadn't undressed further. Even Nadia had been happy to change from the robe she'd been wearing into day clothes, not bothering with a nightgown, though one had been offered. After yesterday's experience, she probably wished to be prepared for anything.

Satchel over his shoulder, he headed to the kitchen door. His shoes tapped out his departure far louder than he would have liked, and he regretted putting them on already. Most of the household—or what remained of the household—appeared undisturbed. Many of the servants had left after the last bombing, expressing the need to seek their family's welfare. Only Nadia's relatives remained—an older gentleman with his wife and two mostly grown sons, and three servants. The lady of the house had hardly spoken since the last attack, but when she did, it was by way of complaint to the wiry woman servant who had stayed and in turn ordered the other two servants about. The older man had been gone most of the evening with his sons. For whatever reason, Nadia seemed content to avoid their company. David got the feeling her relationship with them was not a close one, so he hadn't questioned her.

He paused briefly at the kitchen and eyed the table. There was enough natural light for his chore, but he did not wish to be interrupted. He climbed a flight of stairs and wandered in and out of rooms for a few minutes before locating a library or study. Shelves of books covered two walls while a large desk sat near the window. He drew back the heavy green velvet curtains to allow the morning sun entrance. Brilliant rays washed over him.

David closed his eyes against the glare. And breathed. He would figure a way out of this.

"God. . ."

The word clung to his throat. What right did he have to address the Almighty after these many years? No, he had to figure this out on his own. Like he always did.

After shifting the desk a few feet closer to the window, David withdrew from his satchel the revolver and set it aside. For the time being, he had little use for it. What he sought was the thick envelope Baron Roenne had given him before his death. With everything that had happened over the past couple of days, David had only read over the initial instructions—the ones that had already failed. He needed to know everything available to him if he was to figure out how to leave the country as quickly as possible.

First came a list of names—acquaintances, friends, and family who might be able to offer assistance. Several in Warsaw. One in Lithuania. A couple in London included a name linked with the *Times*—probably a British newspaper—and an earl. David had to keep reminding himself who he'd received this from.

Next was a bundle of British pounds. That would be great if they made it that far. Beside that, he placed a similar stack of *złoty*. There were also German *marks* and other types of money he didn't recognize. The baron definitely hadn't placed all his eggs in one basket.

He obviously knew his daughter.

David set a handful of maps beside the money and withdrew two letters sealed in individual envelopes with the instructions to save them until their arrival in England. One bore Nadia's name and the other her mother's. He returned them to the larger envelope and spread open a map of Poland instead. If they were able to find a car, he wanted to know the quickest route out of the country. Lithuania to the northeast seemed the surest course, as it would take them away from the German advance. Especially if the names on Baron Roenne's list could assist them in continuing on to England.

"Ah, Pan Reid," a voice spoke from the doorway. The baron's cousin, Pan Kaczynski, if David remembered correctly, strode into the room. Though younger than the baron had been, silver peppered his light brown hair and deep-set wrinkles spanned out from the corners of his eyes. "I hope you have found what you require."

"I have." Light and a flat surface had been easy enough to come by.

The man leaned over the desk and looked the map and piles over. "What are your plans?"

"I still only have one focus. I need to get Na—Lady Roenne out of the country as her father requested."

The man's face fell, much as it had when Nadia had first announced to him that her father had been murdered.

"I need a car."

Kaczynski nodded and lowered into the nearest chair, high-backed and upholstered. "I wish I had one to give you, but I do not have a collection as Baron Roenne. My own will have room for only one besides my family."

"Lady Nadia's safety is all I care about right now."

Kaczynski gave him an assessing look.

David asked, "How soon will you leave?"

He settled deeper into his chair, as though a weight pressed heavier over him. "A few days longer, I will wait and watch. I have some hope in our army and air force."

David held his tongue. He didn't share that hope. "I appreciate the offer, but I don't feel I should wait. Not if I can find another way. If not. . ."

Kaczynski nodded. "Then I wish you luck, as you Americans say. Or, more importantly, *Bóg z tobą*."

David nodded his thanks and leaned into his elbows. He wished he did dare to pray and request God's help. At least for Nadia's sake. Instead, he mumbled a thank-you in Polish and packed the money back into the larger envelope. All except the złoty. He would see about buying a car today and the provisions they would need for a dash to the northern border. If all went well, tomorrow morning they would be on their way.

"This is what you need." Kaczynski slid open a drawer and withdrew a bottle of vodka.

David swallowed hard, a thirst rising up. He couldn't look away as two glasses were poured and one pressed into his hand. He breathed it in and felt the burn in his nose. One long sip wouldn't hurt. Just something to take the edge off his headache and the sense of failure that never let him be. One sip was all he needed.

≈

Where was that man? Nadia had been awake for hours waiting for David to return from wherever he had disappeared to. No one seemed to know. She'd eaten the breakfast provided by her hosts, then organized what belongings remained to her. And still waited. The clocks now pushed their hands toward midday, and still no sign. Had he abandoned her? Could she blame him?

Was it bad to have expected at least a goodbye?

Nadia picked up the leather-bound journal she had taken from her father's desk after his death. She opened to the first page only to close it again. The tips of her fingers smoothed over the cover. Not yet—the loss was too sharp, and the thought of reading his words felt like a turn to the blade already planted in her chest.

With the journal again buried in her suitcase, Nadia wandered through the house while trying not to remember yesterday. Nor to consider how dependent she had become on the American in such a short time. She glanced into a music room, a piano and harp on display. Music seemed frivolous now.

The next room was a small library, walls lined with books, a large mahogany desk crowding the space in front of a wide window. She had always been able to escape into books and find the friendships she sought, the acceptance she craved. Even love—or at least stories of it. Strong, deep, and abiding love—unlike what was portrayed in so many romance novels. She had no patience for affairs or lust or run-away passion. She wanted real love, whether between a parent and child or man and woman.

She took a step into the room and inhaled the aroma of pages yet to be explored. Would escape into fiction be possible with her world hanging by a thread?

A groan rose from the other side of the room, by the desk.

"David?" She moved across the thick rug and peered around the back of a large upholstered chair. A head lolled forward, dark hair sticking in several directions.

"David?"

He groaned again but looked up at her, his eyes squinting and hazed.

"What is wrong with you?" Even as she asked it, she caught sight of the bottle of vodka on the floor near his feet. An empty bottle. "Did you drink all of it?"

"Only one glass," he muttered. His face appeared ashen. "Was only going to have one glass." He slouched forward with his head dropping onto the desk.

"But you didn't stop, did you? And now you are worthless to me." She kicked the bottle under the desk and retreated back through the door. But only made it as far as the hall. Should she leave him here? What if the Germans returned with more bombs?

He's the fool who drank himself into a stupor.

She gritted her teeth. How many times had he already risked his life for her?

Nadia turned back into the library and sighed as she looked down at his pitiful display. "I cannot leave you here." She spoke in Polish, having nothing to say to him. She took his leather satchel first and then eyed the revolver staring up at her from the desk. A drunk man and a gun were rarely a good combination, but it was probably his. She tucked the revolver carefully beside the camera.

David's hand was cold and clammy as she pulled him out of the chair. Thankfully, he was conscious enough to assist. A little. Once he made it to his feet, he leaned heavily on her. "All the way down the stairs?" This was ridiculous.

He looked over at her, and she became instantly grateful that at least vodka had no scent of its own. He was far too close, and his breath warmed her neck. She wanted to squirm away, but that would do nothing for their end goal. Every step was a chore. Everything about him was suddenly repulsive. Not only could she no longer take comfort in his presence, but the respect she had begun to feel for the man quickly dissipated.

"I messed it all up again." Each word was slurred.

"I cannot argue."

"I had one job. Keep him safe." He shook his head as though clearing it. "Keep *her* safe."

"I do hope you recognize the difference."

"What difference? Still all on me. All my fault. Dead because of me."

His words made little sense, but he seemed to be more agitated by the minute. Who was dead because of him? Or was he talking about possibility—what might happen?

"You are not responsible for what happens to me."

"Promised. Promised to keep safe. Failed again."

She slowed on the landing. "How did you fail?"

His head dropped forward as he shifted. She almost buckled under him, stumbling into the wall. The weight of him crashed against her, forcing the air from her lungs. His breath seared her ear. "Didn't see him. Wasn't strong enough."

"You seem plenty strong to me." She pushed against the wall to shove David away while still keeping a grip on his arm to keep him from falling headfirst down a flight of stairs, though it would serve him right.

When they finally reached the cellar, she was all too happy to deposit him on his mattress. She felt only a small amount of guilt for the moan of pain he released when his head clipped the edge of a crate. Once he had started his fall, there was only so much she could do to control it. She was more than ready to put distance between them, but curiosity was a horrible itch in one's brain. Once he was sober, he would close up like a clam again.

Nadia rolled David onto his back and pulled the woolen blanket to his chin. Not that he looked like he needed it. Sweat glistened on his brow. "Who is dead because of you?"

His head tossed side to side, a look of torture distorting his face. "I killed him."

Nadia pushed aside the growing guilt for prodding so deeply. "Who? How?"

"Ben." David raised his hand and pressed the heel of his palm against his forehead. "And I'll fail again."

Her strength depleted from the trip downstairs, Nadia settled on the edge of the crate beside him. Her insides felt rather weak at the moment. "I hope not."

"I can't do anything right. That's why they don't trust me." His eyes closed, but he continued his mumblings. "They don't say as much, not anymore. But I see it in their eyes. Disappointment. Get married. Have a family like everyone else. What's wrong with you? You only think of yourself."

Nadia stared at the man. She had been told similar remarks enough times, though worded quite differently. Expectations she had not met. Of course, those were her mother's expectations. Her father never said much about what he wanted for her, leaving her to wonder if he had any aspirations for her at all. What had he wanted? Or had he even cared?

A familiar ache spread through her heart, but this time she pushed it aside with what David had told her. Tata wanted her safe, far away from this—all of this.

Yet here she remained despite his planning. That was not David's fault regardless of his need to take the blame. It was her choice, and she refused to regret it. At least one family would be free from this fear and death. Because of her.

The oddest sensation spread through her center, momentarily pushing aside the pain. The strangest sort of. . .*happiness?*

"They are probably right," David murmured, his voice slurred, and she realized he had not ceased his mutterings.

"Nie. They cannot be."

His eyes opened, and he squinted up at her, his eyes still hazed but holding a plea. There was an almost childlike quality to his expression, one that tugged at her heart.

"Your family is wrong. As are you." Nadia leaned down and laid a hand on his arm. "You could have been in England by now if you only cared for yourself. Yet here you are." She took a steadying breath. "Here we are."

⧨ CHAPTER 10 ⧨

September 5, 1939

Nadia paced the kitchen, not sure what else to do. Even the most interesting book could not hold her interest for more than a minute or two. For two days she had been "sitting tight" as David called it, while he traipsed across the city. First buying a half-rotted car—supposedly it was the only one he could find for sale at the "right price." By the time he had driven the car this far, he had decided it needed a day of work. A new back tire. A bunch of tinkering under the hood. She had nothing to do but watch and wait and hide in the cellar every time the sirens warned of another air raid.

Every day more bombs dropped. More German planes were shot down. And even more Polish planes. Numbers were dwindling. How could the local radio continue to praise their victories both over Warsaw and on the front? David seemed convinced it was all propaganda for the sake of the city's morale, but she wanted so badly for the reports to be real.

Unfortunately, she sensed David was again correct.

Already people streamed into Warsaw with everything they could carry, fleeing the advancing Nazis. Air raids only grew worse by the day. Every day.

Tata and David were right. She needed to leave Poland—wanted to leave. Away from the pounding of guns and the ever-constant fear. Enough waiting.

The sun greeted her with the stunning warmth of lingering summer, and she closed her eyes against its brilliance. And breathed. The fate of Poland was not yet determined, and at the moment she could almost hope.

Then Nadia opened her eyes to the rubble-strewn street. The crumbling and blackened walls across the way. The remains of the German plane after a fire ravaged its body. A crater in the middle of the street from a direct hit.

Her optimism shattered.

The car David acquired looked almost as bad, but she headed toward it. He had hoped to leave before noon, and it was almost that.

No sign of him.

She walked to the end of the block, her muscles tensing with each step. She caught sight of his now familiar jacket half a block farther. He crouched, camera in hand.

Nadia quickened her pace, attempting to see what captured his attention. Her steps faltered as the image came into view. Half the building had been demolished by fire. In the front, a woman rested on the crumbled remains of the wall, slowly rocking while keeping her gaze trained on two young children. The eldest could not have been older than five, the youngest half that. They crouched, grabbing at pebbles, stacking them into a tower or something of the sort. Soot stained their faces, making evident trails left by tears down their full cheeks.

David nodded his thanks to the woman before turning his attention to a family pushing what appeared to be a baby pram piled high with bedding and provisions—probably everything they could bring from their home before they had to abandon it for the sake of their lives. David again peered through his camera.

He took a photograph before noticing her. A hint of red tinged his clean-shaved face, and he headed her direction. She looked back to the people he had chosen to capture. *"Dlaczego?"* The word came out as an accusation.

"Co?"

She could not hold her tongue but switched to English so he could not misunderstand. "Why would you take such photos? Of their pain and humiliation? What reason could you have for wishing to remember them so? Or do you think to sell your photographs and make a profit from their pain?" The words spent, heat surged to her own face, whether from anger or embarrassment of her outburst. Either way, she wanted some distance from the American.

"Hey, wait. It's not like that." He caught her far too quickly and pulled her to a halt. "Listen, I'm not trying to hurt anyone. I would never mock what they feel. I want to help them."

She spun. "How exactly?" These were her people, and she was tired of seeing them used.

"I want to—"

His words were halted by a loud wail of sirens warning of another air raid. David swore under his breath, and she barely held her own curse at bay. Was there no end? Could they not even finish a conversation without being forced back underground?

Nadia tried to keep her feet as David pulled her back toward the house, but a hum of planes grew too close. The bombs began to drop.

David dodged sideways into the nearest building, pulled by a flow of people fleeing the streets. An explosion was followed by a popping sound. Someone screamed. Another cried out in agony. Nadia glanced back as people crumpled or stumbled. Red stained their clothes.

"*Mój Boże*," she cried heavenward. But how could any God allow this to happen?

David jerked her down a flight of stairs into darkness where all they could do was listen as the bombardment continued, overshadowed now by the screams of the wounded and cries of the bereft and frightened. And children. She could hear their young voices as they cried or begged for the bombing to end. Mothers and fathers tried to shield their offspring from both harm and the realization of what happened around them.

Nadia had never felt such gratitude before—that she did not have children of her own. How could a loving parent bear such fear? Her heart hurt on their behalf. Just as much as it hurt at the thought of never knowing such love for someone. And from someone. The life of privilege she had enjoyed did not make her invincible. Neither did the arms of the man beside her. He had no power to truly keep her safe. A bullet could pierce him just as easily as her—just as easily as it had cut down the families on the streets.

"People need to know," David whispered beside her.

"Know what?" she snapped, her anger returning.

"They need to know what's going on. To *see* it. So there can be no doubt in their minds."

Nadia blinked against the darkness of yet another cellar. "That is why you are taking the photographs?"

She felt his nod more than she saw it. "When we get to England, we'll have proof of the crimes being committed here against civilians."

"*If* we get to England." It seemed so very far away right now.

"*When* we get there." His tone held no room for argument.

An eternity passed before they finally returned to the street above. Nadia's feet dragged. *Close your eyes. You do not have to see it. You do not have to look.*

But her eyes remained wide as they stepped out into the sunshine that no longer seemed to penetrate the doom hovering over the city, had no strength to warm her. Men, women, and children lay across the street, gunned down by a low-flying plane. Dropping a haul of bombs on the city had not been enough.

Anger and helplessness warred within, making her breath short and head light. A ringing in her ears was nothing against the wails and cries. She looked toward the smoky sky. Maybe she should target her rage in that direction—at a God who would let such horror reign.

David crouched, his large hands not quite steady as they brought the camera up. She followed his focus to the family they had seen earlier—husband, wife, and children. All dead. Their pram and its load of treasures spilled on the street. A jagged breath from the man at her side pulled at her. His lips pressed a hard line.

Nadia set her hand on his shoulder. Yes, their story needed to be told. The story of fleeing from an approaching army or from a home left in ruins, only to be shot down like dogs in the street. A sob choked her, but she could not let it free. If she let the dam break, there would be no repair.

"What?" David jerked to his feet and jogged across the street toward the overturned pram. He shoved his camera into the bag with hardly a glance at what he did, his entire focus on the pile of belongings—as they shifted. He threw blankets out of the way, then pots and sacks of food. Unburying a child, a young girl, probably no more than four or five.

"Mama!" the girl wailed at seeing him. "Tata!"

Nadia's eyes swam at the anguish in the child's cry. She hurried to the girl, wishing she could protect her from seeing the fate of her family. No child deserved such torment. David was lifting the little girl into his arms when Nadia reached her and placed two hands on either side of her face. Blinders. "It will be all right, *maleńka*." She held the child's gaze while switching to English for David's sake. "Grab a blanket, quickly. Do not let her see."

David handed the child to Nadia and returned seconds later with a wool blanket to wrap over the girl's head so all she could focus on was Nadia's face.

"Can you tell me your name?" Nadia asked her as she walked.

"Krystyna," the small voice squeaked.

"Ah, what a pretty name. Mine is Nadezhda, but I prefer Nadia. I want so very much to be your friend. What do you think, Krystyna, will you be my friend?"

The girl tried to twist in her arms, to look behind. "Where did my mama go?"

"Not far. But she wants you to be safe."

"But the planes are gone. I don't see them anymore." The girl trembled in her arms. "They make big noises. And even Tata is scared, I think."

"They are pretty scary."

"Ryszard thinks we should have stayed home. He's angry."

Nadia's heart throbbed. "Your brother?"

A nod.

"Who all came with you?"

Krystyna's brow bunched. "Mama and Tata. Ryszard and Marcin and Elżbieta."

"Nadia!"

She peered over the blanket, surprised at seeing David with an older girl hanging limp from his arms.

"She's alive."

"Alive?" How? Nadia had seen the child, eight or nine, lying dead with the others.

"The bullet hit her arm, but I think she struck her head when she fell. We must find a doctor."

Nadia cuddled the younger girl against her. "I think there is a hospital only a block or two from here. A maternity hospital." If she remembered correctly. Surely they would be equipped to care for the children. She led the way, grateful to leave the awful scene behind. But what would they do with the children? Were there relatives who would take them in? Would the hospital have room for both of them?

Questioning fell away, sinking like a brick to her feet along with the hope of finding the care the older girl required. The hospital stood before them, smoke rising from several areas, a whole wing crumbling. "Why would they bomb a hospital?" She had not thought she could feel more ill. "Who would knowingly do such a thing? They had to have known. They had to have. You can tell it is a hospital. There are women and babies in there! Who would be so evil?"

The whimpering of a child halted her rant. She bit her lip to stop her mouth until she tasted blood. Her vision burned and blurred. Was there nowhere safe?

⫷ CHAPTER 11 ⫸

Near the steps of the hospital, David laid the girl on the grass, still green with summer growth. The vitality seemed at odds with the cold and gray of winter that seemed to grip his soul. With a pitiful moan, the child rolled her head to the side, and a spark of hope ignited within him. Her arm would likely heal. If only her head injury wasn't too severe.

Nadia came alongside, speaking soft words in Polish. Meant for the child and not him, so easily ignored. He had enough on his mind. How long until a doctor would be able to see the girl, or would there be no one? Her wounded bicep still oozed blood from two holes. A good sign that nothing remained lodged inside. He removed his jacket and ripped the lower part of his shirt, a long strip to tighten around the thin arm. Somehow the bone remained intact.

A miracle.

He could not accept otherwise. But why would God save this child and not her family? His attempt to take a photograph had probably failed due to how shaken the scene had left him. The bitterness of bile still clung to the back of his throat.

The younger girl in Nadia's arms whimpered.

A second miracle.

Neither of the girls should have survived the attack. But they had and would be able to offer each other some comfort.

David tied off the makeshift bandage and laid his jacket over the unconscious child. Again she stirred.

"Take this one," Nadia ordered, thrusting the small thing into his now empty arms. "Wait here with them while I try to find help."

What? He was no nursemaid. Instinct pushed him to his feet. He should be the one to brave the burning, crumbling building while she stayed with the girls to comfort them.

"You do not speak Polish." She must have read his intentions.

"A little," he protested, though not sure why.

"Not well enough. Stay with the children." With that she was off, jogging up the grand stairs to the double doors above. He could not remove his gaze until she disappeared within, and even then it was hard to turn away, a band tightening around his chest. His head throbbed from the ever-mounting tension.

"Keep her safe," he whispered, an all too familiar feeling of powerlessness seeping into his bones.

No other option in view, David settled onto the grass with the youngster on his lap. She looked up at him with wide eyes and a whimper.

"It's all right. I'm not as horrible as I look." He gave a rueful smile, knowing full well she wouldn't understand a word he spoke. "Do you have a name?" He searched his tired brain. *Jak się nazywasz?* When she didn't answer, he pointed to himself. "*Nazywam się* David." His name came out flat, without any attempt to accent it properly.

Her pale eyebrows lifted, but she seemed just as afraid as ever.

"Here, let's do something fun." A bizarre concept after what they had both just seen, but he plucked a thick piece of grass from the trimmed lawn and shifted the girl so she was between his arms with his hands free. He pinched the grass between the tops of his thumbs and the meat of his thumbs before bringing the center to his mouth and giving a blow.

The girl startled at the squeaky sound. He blew again, trying to make it more warbly. "Kind of sounds like an elephant, doesn't it?"

She angled a look at him but said nothing.

"You know elephant?" He brought one arm up to his nose, demonstrating a swinging trunk.

"*Słoń?*"

"*Tak.*" He blew against the grass again and was rewarded with a brightening of her pale brown eyes.

Then her sister moaned, and all attention shifted. David set the smaller girl beside him, knelt beside her sister, and brushed her blond hair from her eyes. She was too young to be lingering between life and death.

No younger than Ben.

He'd felt even more helpless that day.

David pushed the voice away and tried to focus on the present. "Are you going to wake up for me?"

She tossed her head from one side to the other as though with a *no*, but her eyes flickered open. She immediately squeezed them shut against the brightness of the sun above. David shifted to provide a shadow. Her eyes again fluttered open and froze on his face. He managed a smile—or somewhat of one. *"Dzień dobry."*

She looked confused, whether from his horrible accent or her location. If only Nadia was here with her soft voice and soothing words to put the children at ease. The girl said something, but it was slurred and mumbled, and he was at a loss to put the words together.

"Przykro mi," he apologized. Hopefully Nadia would hurry back with or without a doctor.

A tug on his sleeve made him glance at the younger girl standing beside him. She slipped back onto his lap and laid her head against his chest. He couldn't help but cradle her there while his mind traveled home to his nieces. Some would be this age, some older. He hardly knew them—he'd been avoiding the family for too long.

"Why don't you come home more?" His oldest brother and father pestered David whenever he did contact them or show up during a holiday when he hadn't been expected. His youngest sister had been worse until she'd married a year ago. Most of his family seemed to have given up on him the past couple of years. Too many excuses, and they were tired of them. Or maybe didn't buy them anymore, if ever. His siblings had probably gotten tired of having him around anyway. Even when David was there, he sulked on the sidelines instead of joining in the conversations.

Yet suddenly he had the strangest craving to go home.

Dust and smoke added a haze to the air as Nadia hurried through the halls, searching for anyone who looked like a doctor or nurse among the hustle of bodies hurrying in all directions. Some seemed to be searching for loved ones. Others were moving to a safer location on the lower floors.

Some were hunting for help just as she was.

A nurse with a long white apron assisted a woman who cradled a screaming baby in her arms. Another nurse piled blankets on a cart and rushed toward the stairs. She hardly slowed before the smack, smack, smack denoted the cart's descent. Of course the lowest floor, a basement, would be the safest place for their patients. Nadia followed, keeping out of the way of the steady flow of people heading in both directions.

She hurried to the side of a nurse carrying a bundle of bandages. "I need help with a child."

The woman kept walking. "What is wrong with it?"

"Her arm was shot, and she appears to have hit her head."

"Keep pressure on the wound until the blood clots enough. Clean it and bandage it well." She did not slow her steps.

"We need a doctor. Surely there is someone who can help."

The nurse's steps faltered. "We have been working nonstop the last four days to keep these mothers and infants warm and fed. Four babies were born already *today*, one as the bombs fell on this building. Dr. Grocholski was killed in the last bombing. Other people have been flowing through those doors nonstop needing help. We have nothing left to give." She pulled a roll of white gauze from her bundle and pressed it into Nadia's hand. "Clean the wound well with hot water. Alcohol if you have any."

Nadia gripped the bandage as the nurse jogged away. Heart pounding, she glanced around her. The faces of people. Children. Babies. What sort of hell had she fallen into? And yet her feet pulled her farther along the hall, down the stairs. The wailing of infants met her ears and tore at her. Mothers in their nightgowns lined the narrow passage below, their tiny bundles squirming in arms or pressed to the breast. One woman slumped against the wall, her head lolling off to one side in an attempt to sleep while two—*twins* lay in the crooks of her arms.

Another woman, her face as pale as the sheet covering her, lay propped up on a pillow, her babe a few months older than the rest. She stared upward, murmuring what sounded like a prayer until Nadia reached her. "Save my baby," the woman pleaded. "Save my baby."

Nadia knees weakened and she let herself sink to the woman's side. "What is wrong with your baby?"

The mother's dark brown eyes widened, and a light sparked within. "Nothing. He's healthy. But who will keep him safe when I am gone?"

"Gone?"

A nurse pushed between Nadia and the woman and thrust a bottle of milk at the latter before hurrying away. The woman's hand shook as she attempted to feed her baby.

"Let me." Nadia shoved the bandaging into her pocket and took the baby before realizing she had only held one other babe before now, and only for a moment. But instinct pulled the baby to her chest. She took the bottle next, and the child began sucking vigorously.

"Dziękuję," the woman whispered as her eyes slipped closed.

"Are you family?" The nurse had returned and stood behind, hand on hip, while the other held a tray.

"A friend," Nadia replied, trying to remember her station and why she did not need to cower before the large woman with such a dark glower.

"You will take my baby, won't you? Take him far away from this. . .from here." The mother was breathless when she finished her plea.

"I. . ." *can't.* The words blared in her head, but her tongue felt swollen.

"I told you," the nurse interjected. "The baby can be sent to the children's home. The one in the *żydowski* district."

Jewish. The woman was Jewish. No wonder the animosity from the nurse. Nadia wanted to correct the nurse on her own parentage but held back. Who cared what the woman thought? "Is there no other family?"

"The father is dead. They came with the refugees a couple of days ago." The nurse fidgeted as though anxious to be gone. She motioned to the woman. "An infection was well established by the time they came here." Her matter-of-fact description gnawed at Nadia's resolve to remain civil.

"You are above losing your temper. You were born into nobility."

Tata's rebuke rang in her ears, as did her rebuttal. Nobility meant little in Poland in this modern era. But she would honor her father's name all the same. Nadia stood and faced the nurse, adding a bounce to keep the baby pacified as his bottle ran dry. "There is nothing more that can be done for her?"

"With our walls falling down around us and supplies running low?"

"That does not answer my question." Nadia spoke pointedly.

The nurse seemed to shrink back a little. "Nothing."

"Very well. I need a paper and pen. Immediately."

The nurse hesitated only a moment and then withdrew a notepad and pencil. They would have to do. Nadia took them and crouched back by the mother's side. Her eyes were wide, but her breathing was labored. Nadia laid the baby on his mother, leaning near so he would not roll off accidently. Her own hands were less than steady while she wrote out a quick letter, pausing only to ask names.

> *I, Bejla Mazurski, have requested that Nadiashda Roenne*
> *see that my child, Arek, born June 5th, 1939,*
> *is found a good family who will raise him as their own.*

She held the paper so Bejla could scrawl her signature at the bottom. She let the pencil fall to her chest and clasped Nadia's hand. "Please, see that he is loved."

Nadia nodded, not trusting her voice. "I will do everything in my power to keep him safe. And see that he is loved."

The mother's hands fell back, and her focus centered entirely on her small son in her arms. She strained to press a kiss to his downy head. Tears rolled down her face, but her eyes showed peace—hope even. And gratitude as Nadia scooped up the baby.

"Thank you."

Nadia wished she could linger and allow the mother every last minute with Arek, but David was waiting for her with a little girl who still needed medical help. "I have to go. I am sorry."

The mother nodded and relaxed back into her pillow. After one last longing gaze at her baby, she closed her eyes. Fresh tears slipped across her cheek, trailing to her ears.

Nadia felt her own eyes burn as she turned away and started back up the stairs. Why, oh why, had she come down here? Why had she not left before seeing such agony?

The boy fussed as Nadia tucked his flailing arms into his blanket. An unexpected sense of peace penetrated her frantic thoughts.

I sent you there.

Nadia almost stopped midstep, the thought struck her with such power. She looked heavenward again, but this time with a sense of wonder. For a moment, she did not feel so alone.

☰ CHAPTER 12 ☰

Finally back in the relative safety of the cellar, David sank onto a chair and looked over his growing responsibilities. Evening settled over the city. Somewhere to the north, a huge swath of the city burned, flames licking at the night sky, but their section of Warsaw remained strangely at peace, despite the horrors of hours ago. The baby had finished a bottle of goat's milk a few minutes ago and slept in a crib they had fashioned out of the crate and a thick quilt.

Krys, as he'd taken to calling her, lay on her stomach beside her older sister, talking in a quick but hushed chatter. Elżbieta, or Bieta, complained of the pain in her head, but at least she was awake. She'd scared him when she had lost consciousness again while they'd cleaned and bandaged her arm. She was only nine years old while her little sister was four and a half—Krys had looked up at him with a stubborn tilt to her chin when she'd corrected her sister and included the extra six or so months. Bieta had shared much more, allowing her little sister to fill in details about their life on a farm, packing what they could carry, and coming to the city.

Would it have been better for them if they had taken their chances with the German advance? The question had pestered David while digging graves for their father, mother, and three siblings. The whole family accounted for, and no relatives or friends that the girls knew of, what could be done but provide a place for them to stay? Food. A road toward safety.

"Are you angry?"

David looked up to where Nadia watched him far too closely. He averted his gaze. Safer to watch the children than risk her seeing too much. "Very," he said truthfully, "but you might want to be more specific with your questioning."

She cleared her throat. "Are you angry about the children?"

"That their families have been stolen from them by the Nazis? Extremely."

"Is that the only thing you are angry about?"

She seemed braced for him to tell her he wanted nothing to do with the children, but nothing could be further from the truth. Yes, they added complexity and layers of stress he'd never experienced before, but innocence glowed in their eyes. And need. To be loved. To be protected. Even if Nadia didn't insist, he would have felt the same.

"I might be a little frustrated at my incompetence—"

Her brows rose.

"With the Polish language," he hurried to clarify.

She chuckled softly. "Ah, I see."

"You probably think I should have just admitted to plain old incompetence on every level." His face grew hot as he considered waking up yesterday with a splitting headache and remembering bits and pieces of his inebriated state the day before. Worse was looking into Nadia's eyes the past two days, seeing an expression he knew too well. Disappointment. Loss of trust.

"Have you not?" she said with a half smile.

"I suppose so." He glanced at her and was tempted to try holding her gaze for once so she could read his apology. But what else would she see?

Nadia knelt beside the girls and tucked the blankets around them before lowering the wick on the lamp to a low glow—restoring electricity to the city seemed a lost cause at this point. Nadia remained beside them, singing softly until eyes drooped and both girls slipped into slumber. He could well guess their exhaustion, for he felt the same heaviness. He wondered if sleep would come as easily if he lay down. Somehow he doubted it.

"Do you believe in God?"

David straightened. He almost asked where that question came from, but it actually made perfect sense after what they had witnessed today. "I do."

"And what sort of God is He, who you believe in?"

That answer took a few more minutes to formulate. David wanted to describe the kind and good Father he had believed in as a child, still wanted to believe in, but watching a city slowly get pummeled to nothing gave him pause. "I don't know."

"Then how can you believe in Him?"

David released a tight laugh. "I guess it's just been a while since I gave it much thought." Gave *Him* much thought. "I've been taught my whole life that God rescues, saves, and loves His children. That He answers prayers. But I also know He allows bad things to happen—for some reason He allows stupid people to do stupid things."

"Speaking from personal experience?"

Every muscle tensed as though they could propel him far from this conversation.

"You spoke of someone while you were. . ." She glanced at the children and gave a tight smile.

"When I was thoroughly sauced?"

Her blue eyes narrowed. "I am assuming that is slang for being inebriated."

David set his jaw. "What did I say?"

"You mentioned Ben."

The name struck David like a blow to the chest. Strength fled while failure echoed through his head.

"Who was he?"

"My cousin." He tried to swallow, but his throat felt swollen. "He was about my age."

"What happened?"

Silence hugged the question. Nobody asked that. Either they knew and never spoke of it or they would never know.

Tell her.

David shook his head against the thought. She would only hate him like everyone else who knew. She'd realize she was better off without him. That scared him most of all. He didn't want to lose her.

What do you mean, lose her? he chastised himself. *You've only known her a few days. Your task is to get her to England and then leave. No connections.*

But in actuality it felt like weeks had passed since meeting at the dinner party. Not just the world was different; they were as well.

"You do not have to tell me." Nadia stood, pressing her skirt smooth with her palms before slipping from the cellar, her silhouette disappearing into the light from the kitchen. Leaving him feeling emptier and more a failure than before.

A moment later, she reappeared, jogging toward him. "David, where is the car?" Though she spoke in a whisper, tension formed each word.

"It's parked right out front. Everything is ready for us to leave in the morning."

Her head wagged. "Nie. The car is gone."

"What do you mean?" David pushed past her and raced to the street, now lit only by moonlight. Gone. All his hard work. Again. He felt in his pocket, and the keys jingled.

"How?" Nadia had caught up.

"Probably hotwired it. We shouldn't have waited. We could have been in Lithuania by now."

"When? When would we have left? Before or after we found the children? Before or after burying their dead? There was no time." She touched his arm. "David, this is not your fault."

Then why did it feel that way? He glanced down at the hand on his arm. "We could have loaded up the children as soon as we returned. I could have driven all night. We'd be there by morning."

She squeezed his arm. "A little optimistic for that car. And assuming the Germans left all the bridges intact. Do you really believe we should have raced to the border in the middle of the night, keeping our lights dark so as not to attract a Nazi bomber?"

He wanted to groan but bit it back. "I don't know."

"Neither do I."

Frustration forced him to step away from her. "There must be something I could have done differently."

"*Zatrzymaj się*! Sometimes there is nothing we can do. Nothing *you* can do. You cannot bring your Ben back any more than I can save my father." She circled him, cutting him off, compelling him to meet her gaze. "Any more than you can save me. David, you are not God!"

Her shoulders trembled, and her hand rose to cover her mouth and a scream that seemed torn from her soul. Followed by a weaker one. Then a breathless whimper. She sobbed and fell against him, tears flowing.

David brought his arms around her, needing to hold her probably just as much as she needed to be held, to not feel so adrift, helpless, lost. He couldn't remember the last time he'd held someone like this. Even his mother, not even a brief hug since Ben's death. And his siblings—he'd kept them at arm's length too, convinced they didn't want him anyway. It was easier to keep his distance than risk being turned away.

David closed his eyes while his sinuses burned across the bridge of his nose to the corners of his eyelids. Men didn't cry. He wouldn't let himself. No more thinking about the past. The future seemed just as grim. But the present—he could hold on to this moment, drink it in, and live it while he could, live like he'd never allowed himself before. The woman in his arms needed him, maybe even wanted him. . .for now at least.

He brushed a finger across her wet cheek, sweeping strands of silk behind her ear. A perfectly shaped ear, ridges and grooves. His study seemed to gain her attention, and she peered up at him through the moisture in her eyes. Her lips trembled as they pressed together. If they might not last the next bombing, what harm could a kiss do? Why not seize the moment and what life they had left?

He lowered his head, closing the distance between them. Felt the brush of her mouth against his. Soft and smooth.

A hunger gnawed in his chest, an intensity giving strength to his arms as he drew her against him. He closed his eyes and drank her deeper, shoving away the warnings in his head. Enough thinking. For once he wanted to *feel*. Accepted. Needed. Wanted.

Nadia jerked away. "Nie." She stared at him as though he'd tried to hurt her.

Maybe he had. How could he have let himself believe, or even hope, it would be different this time? He broke everything he touched.

"Przykro mi." David turned on his heel and started away from her. What had he been thinking? What sort of fool. . .? He turned down the next street, needing distance, his thoughts and body craving something to wash away the sensation he should have known was on the other side of a kiss. Ah, sweet rejection. Failure. Flawed. Never enough. A hot thirst burned the back of his throat, the need for something strong enough to drown in.

Don't do it.

He quickened his pace but couldn't escape the craving or the memories. His sobbing mother whose sister had told her they would happily never see them again. Her pain was his fault, so maybe he could bring some comfort. He hungered for it himself—assurance that he was still loved despite everything. He went to her side and stretched his arms around her, burying his face in her shoulder. Her hands, so strong and unyielding, pushed him away. She walked away, abandoning him for her bedroom. Her sobs echoed through him even now.

A boisterous voice sang what sounded like a folk song—an inebriated folk song—and David started toward the several men gathered near a bench. Two held bottles. He couldn't tell the color of liquid flowing within, but he didn't care. Judging from the men holding them, either would serve his purpose.

"Witaj." He lightened his tone for the greeting and dug in his pocket for some coins. "Is there enough to share?"

Their eyes brightened. *"Amerykanin?"*

"Tak."

The older of the men, thick brush on his chin, thrust the bottle into David's chest before he could offer payment. He nodded his thanks. Gripping the glass, warmed from the man's hands, David raised it to his mouth and breathed deep through his nose, anticipation making his skin tingle. One long drink—that would be enough.

The image of Nadia halted his hand. A baby boy who needed goat milk to survive. Two little girls who looked at him as though he could keep them safe.

No, Nadia was right. He couldn't protect them from so many forces out of his control, so much bigger than him.

He tipped the bottle and felt the burn on his tongue. And coughed. Gagged.

Laughter roared in his ears, and someone yanked the bottle out of his hand. The weak American who could not handle their liquor. He heard their jests, understood enough. Little did they know this was nothing compared to some of the drinks he had buried himself in, leaving himself for dead. What they didn't know was that what he couldn't stomach was the thought of causing any more pain to those children. . .and that woman.

Even if she didn't want him either.

———————⁓———————

Nadia stiffened every time one of her relatives or the remaining servants entered the cellar, braced for David's return. She gritted her teeth, hating what he had done to her. Her stomach was in knots and her thoughts as hot and messy as a bowl of *bigos*. Why had he kissed her? What gave him the right? And why did she want more?

She took to pacing with Arek in her arms, which he seemed to appreciate. Though with how wide his eyes stared up at her, her tension was probably not so well disguised. But she had never been kissed before, in all her twenty-five years.

Nadia huffed out a breath, still unable to chase the nervous tension vibrating through her. Young men had made the attempt before, but she had always been able to avoid it. They had only wanted her connections or wealth, and she refused a relationship based on either of those. Matka had cursed her novel reading, but it was not as though she indulged in romance. She had no need to. Love was scattered through most of the great works, from *War and Peace* to *Great Expectations*.

But even hundreds of works of fiction left her woefully unprepared for the sensation that still made her lips tingle, the racing of her heart, the hunger for more. . .and the look of need in David's eyes.

Footsteps turned her to the entry, and the dark form headed toward her. Strong, determined steps. And a bottle in hand. Of course. Liquid courage. Bitterness and disappointment fought for dominance.

"Here," David shoved the bottle into her hand, taking the baby in the next motion and raising Arek to his shoulder.

She stared for a moment, her rebellious gaze flitting over his mouth before finding the presence of mind to look at the bottle. Of milk.

"In case he gets hungry in the night."

She wanted to thank him, but she also wanted to hold on to the anger she had been so carefully nursing.

"There is something else you should know."

She squared her shoulders, readying herself for whatever he

might say next.

He stepped closer and lowered his voice, a whisper in her ear, close enough to feel its warmth. "I'm not giving up until you and these kids are out of Poland."

The fight fled before his conviction, and her heart gave a painful thud. "Very well."

David gave a nod and stepped back, his focus now completely on the babe in arms. For a moment, Nadia allowed the pang of regret. Maybe she should have kissed this man in return.

⊰ CHAPTER 13 ⊱

September 6, 1939

David walked quickly while sidestepping rubble and other pedestrians weaving through the streets. It was midmorning, and he had nothing to show for the hours of hunting, working his way down the list of resources and acquaintances the late baron had supplied. Ahead of him, bricks and stones were piled to form a barricade to slow the Germans and their tanks if they arrived. *If?* David shook his head. Nearly a week had passed since the Germans had invaded, and the city fell more to pieces every day. Still, the Polish government tried to convince their civilians there was hope, that the Polish army was holding their own.

After spending over an hour this morning laboring on a similar barricade, David had decided this was far more preparation than precaution. Only a matter of time before the Germans arrived.

"*Przestań!*"

David glanced at the Polish soldier hurrying toward him, rifle in his hands. At this rate, David wouldn't make it back to the house until dark, but it was too late to turn back and try another street.

The soldier met him, motioning to where a half dozen other men worked, one with a loaf of bread tucked into his jacket for safekeeping. His poor family probably wondered about his delay. The soldier rattled off orders, but David shook his head.

"I'm sorry, I don't speak Polish." David raised his hands innocently while sidestepping the soldier. The gun lowered a fraction, giving David courage to keep walking. No one called after him. He was free to go. *Hallelujah.* It was only a matter of time before Nazi planes began their daily bombardment, and the thought of being away from Nadia and the kids was like an itch he couldn't scratch, a need tearing at his insides when he was away from them.

He successfully avoided one more barricade in construction and the press gang. Within an hour he reached the grand house they had been staying at most of a week. A dark burgundy car was parked just outside, engine humming. David circled, impressed by the lines of the Sunbeam with Weymann body that would have been imported from France. Not a large car, but a second seat would hold more than Kaczynski's wife and two sons.

David quickened his pace, meeting Pan Kaczynski at the door. The man brushed past him, suitcase in hand. David followed to where he shoved it into the truck with other bags and supplies.

"Maybe you can speak sense into Nadezhda." The man slammed the trunk closed and turned to David. "Her father would want her to come with us."

"Yes, he would." David offered a tight smile and turned back to the house. "I'll see what I can do." Even if he had to hog-tie her to get her in the car.

Inside, Pani Kaczynski ordered about her remaining servants on what to pack and what to lock away for safekeeping. In case they returned. In case anything was left of the house when they returned.

As David took the stairs down to the kitchen, the weight on his shoulders seemed to ease. All he had to do was convince Nadia to leave with her father's cousin and his task would be complete. She would be their responsibility.

Nadia looked up as soon as he appeared in the doorway, and her gaze narrowed. She held Arek to her shoulder while watching the girls construct a tower out of empty tin cans, but he could sense her bracing for battle.

"You should be packing your things."

She arched a brow at him. "You found *us* a ride out of Warsaw?"

He forced himself to hold her gaze. "You know what I'm talking about. This is your chance. You need to go."

"So anxious to be rid of me already?" The corner of her mouth turned up, but her blue eyes held ice.

No. In fact the thought of her leaving, of never seeing her again, did unpleasant things to his chest that he refused to contemplate. *One task.* "Yes."

Her gaze flickered away, and the smile vanished. "I will not leave the children."

"I can care for the girls. I'm sure they will allow you to take Arek." It wasn't as though the baby would take up any extra space.

Nadia boosted him higher on her shoulder and began pacing. "They prefer I return him to the hospital so someone more. . .qualified can look after him. Pani Kaczynski has her headaches after all, and the journey will be several days."

David released a breath, and some of the fight left him. "I can speak with them again. Surely they would prefer you go, even with the baby."

"It is not only that he is a baby that they dislike. But what *kind* of child he is." She faced him. "I am not leaving, David. Not without these children. *All* of these children. And. . ."

Nadia turned and started pacing again, a motion the baby seemed to enjoy, leaving David without an argument but with a little hope. He tried to push it down, but the question remained. Had she been about to include him in her list?

David turned his attention to the girls' tower just as it collapsed. He showed them how to stack it with a solid base—a peculiar activity for the middle of the afternoon while others rushed to evacuate. For a moment, he needed the simple distraction. Both from the war and the woman across the room.

It was impossible not to watch the man kneeling beside the two girls, impossible not to marvel at the relaxed way he played with them. Yes, his shoulders and the corners of his eyes still held a tightness that belied the burdens he carried. The ones she only added to.

Hardest yet was not to admire the subtle curve of his mouth as he talked with the girls in a mix of English and Polish.

She shook the thought off and headed for the stairs. She had been inside most of the day and craved fresh air. Pan Kaczynski met her at the top of the stairs but jerked at her appearance. "You have changed your mind?"

"Nie. I am sorry."

He grunted low. "I cannot feel good about abandoning you here."

"Not abandoning me. Pan Reid will keep me safe. I trust him."

Another grunt. "Very well." He nodded his farewell and started away. Nadia followed as far as the doorway and watched as he joined his family in the car. The door clicked closed, and a momentary flicker of doubt kicked at Nadia's resolve. The wheels spun against the cobbled stone.

"Nie." She whispered against the fuzzy head of the child she held. He squirmed in her arms, and she held tighter, finding his tiny hand with her own, encouraging his fingers to wrap one of hers while she smoothed her thumb over his impossibly silky skin. How could they have asked her to leave this precious baby behind? Maybe it had only been a day since he had come into her care, but each hour had wrapped him into her heart with a strength that left her breathless. She loved him.

Tears pricked her eyes at the intensity of the feeling, the wonder of it. Her experience with love was not very extensive, mostly imaginings from stories read. Not enough to prepare her for this—or for any of her experiences in the past twenty-four hours.

"No turning back."

Nadia's pulse sped at the voice behind her, but she held herself in place, refusing to look at David. "I was thinking, some changes can be made now that we have the house almost completely to ourselves." She was not sure if anyone would remain now that the masters of the house had fled. "Perhaps more comfortable sleeping and living arrangements. But on the ground floor, so we can move quickly when. . .needed."

"The only quarters on the main floor are in the back." David stepped nearer. Too near.

"Yes. The servants' quarters. Which provide a quick route to the cellar." She would not be affected by him. She would not pull away this time.

"If you wish it."

Nadia continued staring out at the street though she ached to glance back. How was she so aware of him, his every move and breath? "You have no arguments?"

A low chuckle rumbled from his chest. "Wouldn't that be a waste of my breath?" He started away. She would usually count his retreat a victory. . .but in this instance it felt like a defeat.

⧽ CHAPTER 14 ⧼

September 9, 1939

On the first floor, in a bedroom abandoned by the servants, David leaned over the paper, another line through yet another name—contacts of the late baron, people he thought would help. Either they had already fled the city like their hosts, or they couldn't assist more than in the most menial of ways. A little more money. Some food for the children, keeping them away from the breadlines that got longer each day. He shook his head. They spent hours each day tucked away in a cellar that no longer contained enough of the daily basics needed. Especially for a baby.

David frowned. He really should have hog-tied Nadia and forced her to go.

An upset cry pulled him up and across the room to Krys, who tried to retrieve a ball out from under a large, upholstered chair. Nadia had brought down several toys from the well-equipped nursery, and the youngest girl hadn't allowed the ball out of her sight since.

David crouched and snagged the ball, then rolled it back to the little girl. Her sister looked up from the picture book on her lap, watching as she often did. She understood much more than Krys did, and the weight of that knowledge had stolen far too much innocence from her. Even with that, if David had looked in on this scene, he might have suspected an ordinary life, not the horror these children had lived through.

When Bieta's attention turned back to pictures of woodland elves,

David fished his camera out of its case. He peered through the lens at the girl with her book and bandaged arm. Something felt different about this photo than the others he had taken that morning of the broken city of refugees who told quite different stories than the local newspapers and radio.

Radio.

David clicked a second photograph of Krys cradling her ball as though a baby and then pushed the camera back into the case. He eyed the list of names again, but instead of focusing on those in Warsaw, he shifted his attention to the short list of London contacts. Lord Wintour, the Earl of Selborne. David had no idea how to contact him. But Thomas Kent of the *Times* might be another matter.

The door clicked open and Nadia stepped in, greeting the girls, whose faces brightened. "Arek is still asleep?"

David nodded toward the cradle they had also scavenged from the upstairs nursery. "How was your visit with"—he had to glance at the sheet—"Władysław Raczkiewicz?" He'd probably butchered the name.

"He and his family are halfway to Romania by now." She set her purse on the desk and glanced over his shoulder at the dwindling list. "Tell me what you have found." She perched on the end of the desk and tapped the paper.

"I need a radio. Two-way. Something to reach London on."

Nadia's finger tapped out a steady beat. Several minutes passed before she answered. "I might know someone. An old military general who dined with us on occasion."

A distant siren announced German planes, and David grabbed the sheet of paper and his satchel while Krys threw herself against his leg. He swept her up in one arm while taking Bieta's hand with the other. Nadia met them at the door with the baby, and they hurried downward together as though well-rehearsed. The few remaining servants, one who had been joined by his family, which included several older children, joined them in the cellar but mostly kept to themselves. Minutes later, the pounding began in force, like huge hail from the heavens determined on flattening every last building in Warsaw. The city was becoming a death trap. Even if they walked to the Lithuania border, it couldn't be worse than this.

"How close do you think they are—the German army?" Nadia bounced the fussing baby, probably trying to settle him back to sleep or work the nervousness from her own body.

David lowered to their crate and pulled Bieta in beside him. At least English gave them freedom to speak without frightening the children—as long as they could keep the tension from their voices. "Closer than I want to think about. I've read enough reports on the German army—we're seeing its strength every day over our heads—to know the Polish defenses won't hold much longer. Even the government can't hide it anymore. They are fleeing as quickly as the refugees flow in."

Nadia took a measured breath.

A plane roared above them. *Tat-tat* of machine guns. Bieta flinched against him, and he tightened his hold. Krys burrowed against his chest with enough force to restrict his lungs.

"And when they do arrive?" Nadia pressed her mouth against the dark peach fuzz on Arek's head. "Do you really believe they will treat the Jewish Poles so much worse than the rest of us? They seem to hate us all."

That they did. He considered his words. "They don't appear to care much for the life of a Pole. But I think they, or at least Hitler, would gladly annihilate every Jew from the face of the earth if he had the power."

Her jaw dropped and her hold tightened on the baby until he protested. "You cannot mean that. Or know that. They have been treated unfairly and lost businesses. But genocide?"

"It's in Hitler's book. What does he call them? 'The personification of the devil' or 'the symbol of all evil assumes the living shape of the Jew.' "

"You have read *Mein Kampf?*"

"No! I can't speak much German, never mind read it. Your father shared those passages with me. And more. Hitler sees Jews as capable of destroying civilization. Your father had friends in Germany, Jewish friends. They'd written to him of their frustrations and the injustices committed against them. And then, over the past year, thousands of businesses and homes have been destroyed and people have been hauled away like cattle. Some have disappeared completely. Others are interned at work camps like criminals." He had to pause to catch his breath and rein in his passion.

Nadia's eyes narrowed, but not with a challenge this time. Perhaps only suspicion. "I did not know my father watched that particular situation so closely. It is interesting that you feel so strongly about the Jews while so many hold animosity toward them, David Reid."

She stressed his last name. What was she searching for? Did she guess?

"You are not Jewish."

And there it was. Push his feelings aside and pretend he was just as Christian—or as non-Jew—as the rest when anti-Semitic sentiments or jokes arose. He didn't want to hide who he was from her. "Not religiously."

Her mouth opened.

"My father is a wonderful Irish, English mix with strong Christian beliefs and roots in the United States that go as far back as its independence. My mother is Jewish, her parents, immigrants from Poland."

Her expression softened. "Aah."

She said the single not-quite-word as though she suddenly understood everything about him. And yet she remained a mystery in so many ways. Something lingered behind her expression. . .

A deafening boom shook the building, and David bent over the children. Someone across the room screamed. The baby wailed, wide awake now.

"Were we hit?" Nadia had ducked down beside him.

He tried to listen, but two men were shouting to be heard over a woman's wail. Another explosion. Plaster rained down on their heads. "I'll go check."

Nadia slipped into his place on the crate, and David set Krys beside her. The little girl struggled to retain her hold on him, and he had to pry her off. "I'll be right back," he whispered to her in Polish. "I'll be back."

Nadia wrapped an arm over Krys and spoke calmly, as though nothing were wrong. But already he could smell smoke. He ran up the stairs, another man on his heels, and out onto the street, with only a second's pause to make sure no planes were directly overhead. He backed away from the building, where smoke billowed from the top two stories. The man beside him cursed as the roof and third floor gave way and crashed down to the second story. David pushed past the man to race back inside. "The building's on fire. We have to go."

Krys grabbed David's leg, and it took all his strength to pull her into his arms where she clung around his neck. Bieta pressed against his side while they were forced to wait for the others ahead of them. He met Nadia's wide eyes and motioned her forward up the stairs and through the kitchen. "Stay close to the wall once we reach the street," he warned. "The skies aren't clear yet."

He felt Nadia's hand grip the arm he held on to Bieta with. The contact steadied the racing of David's pulse. They were together. Somehow they would figure out what to do next.

They moved down the streets, past the fresh graves dug into once pristine lawns. Another plane roared overhead, and David jerked Nadia into a doorway with him. The force of the blast stung the back of his neck as he tried to shield his makeshift family.

As the air settled, so did the thought into his chest. Despite the shortness of their time together, they were no longer strangers. Overseeing them was no longer just a duty or to prove himself. He cared for Nadia and the children. Maybe too much.

He again found Nadia's gaze. It also didn't matter if she ever returned his feelings. He didn't need a promise of forever. He just needed her to stay alive.

———— ≈ ————

Nadia stood frozen, the children sheltered between her and David, her head lifted to meet his gaze. He stared back at her with an intensity she'd not seen before. As though he had just uncovered some great secret that would change the course of the world—or perhaps just their lives. Whatever remained.

A sneeze exploded in her nose, breaking the contact. She squeaked an apology, still shaken from their escape. She felt Elżbieta press against her, and she wrapped an arm around the child. Had it only been a week ago that Nadia had lounged in her grand home, her frustrations nothing more than minor discomforts or preferences? She felt like a different person somehow. Maybe because she finally had a purpose. And these children, who had so fully engrained themselves in her heart.

And David?

"We can't stay here." He led her back onto the sidewalk and along the wall, dodging obstacles as they went.

"Where are we going?"

His steps slowed, and he hefted Krystyna higher. Her small arms wrapped his throat with such force she was surprised he could breathe. "The war hero. With the radio. Where does he live?"

The far western side of the city. At least an hour's walk. But what choice did they have? Even if they had a car, most streets were strewn with rubble and now barricades. "This way." She brushed past him, taking the lead. With the cautious pace and the children slowing them further, the sun would probably have set by the time they crossed the city, but there was nowhere to come back to.

Her step faltered. In the house, in her suitcase. . .Tata's journal. Nausea roiled within her.

David paused at her side. "What is it?"

Nadia clamped her teeth on her tongue. She could not ask him to risk his life. The house was collapsing, and the skies were still filled with bombers. "Nic. Nothing." She started walking again, forcing one foot in front of the last while pressing a kiss to Arek's head. Life—that was what mattered. Not the past, not what could never be changed. Even with resolve pushing her forward, Nadia felt as though she were being ripped in two.

⋛ CHAPTER 15 ⋛

September 10, 1939

David awoke to the rumble of voices over static. He blinked, but the room remained dim, the oil lamp at his side down to the smallest flicker of flame. He straightened away from the desk he had fallen asleep on and turned up the wick. He then massaged the throbbing pain lurking under his temples. His eyes burned, but he focused his attention on the radio in front of him. With the flow of soldiers arriving from the western front and almost constant air raids, they'd arrived late in the evening, leaving little time for introductions to the old general and his family before needing to get the children settled for the night.

Static muffled words over the radio, and David grabbed for the handset.

"Hello, are you still there?" Despite the lateness of the night when they'd arrived and the almost continuous air raids, David had asked to remain upstairs with the radio. London was earlier in the evening, and someone might still be awake at the *Times*.

More static and then a voice. "Yes. This is Thomas Kent. I was told you needed to speak with me."

"Yes, yes." David tried to clear his mind enough to formulate what he needed to say.

"You're American?"

"I am."

"What are you still doing in Poland? I was told you're in Poland, correct?"

"I'm a photographer. I was over here working on a project when the Germans invaded."

"Who do you work for?"

David grimaced. The man probably expected to hear the name of the big newspapers or magazines in America, not a couple of the small-town papers he had on his résumé. "I work on spec."

"Have anything good?"

Images flashed through his mind. Death. Gore. Heartache and horror. Nothing *good* at all, but they were images that could help him build a name for himself. More importantly, they needed to be seen. "They show what's going on over here. Up close and personal."

"Then send them my way. I'm interested to see if there is anything we can use."

"I didn't contact you about the photographs. You are welcome to them, but I need to get someone, several someones, out of Poland."

"We're not a taxi service." His voice was blunt.

David plowed forward. Too much was at stake. "I was told you knew Baron Roenne?"

His question was met by static. In the distance, a siren wailed. Had he lost the connection? Panic pushed David forward in the chair. "Are you still there?"

"Yes. And yes, I know the baron. Why isn't he the one contacting me?"

"He's dead. Murdered by the Nazis on the thirty-first."

"Thirty-first? I thought the invasion began on the first."

"It's a long story." Not one he could tell over a staticky radio. "I'm trying to get his daughter out of Poland."

"Lady Nadezhda? Where in Poland are you?"

"Warsaw."

The crackle of static. This time David waited until the voice returned. "I heard it's getting pretty rough over there."

"Yes, it is. We're running out of time."

More static

"We need help."

". . .don't know if I'm the right person to ask, especially since there's hundreds of refugees pouring out of Poland. The focus has been getting British nationals and government officials out."

"I understand that." David leaned his elbows onto the desk and again massaged his temples. After a night of sleeping hunched in a chair, his head felt like it would burst. He needed this to work.

A long pause, and David sent a prayer heavenward on Nadia's and the children's behalf.

"Let me make some telephone calls. See what I can come up with."

"I'd appreciate that." He leaned back and stretched his neck. His muscles protested. Somewhere within the vicinity, an explosion rocked the earth. "The quicker the better." Ten days since the beginning of the invasion, and he could feel the Germans breathing down their necks. If the Polish government had already fled the country and soldiers poured in from the front, how long did they have? Days? Hours?

Another explosion made David flinch. The Poles had lost their air support, making the city an open target. There might not be anything left by the time the ground forces arrived.

The static buzzed in his ears and his brain. More waiting. What he wouldn't do for a drink right now, something to take the edge off the headache and stress.

David pressed both hands back over his head, sweeping his hair away from his face. Then reached for the glass of water Nadia had left for him on the desk before retiring with the children for the night. It was warm and the flavor was off, but it soothed the back of his throat and took the edge off his thirst. He blew out his breath.

"A lot on your mind? I was in your shoes at the start of the last war." Pan. . .or *General* Czelusniak walked into the room, leaning heavily on his cane. "Children. A young wife. Duty." His accent was thick but understandable.

David was too tired to correct him about the wife. The children would probably claim him, but to Nadia he was only a means to an end. He needed to remember their first meeting. She saw herself as superior in every way. The daughter of a baron. Born to privilege. If she didn't need his help to get herself and the kids out of Poland, she'd probably have nothing to do with him. He should've never kissed her. He shouldn't want to try again.

"Times come when there is nic—nothing you can do." Czelusniak stepped to the corner of the desk and sank into a wooden chair. "Not of yourself." His folded fist rested on the desk. "You must give them to *Bóg*."

Tension spiked across David's shoulders. While he'd prayed for them, *giving* them to God sounded too much like allowing them to die, letting God take them home. David wasn't ready to give them up.

"You believe in God, *no*?"

"Tak." Yes, he believed. But trust was another matter, though he hated to acknowledge it. David didn't doubt that God could do amazing things in people's lives and answer prayers. . .just not his. Too many of *his* prayers had been ignored. Prayers that he could swim faster. That Ben would take a breath. Prayers that his family would forgive him. Prayers to stop failing.

"You will see. You have no control. Can do nothing. *Tylko Bóg powyżej*." Pan Czelusniak's weathered hand reached over and patted David's before the old man stood and hobbled out of the room.

Only God above?

David glanced at the plain ceiling, specked with fly droppings and strands of dusty webs. God seemed woefully far away right now. But the man was right. With bombs daily pummeling the city and the Germans closing in, God was the only one with any power to save.

The echo of the air raid continued in the distance.

David glanced to the door to be certain he was alone and then slipped to his knees. Hands clasped on the chair, he tipped his head forward and cleared his throat.

"Oh Lord. . ." The awkwardness settled around him. He hardly remembered the last time he'd knelt to pray or when he'd truly begged for anything. "I know You don't think much of me. I don't deserve Your consideration or help, but I'm not praying for my own skin. That baby, Arek. And Krys and Bieta. They are young and innocent. I want them to live, Lord. And Nadia." His eyes burned and he gritted his teeth. "I'll do whatever it takes to get them safely away from here, but I *need* help. Even if I don't make it. I don't care anymore." Yes, he wanted to go home someday, to see his family. He'd love to watch these kids grow, to introduce them to America, make sure they had good lives—help them forget everything they'd seen and lost. And Nadia. . .

An image of her smiling, her crystal-blue eyes sparkling as they had when they danced, sucked the breath from him and made his chest hurt.

He only saw her frown now, her eyes shadowed with pain. He wished he could see her happy.

A pang struck his chest with more force and the truth he wished he could ignore—he wished he could make her happy.

The floor creaked, and he jerked up, searching the doorway for an interloper. Nothing. Emptiness. Spreading through him. He hastily ended his prayer and pushed back to his feet feeling more defeated than when he'd begun.

———— ≈ ————

Nadia leaned against the wall beside the door, hoping she remained unseen. The sight of David kneeling, uttering a quiet prayer for the sake of the children, and even her, burned into her mind, promising never to be forgotten. Oh, that she had the faith to truly petition God. To truly believe He existed, never mind cared.

Nadia stole one last glance at David as he pushed to his feet and settled into the chair. She tiptoed away, grateful for her stocking feet, as she hadn't wanted to wake the children while she checked on David. Her intent was to encourage him back downstairs until the air raid ceased—a mission she had abandoned for the time being. She did not want him to think she had overheard him, and the planes seemed more distant now.

She slipped back down the stairs to the cellar—again. Almost enough to make a person feel like a ground squirrel or mole. Could God really be a part of all this—or did He simply sit back and entertain Himself with the doings of His creations? If so, she was not sure she wanted anything to do with Him.

Arek squirmed on the mattress where she had tucked him be-side Elżbieta—or Bieta. She liked the pet names David had chosen for the girls and the easy way he played with them. It was hard not to feel a little jealous. Not for his attention but over wishing her father had engaged with her in such a manner. She had tried for so long to please him, to convince him to really see her, and to not be so disappointed that she was not an heir to carry on the family lineage. But no. He had found his joy elsewhere. And she had finally given up.

Nadia scooped up the baby and jostled him back to sleep. How could a parent not love and treasure any child they received? Arek was not even her baby, and already her heart ached with love. So how could her mother hold her constantly at arm's length? How could her father's affection be so hard to gain? Was she simply undesirable?

Now that she had lost Tata's journal, she would never know. Her eyes watered, but she blinked them clear. Someday she would let herself drown in the pain, but not now with the children watching, needing her to be strong.

Footsteps on the stairs fortified her resolve, and she swiped at the remaining moisture. Then turned as David poked his head into the small room. He gave the sleeping girls a quick glance and seemed to relax. "Just stretching my legs and wanted to make sure everything is good here."

Good? How did that fit at all in this situation? But Nadia managed a smile. The children were safe and, despite their nightmares, seemed to be coping. They had food and did not have to risk standing in breadlines yet.

And they had each other.

"Yes, we are good. And you? Did you sleep at all?" Probably not much, judging from the darkness under his eyes and droop in his shoulders. "Any news?"

"I spoke with your father's contact at the *Times*. He might be interested to see my photographs but will get back to us on whether he can help us." David shrugged, but there was a stiffness in the motion. "I should go back. I don't want to leave the radio for too long."

"Tak, but you will come down when the. . ." She glanced at the girls, who stirred. "When bombers come close?"

"Yeah. Sure."

He didn't sound very convincing.

"I need you to be here," she said softly, wishing she did not have to voice her fears.

A brow rose. "You're safer down here whether or not I am. And it's not like the Germans are taking many breaks today."

No, the raids seemed almost constant. And every time she heard them, she worried about him—she could not help it. Nadia motioned to the girls. "I cannot do this without you." The words sank through her, the depth of them startling. She needed him. And not just to get them safely away from here.

⊒ CHAPTER 16 ⊑

September 11, 1939

The city had become a maze of antitank fortifications and barricades, making movement difficult. David skirted a handful of Polish soldiers arguing. He caught snippets about the German advance into the suburban communities of Warsaw. Even without almost constant air raids, the low rumble of battle echoed from the southwest. Not that there was much pause in the planes swarming the skies overhead. Yesterday he'd taken to marking each raid, a small tally with a broken pencil as he waited for word from London. By nightfall David had counted seventeen. Pan Czelusniak reported this morning that his contacts in the army had counted upward of seventy planes throughout the day before—the Sabbath day.

"Please, let there be word," he mumbled under his breath at the sight of a crude graveyard forming on an open patch of dirt that had probably served as a park or garden. It was impossible to tell with the mounds of dirt and new holes being dug. Several bodies waited for their rest.

He gripped the small bottle of milk he'd been able to trade for and quickened his pace. Nadia had planned to go, but David had encouraged her to sit by the radio instead. Not safe but better than risking the streets.

A shout went up, a man waving his arms frantically for any who would listen. Something about the Germans. Very close, if David understood correctly. But how close? How much time did they have left? David made his way past the building where Nadia and the girls waited for him and walked due west through the already war-worn street. Refugees from the countryside and suburbs continued to flow, moving deeper into the city with what they could carry.

Only a couple of blocks from the edge of the city, David decided to scale a pile of stone into a bombed-out residence, through the open wall, and up mostly intact stairs to the third floor. He didn't have to find a window because most of the western wall had been removed by fire. The floor creaked as he put his weight on it, so he shifted toward the eastern wall and made his way slower. Most of the support timbers had been completely incinerated or at least weakened by the flames. Just enough remained that he could get a decent view of the west part of the city and its suburbs—or what remained after a week and a half of bombardments.

The horizon was strewn with the returning army—no, it wasn't brown they wore but tones of green and gray. And tanks, rolling between buildings, down streets in endless lines.

"Oh, Lord, now what?" David gritted his teeth while panic crawled up his spine. He had to get back to Nadia and the kids, had to get them away from here with or without help from London. They would hike to the Lithuanian border on foot if that was their only option.

He scaled down the ruins, less cautious than before, scrambling over the piles of brick and rock with hardly any thought to the milk bottle in his jacket pocket. As soon as he hit the ground, David sprinted past every other obstacle in his way, whether it be a person, military vehicle, or rubble.

When he burst through the door of the apartment, Nadia jerked to her feet. "What has happened?"

"The Germans are in the suburbs but barely held at bay." He leaned over a chair to catch his breath. "We can't wait any longer. I'll try England one last time while you gather the children." He maneuvered past her and dropped into the chair beside the radio.

Nadia shifted out of his way. "They already contacted us. They will send a plane."

Hallelujah. God had given him a second chance. "Where? When?"

Before she could speak, Pan Czelusniak pushed into the room, addressing Nadia in Polish. The conversation pinged back and forth between the two, becoming more adamant with each rebuttal.

"What is he saying?" David interjected, his brain too much of a hum to keep up.

"He will not come with us. He plans to stay here with his wife." Nadia's terse tone suggested she had not yet accepted his answer.

The old man spoke again, this time his voice softer.

"He says he has seen enough war to last a lifetime. He would rather die at the beginning than endure more." She echoed the sorrow. She asked something more, and the old man replied with a nod. She translated. "He wants us to take his daughter-in-law and grandchild with us. His son is in the army, but Pan Czelusniak would like to know his grandchild will survive this."

"None of us are going to survive if we don't leave here now. What did Mr. Kent say?"

Nadia rotated to him, her eyes hooded and her jaw tightening. "Seven o'clock in the morning Warsaw time. On the thirteenth."

That gave them almost two days. "Where is the meeting place?"

"He did not want to give all the information in the same message. He will transmit the location this afternoon." Her eyes mirrored his own fear. "But we do not have that long, do we?"

David shook his head and reached for the handset of the radio. He had to contact them now, get them to give the location. The radio itself, they might be able to take with them, but the battery pack and generator that gave it life were too heavy and large to be transported. Not with the children and supplies also needing to be carried.

But the next fifteen minutes offered no answers except that Thomas Kent had left for a meeting and no one knew when he would return. No one else had the information they needed.

A curse escaped David's mouth before he remembered Nadia, and now the children, huddled behind him, waiting to leave. The booming in the distance grew steadily nearer, but this time it was not accompanied by air-raid sirens, though those were still frequent enough. "I'm sorry," he murmured, both for Nadia's sake and God's. His dependency on the latter grew with each minute.

What now?

"You must go," said Pan Czelusniak, as though hearing his prayer. He continued talking in Polish, but David found it hard to focus on what he said. The old man stood beside his sweet-faced wife, whose pale blue eyes seemed to twinkle despite everything. There was something about the woman that made it hard to look away, harder to walk away and leave them to whatever fate the Germans brought. Perhaps because she reminded him of his own *babka*.

"We will meet his daughter-in-law at their home four blocks east of here. He has given me the address," Nadia supplied after a moment. "He has sent a message to her. And the radio. . ."

The old Pole was still talking.

"He has a friend who may be able to help us. We must take the radio with us. He will provide the directions. But we must go now."

Her words were punctuated by a tremble of the ground and thunderous symphony of explosions.

Nadia leaned against a wall, gathering strength and her breath, while David collected Zoita and Aleksy Czelusniak. They had made good time the first few blocks, but already Bieta's feet dragged and the weight of Arek burned Nadia's arms. She began to have doubts if they would make it across Warsaw, never mind halfway to the Lithuania border as David began to suggest.

Arek fussed, and she bounced him, the movement cinching tight the muscles in her shoulders and neck.

"Will they catch us?" Bieta asked, looking behind. "The Germans?"

"Nie." Nadia touched her cheek, wishing both arms were free to pull the girl into an embrace. "We will not let them. We will go far away. Where there is no more war." Oh, that she could keep that promise.

"I don't want anyone else to die." Bieta's eyes pooled.

"I no want to die," Krys piped in from beside her, not quite coming as high as her sister's shoulder.

"We will keep you both safe."

Bieta stared up at her, hope struggling with the fear in her honey-brown eyes. "That is what Mama and Tata said."

Nadia breathed in resolve. No one would hurt these girls even if it cost her life. Even if she was compelled to take a life. She pictured the German officer who had caused her father's death—it hardly mattered that he had not pulled the trigger. Would she be able to actually kill a man—kill *him* if he threatened them? She wanted to answer yes, but her gut flip-flopped at the thought. Despite the anger and hate. . .

David's return saved Nadia from finding an answer to her own question, never mind Bieta's. At least for now. David gave her a questioning look and then took Arek from her arms despite already carrying a backpack with the radio and other supplies and his camera satchel. He nodded toward a middle-aged woman and her son. The blond-haired boy was probably only a couple years older than Bieta though tall and lean. "This is Aleksy and Zoita, who will be joining us," he provided.

Nadia nodded her greeting, too tired for etiquette. Thankfully, with the backdrop of explosions, no one required anything more, and they were soon trekking along with the flow of bodies toward the center of the city. Zoita led the way, more familiar with the city than the rest of them. Her son followed, then Nadia and the two girls, holding hands in a line. David brought up the tail, Arek in arms until Krys began to whimper her exhaustion.

"Come here, *myszko.*"

The endearment was common enough, but used with English and with David's accent, the word tickled her heart. "Mouse?"

The corner of his mouth tipped up, but he made no reply as he handed the baby into her waiting arms. He lifted Krys onto his shoulders. Her thin arms wrapped his neck while her chin rested on the top of his head.

It felt as though they had walked an hour or more when a group of planes roared toward their area of the city and they took shelter in the closest building—or half of one, the top already gone.

"At least we won't be a target," he said with a half smile directed toward Bieta. He lifted Krys down and opened an arm to the older girl as well. She climbed into his embrace.

Almost used to the pounding overhead and the strangers taking shelter with them, Nadia took the time to rest her feet and feed Arek. She sat on the floor but could not help but steal glances at David, who placed a child on each knee, distracting them with English words. Crate. Wood. Shelves. Spider.

Nadia cringed and focused on the baby with his full cheeks and the perfect dimples on his knuckles. His dark hair stuck out from the small cap she had positioned on his head. He smiled with perfect innocence, no concept of what was happening around them. All he knew was warmth and love. Oh, to own such naiveté! No sense of loss. No tears for what was left behind. Only the present moment.

A smile, slight and strained, and for Arek alone. She clicked her tongue and he giggled. Her heart melted.

Someone moved beside her, and she glanced to David and the look of wonder in his rich brown eyes. Half Jewish but a Christian. An American with Polish roots. Strong. Radiating warmth. How she wished she could hold to that and forget everything else. Forget her lineage and the expectations that had been engraved into her brain. Forget who she had been raised to be. What did it matter anymore with her father and mother gone and the lone goal to flee Poland?

"My babka used to call me that." David kept his gaze on the baby. "Her myszko."

"I can see why."

His head snapped up, and she fought to bite back a smile at his expression. "You think I look like a mouse or simply smell like one?"

"Well, if I were speaking straight from the bridge. . ."

"Being honest?"

She nodded. "It is the way you scurry around. Really quite impressive."

He chuckled, and Arek echoed with a throaty laugh.

"At least someone is happy," David said, reaching to tickle under Arek's chin. The baby ducked his chin and laughed again, drawing the same from Nadia. The girls shifted closer, and Krys smiled.

Happy?

Nadia's brain protested. How could one be happy in the middle of such horror and fear? The city was literally crumbling around them, and their chance at safety dwindled with each passing day. Yet the smile pulled at her mouth as a deeper joy infused her soul in a way it never had before, even when surrounded with every comfort. She was no longer lonely. She was wanted and loved. She had a purpose. And in a way, yes, she was happy.

⬗ CHAPTER 17 ⬗

"And now?" Nadia whispered, not wanting the children to think too much on her words.

David blew out his breath, his head shaking at the empty house—miraculously still intact. It wasn't shelter they needed. "I wish I could say I was thinking of a solution and not stuck on those same two words." He offered a half smile, but she had never seen his eyes more somber.

"We cannot stay here. Not with the Germans so close."

"I know. It won't take long before they either plow through or surround us. We need to leave Warsaw tonight." His smile flattened into a grim line.

"And the radio? We still do not know where to meet them."

He pulled Bieta to his side, his arm around her shoulder, careful of her bandaging. "We'll head toward Lithuania. Maybe some of the towns along the way will still have electricity or a generator. We can only pray we're headed in the right direction and have time to meet the plane. If not. . ."

"If not, we figure something out?" She did not mean to say it as a question, but she could not take it back.

"Yep." He gave a firm nod. "Can you explain things to Zoita?"

"You do not want to? I heard you with the girls. Your Polish is improving." She allowed for a hint of a smile.

His reappeared, a little wider than before, making the effort worth it. "Yet it will always be inferior to yours."

"As is your English."

A chuckle.

Nadia savored the warmth in her center, though turned away to address the older woman.

She tried to hold to the warmth as they headed toward the north-eastern borders of the city, but the mounds of rubble and the looks of desperation or destitution on the faces of her fellow Poles drew it from her. Pain radiated through her feet, growing with each step. Her arms felt numb with exhaustion from carrying her precious bundle. Hope slipped from her at the thought of the two hundred miles between here and safety.

Unless they could contact London again.

Please, God, let us find power for the radio. She closed her eyes for a moment, feeling the plea deep in her heart. If only God would hear. If only she had more confidence of His existence. But the frequent worship at a grand church near her ancestral estate had not really been about God or worship at all. Only appearances and social expectations. She wished for David's faith. . .his hope.

"We might as well keep walking. Try to make it beyond the city tonight." David motioned for Zoita to continue.

"One moment." The woman stepped to Nadia, the kindness in her eyes startling. They were strangers, with years separating them. "That is no way to carry a baby. Not for any length of time." Zoita pulled a scarf from her shoulders and wrapped it around Arek and then Nadia, fastening the child snug against her and removing the weight from her arms and shoulders. Blessed relief.

"Dziękuję." Nadia hoped her eyes conveyed her gratitude. Not long ago, she would not have thought to thank someone like Zoita for such a simple offering. It would have been expected. But rank and birth seemed nothing now. Only the flesh and bones of very fragile lives.

Their small group continued toward the northeast of the city. Street after street they walked, the crowds diminishing the farther east they traveled. Some streets were mostly intact, with only a house or two demolished. Others had nearly burned to the ground. It did not seem to matter what area of the city, upper class or lower—the Germans apparently were no respecter of Poles and wanted them all to suffer.

Zoita came to a stop, and Nadia lifted her eyes to the bridge crossing the Vistula River. Or what remained of it. Part of the center had been struck, collapsing the main structure. Enough remained that people were making their way across on foot in single file, but that required sitting to slide down a length of wood to the collapsed section, and then scaling up the far side.

Nadia glanced at David to find him watching her. "Wait here. I'll cross with Bieta first and then come back for Krys. When they are across, I'll help you with the baby."

Zoita turned to them. "I help," she said in English before switching to Polish. "I will help you with the children." She reached for Krys, who pulled back and clung to David.

"Bieta, you go with Pani Czelusniak," Nadia directed. "We will all be with you."

The older girl looked to David for confirmation, and he gave a nod, apparently following the discussion. "I'll be right there," he offered. *"Nie przejmuj się."*

Nadia looked up, and he offered a slight smile, as though repeating the admonition not to worry. David set out with Krys first, Aleksy on their heels. Zoita moved slower with Bieta's hand in hers. When they reached the drop, David slid down and then held out his arms for Krys to jump down to him. Once Aleksy joined them, David waved the two children to go a little farther while he waited to catch Bieta. He gave Zoita a hand down and then looked to where Aleksy already pushed Krys up to the last portion of the bridge. Bieta and Zoita soon joined them on the far side. David remained in place, his gaze now on Nadia. He waved for her to join him, so she started out across the bridge.

Nadia braced Arek with one hand, needing to be certain he was secure against her, while her other ran across a length of railing. She glanced down to the rushing water as it struck the collapsed portion of the bridge before rushing under and around. Her pulse sped. What if she lost her footing or the bridge gave way? She could not swim with a baby.

"Nie przejmuj się," David called.

"You are only saying that because you do not know how to say anything else!" she shouted back over the rush of the river.

"Maybe. I have heard that phrase a lot this week."

"A poor argument for telling me not to worry."

"Przykro mi."

"At least your accent has improved," she teased, grateful for a momentary distraction from her fears.

"You should have heard me try to speak when I first arrived. I have learned a lot in a few months."

"You may speak like a native one day." She was close now, almost to the drop.

"I would like that. But I would require a patient tutor." He reached up and gripped her hand.

Her gaze froze on his as she tried to read the question written in the dark depths and in the creases between his eyes.

Could you ever care for me?

Nie, that could not be the question. Just her imagination reflecting her own thoughts.

She dropped into his arms, and he steadied her onto her feet, the baby tucked between them. *Could you ever truly care for me?* Heat infused her cheeks. What if he could read her thoughts easier than she read his? Stupid, stupid thought. There was no time for this. The middle of a war was neither the time nor the place to explore the stew of emotions churning within. And this was not the man to allow into her heart. She could already hear Matka's lectures.

Not that her mother's opinion mattered anymore. It might be satisfying to encourage the relationship just to spite her mother.

Nadia inwardly chuckled but then noted the intensity of David's gaze as he studied her—probably wondering why she had not pulled away. She jerked back and tried to step past him, but her foot did not follow, snagging on a broken plank. With no railing to break her fall, she dropped sideways. David's hands grabbed for her, his fingers brushing hers before the water closed around her. The cool water swirled, dragging her down.

Arek!

She had to get above water—had to save the baby.

A pressure spread around her waist and propelled her upward. Her head broke the surface before she realized David was beside her, water running down his face. Nadia grabbed on to the edge of the bridge as David tugged Arek free from his bundle and pushed him against his own shoulder. A high-pitched scream penetrated Nadia's panic. He was alive. He was breathing.

Sirens wailed.

A low hum moved across the skies.

"Nie, nie, nie. Not now."

David gripped the bridge beside her, and she followed his gaze to where the girls waited for them at the end of the crossing. They vanished a second later, hopefully finding cover.

"Trzymaj się."

Her head snapped to David. "Let go? This is not the time to practice your Polish."

"Do you really think it's the time and place to nitpick?"

"I do not know what that means!"

An explosion behind them turned both their heads. The roar of a bomber swooping low. Nadia ducked, though there was nowhere to go. The popping of gunfire rattled the bridge. Someone screamed in pain. From the west shore. But all she could think of was her little girls up there somewhere. Surely God would not have protected them before only to kill them now.

The thought sent dread through her like none she had experienced. She needed to know that her girls were safe—she needed to see them. Now.

She pulled herself over the edge of the bridge, kicking against the water to gain momentum. Only to be dragged back into the river.

She tried to squirm away from David. "Let me go."

"There are more coming. We have to stay low."

At his words, three planes roared toward them, growing nearer, lowering with each passing second.

"Let go of the bridge."

She felt David's hand on her arm, caught the look of determination in his eyes. She released her hold on the bridge, and in a single motion he swept her under the shelter of the slope she had just slid down, and her feet touched something solid under the water. A strong arm wrapped her, securing her in place beside him. His warmth seeped into her despite the coolness of the water embracing them.

The planes thundered past, dropping their bombs over the city, their destructive symphony almost familiar now. The horrid guns peppered the ground surrounding the bridge. She closed her eyes and saw her girls in the darkness. Saw them hurting, bleeding, needing her. The need to scream swelled painfully in her throat. David's arm wrapped over her shoulders as he pressed Arek between them, as though trying to cocoon them both. If only he could offer any real protection. But in reality, he was just as mortal and prone to death as any of them.

≡ CHAPTER 18 ≡

David had never struggled so hard to let go. Even with Nadia tucked up on dry land and sheltered by the massive concrete slab of bridge slopped down into the water, he felt his muscles constricting in their need to provide more protection. Fear, red and hot, burned in his gut.

"There are still planes." Nadia had Arek tucked against her, though he still cried. "Where are you going?"

"I need to know the girls are okay." He held her gaze a moment longer, sensing the same need in her. "I'll be careful."

This time she offered a short nod, and he turned and dove into the river. The fallen bridge acted much like a dam and slowed the current, but an undertow held strength. He tried to keep his body on the surface while swimming hard, driven by the need to hold his girls, know they were safe. The image of their faces drove adrenaline through his veins, strengthening his arms. Still, it seemed far too long before the shore came within reach, and he pulled himself onto the bank.

With the sky rumbling, David stayed close to the cover of the bridge in case a low-flying bomber returned with another round of gunfire. The dirt and rock shifted under his feet, and he grabbed handfuls of grass to pull himself upward. Finally, he reached the top and searched the area for the girls and Aleksy and Zoita. He caught sight of something blue in a nearby stand of trees on the other side of the road. Zoita's dress.

He scanned the skies before darting across the open area separating them. His breath was short by the time he reached where Zoita huddled with the two girls and her son, like a mother hen and her chicks. Bieta ran to him, hitting him with enough force to hurt. Her good arm wrapped around his waist and her shoulders began to shake. Abruptly her head jerked up, eyes wide.

"Where?" The single English word spoke all her fears.

He combed his fingers over her hair. "Nadia and Arek are hiding under the bridge."

Her body relaxed the smallest amount before Krys crashed into them with her arms wide. David stooped low, and her arms wrapped his neck, choking him. Yet at the same time, he felt he could finally breathe.

An explosion behind them vibrated through the ground under their feet. David twisted. Iron groaned. Concrete rained down in chunks. The bridge. The bridge had been hit again. The blood drained from his head, making his brain fog up.

"No." The word left him on its own accord, as did the air from his lungs. Not Nadia. Not Arek. He had left them behind to protect them—not to sentence them to death.

Do you still think you have any power over life and death?

He couldn't even answer the question lingering in the back of his mind. He tried to pry Krys' arms from his neck, but she clung tightly. "I need to go get the others, Myszko. You have to stay here. Stay safe. *Czy pan rozumie?*"

Bieta nodded solemnly, her hands moving to her sister's shoulders. Krys said nothing but eased her hold. Tears glistened in the girls' eyes. David glanced to Zoita, who already gathered the girls in her arms. He managed a nod and then spun back to the bridge, this time hardly glancing upward as he sprinted back across the open terrain. Two bodies lay near the far end of the bridge, which had collapsed into the river.

"No, no, no."

Nadia couldn't still be under there, crushed.

David jumped down to the lower length of bridge and sprinted across, choking on dust and stumbling over chunks of concrete and twisted iron. He lunged sideways at the end, dropping into water up to his waist. Before pushing through it, he looked up and froze at the sight of the most beautiful woman he had ever seen, crouched against the fallen section of bridge, as though it could protect her. A heavy layer of dust covered every inch of her and the baby tucked against her chest, and a black smudge stood out against the pale skin on her chin, but she was alive.

For a moment, he couldn't release his last breath, and it burned in his lungs. He trudged the final distance through the heavy water, then up the bank where she stood to meet him. His arms acted on their own, pulling her and the baby against him until he could finally manage to fill his lungs again. A tremble moved through him, and a numbing pain spread across his sinuses.

Another plane rushed overhead, and he found the presence of mind to crouch with her against the side of the bridge. "I shouldn't have left you."

"What would you have done? Been crushed with us?" Nadia searched his gaze and he looked away. "The bridge missed us by inches. It did not collapse at once when the bomb struck. It started to let go, and I was able to get out from under."

David was unprepared for the strength of the gratitude that poured through his veins. *Thank You, Lord.* Nevertheless, the thought of what could have been left him ill. "I should have taken you with me. I almost killed you."

"It would not have been your fault, David. You cannot control everything. We could just have easily been shot crossing the bridge with you."

He clenched his jaw, not allowing himself to accept her words, even if they were meant to comfort. They didn't. They made him weak and powerless, and he refused to accept that.

"The girls?"

"Safe with Zoita." He managed the words and forced his brain forward, to solve the next problem, to make a plan. Really, there was nothing they could do but huddle here until it was safe to cross again. He focused on the skies, which seemed remarkably calm now. A low hum in the distance but nothing close, nothing moving toward them. "Let's go."

He pushed her onto the bridge and pulled himself up. As they made their way across the more damaged part, he kept a hand on her arm. Only a few steps brought them to where he had shrugged off his satchel and the bag holding the radio before diving in the river after Nadia. The soft leather satchel appeared undamaged, and he hooked it over his shoulder. He would have to check the camera once they were across.

"Oh, David."

He glanced to where Nadia stood over a block of concrete that had broken free during the explosion and crashed down over the radio. David shoved the boulder aside, but he didn't bother with the bag or any of its contents—crushed beyond repair. He shifted his gaze to Nadia and her stricken expression. Again, he had failed her.

When they reached the trees, the girls ran to meet them with cries and vice-like grasps, as though they would never let go. Right now, David was fine with that. He needed them close—needed everyone close. He lowered onto the ground so he could better hold the girls. He couldn't afford to lose any of them. Not just because of duty or promises made but because of a deeper feeling filling his whole being. He loved these girls and that baby. And Nadia. He'd never felt anything so frightening in all his life.

You'll fail them.

"David."

You'll get them killed.

This is why he had avoided giving his heart away in the past. It was too much of a risk.

"David, take the baby." Nadia lowered to her knees beside him, her face pale under the dust.

He maneuvered his arms free from the girls so he could reach for Arek, still wet from their swim. Zoita met him with her scarf, wrapping the child in its warmth. David was hardly aware of her motions, his focus on Nadia as she tugged at the edge of her blouse. "What's wrong?"

Instead of answering, she freed her shirt from the hold of her soaked skirt and drew it up to her lower ribs, turning enough for him to see an angry welt the width of his hand and twice as long. Already shades of blue and purple marred her skin.

"What happened?"

"I may have not made it as clear from the bridge as I said. A beam caught me as it fell." She shivered, whether from pain, the realization of how close she came to being crushed, or the chill of her damp clothes.

"Come here." He opened an arm while the girls shifted to make room for Nadia. She lay down and rested her head on his leg. The girls curled around her, cuddling into him. He relaxed Arek into the crook of his arm, the baby quieting in his warm cocoon. They all seemed to crave a moment to pause, rest, and hold on to each other.

———————≈———————

Nadia awoke slowly to soft light and shades of pink in the quiet sky and the distant hum of voices. She was a little cool, damp in places, but no longer as soaking wet as she had been when she settled beside David and closed her eyes. She slowly withdrew her arms from around Krys, who had cuddled in at some point. Only then did Nadia become aware of the heavy hand against her shoulder. She looked up into David's face, the shadows deepening the worry etched around his eyes.

"We need to keep going."

"Tak. Of course." They could not spend the night out here without even blankets to warm them from the chill creeping into the evening air.

As she sat, a sharp pain bit her ribs. She gasped for what little air her lungs would accept.

"You all right?"

"I will be fine." She straightened, more conscious of her injured side. Any other situation, she would have ordered a doctor to be summoned while she remained in bed to recover. Instead, she steeled herself against the discomfort and reached for Arek.

"I'll carry him," David said, keeping the baby under his jacket. He shifted and shook the girls awake. They groaned but quickly rose, looking about to see how much the world had changed since they'd fallen asleep.

Zoita and her son joined them, their bundles already slung over their shoulders. Nadia felt a pang of regret. Other than David's camera satchel, they had lost everything. Because of her.

"We can't stay in this city another day." David looked toward the sinking sun. "Or another night."

"Where will we go? How—"

"We'll walk. All the way to England if we have to."

"A little difficult with the English Channel to consider."

The corner of his mouth twitched in a weary, almost rueful smile. "Men have walked on water before."

Nadia groaned. "We are not quite so holy or divine."

David stood in place, as though actually considering her comment.

Two crevasses deepened between his eyes, which stared at nothing. He appeared. . .broken.

Then he spoke, his voice low and almost resigned. "You're right. I can't do this on my own." He glanced down at the girls, his hand brushing Bieta's hair back from her face before cradling her cheek. "There is no way we will survive this without a miracle. And I would be an ungrateful fool not to acknowledge the ones God has already given us." David glanced at Nadia. Though there was nothing condemning in his gaze, that is what she felt.

She shifted, as though she could step away from the sensation. "We best start walking."

Something akin to relief flashed across David's face. Perhaps he had braced for more argument. But he was right. They couldn't stay. They would figure out the rest as they went. Maybe God would have mercy on them and help them find another radio. Or perhaps they would have a long journey ahead of them. As long as they could stay ahead of the Germans—something becoming more difficult with each day.

≣ CHAPTER 19 ≣

September 12, 1939

The axle creaked a steady rhythm as the small cart dragged along a dark road. They had left Warsaw hours ago, and Nadia held on to the edge of the cart, in part to help push, but mostly to keep herself from crumpling to the ground in a pile of sleep. They had found the cart abandoned near the bridge, probably by someone bound for the far side of the river. A miracle? Because of David, she analyzed everything now, wondering what was from God or if everything was simply coincidence.

Nadia shook her head. As exhausted as she was, how could she expect to understand the workings of a God she did not know? Sleep beckoned her, and she allowed her eyes to close for a minute. Oh, to fall into silken sheets and bury her face in the downy softness of her pillow back home.

She stumbled over something—perhaps her own feet—and focused again on David's back and putting one foot in front of the other. The girls were wrapped around each other in the cart, Arek in the center, all fast asleep. A relief from the miles she had walked with the baby strapped to her. The muscles in her shoulders still ached, as did the welt across her ribs. The understatement of the year. Her whole body ached! She had never experienced such exquisite and painful fatigue.

"What was that?" Zoita whispered from beside her. Her son walked behind them, his feet dragging with each step.

"What?" Nadia straightened, listening to the sounds of the night.

A low growl shifted into a howl, rising from the darkness to their left. The cart rolled to a halt.

"You don't have wolves out here, do you?" David redirected the small torch, or flashlight as David called it, that Zoita had provided. A puddle of light spilled against the bushes several yards away.

"I hope not." Nadia felt her thoughts clear as her fingers tingled with sudden adrenaline. The light shifted until it glinted against two eyes growing green against black. Feet bounded toward them. She wanted to scream, but it caught in her throat.

Th-thump, th-thump, it raced toward them. Should not a wolf fear the light?

David stepped between the cart and the animal, momentarily blocking her view of the glowing eyes. The light wavered while his hand yanked something from his jacket the same instant the animal lunged. A revolver's discharge cracked in her ears as the light flew from his hand, tumbling into the grass.

"David!" Nadia darted toward the flashlight, needing to see what was happening.

David stumbled back, then dropped low.

One of the girls cried out, and Arek wailed.

"Easy boy, easy boy," David crooned, and Nadia jerked the light in his direction, where he knelt beside a hairy beast with a long tongue and heavy pant.

"A dog," Aleksy breathed, echoing Nadia's relief. She leaned over the side of the cart to hush the girls and baby back to sleep.

"What is a dog doing out here?"

"Probably protecting his home," David replied with a strained laugh.

She disagreed that there was anything humorous in the situation. The animal had given her a fright and roused the children. She would chase the wretched hound away and curse its existence if she had the energy. Thankfully, the children quieted to low whimpers.

"There's probably a farm nearby." David scratched the dog's head and asked it where its home was.

"You really believe that dog understands your English?" Nadia snapped before she registered how ridiculous she sounded. But with David's brows arched at her, she could not back down. "Fine, boy," she said in Polish. "Where is your home?"

The dog yipped and spun back the way he had come, taking off at a jog.

David's brows rose even higher. "It appears you're correct about his preference of Polish." He shoved to his feet and started after the animal. "I'm going to see where he leads. Maybe there's a place for us to pause for the night and get some rest."

Just the word *rest* incited such a yearning in her. Nadia moved to the cart's handle and waved for Zoita to assist. Aleksy leaned into the back, and the cart rolled forward, off the road, trailing David and the dog. Only a few steps confirmed that they were not going across country but had turned off onto a beaten path wide enough for a wagon. Perhaps a farm was nearby after all. With how dark the night was, they were only feet from the small house before they saw it, heavy curtains blocking any light from slipping through the windows. David followed the dog to the door and knocked.

A moment later, the door cracked open. "*Kto tam?*" a young man demanded, holding up a candle, hand cupped to shield the flame.

Nadia pulled Arek from the cart and hurried forward. "We are fleeing Warsaw and hoped to find a place to rest for the night."

"It's already halfway to morning," the dark-haired youth stated, peering past her to Zoita and the children who sleepily peeked their heads above the sides of the cart.

"We are exhausted. Especially the children," Nadia replied, unable not to plead their case. The longer they stood there, the more her eyes burned.

"Wait here." The youth disappeared, and the door slapped closed behind him.

And wait they did.

Nadia closed her eyes and felt herself lean against David's side. A warm arm slid around her, bracing her. It may have been only a few minutes, but it felt much longer before the hinges announced the boy's return. Only it was not him, but a woman in a nightgown, wool shawl around her shoulders. She looked at their small group and waved them inside.

"My own children are asleep in their beds, but I have sent Binjamin for extra quilts. You may stretch out on the floor for what is left of the night."

"Thank you." Zoita was the first to reply, moving past with Krys on her hip. The girl was mostly limp in her arms, limbs hanging loose, head lulled in sleep. David brought up the rear with Bieta, who was a little more conscious but quickly settled on a quilt at his side. Krys woke just enough to curl up with her head on his other shoulder. Their hostess laid another blanket over them before making up a place for Zoita and her son, and finally Nadia.

"You are so kind," Nadia whispered, not wishing to wake anyone else in the small house. Tears swam in her eyes. Maybe because of the woman's generosity. Maybe because she was simply too depleted.

The woman's eyes settled on her, the candle flickering in them. "Sleep now. The morning will be here soon."

Nadia sank to the floor beside Krys and tucked a sleeping Arek to her chest. The room soon slipped back into darkness. A door clicked, signaling that the woman and her son had returned to their rooms.

Never had a floor felt so welcoming. "Thank You," she whispered toward the ceiling above. Her words might never reach farther, but they felt warranted.

———— ≈ ————

David awoke to tingling pain in his fingers and a moan from beside him. He slipped his arm free from Krys' hold and rotated to comfort Bieta—but she lay peaceful on his other shoulder, while Nadia's breathing came in short gasps. Her head rolled from one side to the other, the low morning light enough to show the pinch between her eyes and grimace of her expression. Thankfully, Arek remained asleep a few inches from her, but that probably wouldn't last long with the storm brewing beside him.

Slipping free of Bieta and the quilt covering them, David maneuvered to Nadia's other side. He knelt and gave her a little shake. Her eyes shot open, as did her mouth with the start of a scream.

David clasped his hand over her mouth, cutting off the sound, but her panic-filled eyes stared up at him. She blinked, and the panic was replaced by relief and a gasp for air. He pulled his hand back as a tremble moved through her body.

"It's okay now," he whispered to her. "You're okay."

She shook her head, squeaking with a muffled sob. "You were dead. They shot you. I saw them shoot you just as they did Tata. They were going to kill us all. One at a time." Tears rolled down her face, and David slid onto his side beside her, his hand returning to her shoulder. Nadia pushed past his meager offer of comfort, her arms wrapping him, her head pressing to his chest. "You are alive," she trembled against him.

"Yes, we're safe." For now, at least, but even his pulse quickened at the imagery of her dream.

"I do not want you to die," she mumbled against his shirt.

"I appreciate that," he whispered in return.

She pulled back, looking up at his face. "I do not—I am not in jest. How many people have lost their lives in the past week? My own father." A tear rolled across the bridge of her nose, angling across her cheek. "Death has surrounded us."

"But we made it out. We'll make it to Lithuania. And then to England."

"We hope."

He wanted to argue, to convince her that nothing could stop them, but reality was not so certain. "We hope."

Nadia started to lower her head back to the floor, so he maneuvered his arm to provide a pillow. She relaxed against him, but he could still sense the lingering tension in her body.

"What do you think it is like to die?" she whispered.

David's chest tightened around his heart, but that probably didn't account for the ache growing in his center. "I'm going to get you away from here. I promised, remember?"

"Maybe. Maybe not." Her head shook. "But sooner or later we all meet death. Like my father. But then what? Is it black and cold, or nothingness? Is it an end? Or something more?" Nadia shifted to look at him, her face inches from his. Her eyes large and searching. Her mouth pursed. Strands of blond lay like lace over her cheek.

He moistened his own lips and struggled to focus his thoughts back on her questions. Death. What did he really believe about death? "I don't think death is the end." He had considered the possibility as a youth, but it was too bleak an outlook. To believe that his cousin, grandparents, and other people he loved simply ceased to exist—that there would never be a chance to see them again, to speak with them, to apologize? He closed his eyes to better focus on something other than the woman whose breath warmed his neck. "When I imagine death. . ." David searched his mind and heart for the right words. "I imagine a beginning."

"A beginning?"

He didn't dare glance at her for fear of losing the images in his head. "I imagine death is like stepping into a warm embrace. Like walking through a doorway away from pain and hurt into the waiting arms of those who are already gone. Family. Friends. Jesus. . ."

The painting of Christ that hung in his parents' home smiled at him from his memories, and warmth spread throughout his entire being with a strange tingling feeling. Not painful like the nerve pain of waking up with a child sleeping on your arm, but pleasant.

"You really do believe in God? In Jesus?"

He nodded, clinging to the feeling of belonging and hope beyond the fear of this world. "I do. I believe in Christ." The feeling intensified. "That He lived. That He suffered for our wrongs. . ."

I do.

The two words burned through him, making it hard to breathe. But how could he fight against the truth of it any longer? Jesus had suffered for every misstep, every sin. Every careless decision that had brought pain to others. Jesus had atoned. Why keep pushing Him away?

"David?"

David rolled onto his back, keeping his eyes closed so she wouldn't see the tears pressing behind his lids. "I would like to think that death is stepping into our Savior's arms. That He is waiting there, in that moment, for us." He choked on the last few words and was grateful he didn't need to manage more than a whisper.

"I hope you are right." Nadia sighed beside him. "It makes losing my tata easier, picturing that the other side of death is not so bad. And those people, all those people who have been slaughtered in the bombings and the advance of the Germans, to picture that each one of them simply stepped through a veil into the embraces of loved ones. . ."

Arek whimpered, warning that he was waking and growing uncomfortable. The weight left David's arm as Nadia rolled back to the baby. He remained in place, clinging to the lingering feelings he'd experienced. The words he'd heard in his heart repeating still.

I do forgive you.

I do wait for you.

I do have a work for you to do.

Help me not to fail, Lord, David silently prayed with growing resolve.

Because if he was right about death, why try to avoid it at the cost of a greater good?

He opened his eyes and looked to where Nadia climbed to her bare feet with baby in arms. That would be his one regret if he died—not having more time with her. Because he would do everything in his power to make sure she didn't follow him through that veil. He still needed her to live.

☰CHAPTER 20☰

Stepping into an embrace.

The thought would not leave Nadia as she tipped the bottle so Arek could drink the last of the milk David had brought. Uncertainty of where and when they would find more milk for the baby gnawed at her. She had never wanted for anything in her life, had never experienced this fear, especially on someone else's behalf. A baby could not subsist long without milk.

Stepping into an embrace.

Nadia shoved the thought away. She had more pressing matters than comprehending the afterlife. Life itself stacked a list of demands she needed to focus on solving. Diapers were also in short supply since their incident at the river. The baby wore a makeshift one now that had been saturated during the night, and the spare desperately needed a wash. She cringed at the thought but would make it a priority as soon as the child was fed.

A bedroom door creaked open, and the woman of the house swept through to the kitchen, dark hair twisted into a tight bun on the back of her head, a kind smile on her round face. "*Dzien dobry,*" she whispered, casting a glance at the sleeping children. David had stepped outside, and Zoita lay awake beside her son, probably questioning if it would have been better to remain in Warsaw.

"Dzien dobry," Nadia returned the greeting. She set the empty bottle aside and shifted Arek away from her just enough to keep his moist pants from soaking her as well. "Thank you for allowing us to stay the night.

I do not know how we would have kept going."

"Of course, of course. You are very welcome." Though the beginning of wrinkles showed when she smiled, in the morning light she appeared a little younger than Zoita, perhaps in her late thirties. I hope you will break your fast with us before you continue your journey. And your baby." She looked from the empty bottle to Nadia. "You were not able to feed him?"

"He had some milk this morning, but. . ." Nadia's explanation died as understanding struck. "Oh, you mean. . . Nie. He is not mine. He *was* not mine. His parents are dead."

Compassion touched the woman's light brown eyes, and she stepped near. "Oh, poor child. You are good to care for him."

"I do my best." Nadia shifted him in her arms as he grew heavier with each minute. "I do not know much about babies."

Dark eyebrows rose, and she opened her arms. "May I?"

"Of course." Nadia released Arek to her, immediately feeling both relief and apprehension.

"Oh, what a fine boy. With such a wet bottom. Have you no clean diapers?"

"We lost what we had."

"Not to worry," she crooned to the baby. "I have plenty to spare." She slipped from the room, Arek in arms. Nadia moved to follow, then thought better of it and forced herself to sit. The woman seemed to have a kind heart, and she would not be gone far. Nadia looked around as the morning sun spread through the room, chasing shadows. A small tapestry of grapevines and flowers hung over a shelf holding an assortment of candles, but the writing was not Polish or any language she recognized. Children's coats, not a few, hung from hooks near the door. A cream-colored shawl hung separate, dark stripes and tassels setting it apart from the fashions usually seen in Poland. A book on the corner of the table confirmed her growing suspicions—the Tanakh, Hebrew scripture.

The woman returned, Arek relaxed in her arms, his clothes and the small blanket surrounding him as fresh as the diaper. "Here he is, dry and happy." She made no move to return the baby to Nadia. "I noticed something that made me wonder. Are you Jewish?"

Nadia's jaw loosened a moment before she caught herself. "Nie. Not

I. But you are correct—Arek is. And you are."

The woman nodded, eyes thoughtful before a cry called from the bedroom. She seemed to hesitate but handed Arek back to Nadia and hurried away. While she was gone, Bieta woke and climbed onto the nearest chair and leaned sleepily into her arm. Zoita stood next and took a couple minutes assessing the small house and kitchen before Aleksy started toward the doorway and she accompanied him outside.

Only Krys remained asleep until the woman reappeared with a toddler on her hip and sent out a call for her family to awake. Two boys in their teens climbed down from the loft, followed by a girl about Bieta's age. Everyone stared shyly at each other across the table.

"Binjamin you met last night," the mother said, motioning to the oldest boy, who was only a year or two before manhood. "The others are Aszer and Cyna."

"We are pleased to meet you all and grateful for your hospitality, are we not Bieta?" Nadia quickly offered their names, including David, who was still outside somewhere, and Krys, who pushed onto the chair beside her sister. "Forgive me if you introduced yourself last night, but I cannot recall."

"Ah, I probably forgot. I am Frajda, and this happy boy is Efraim."

Three younger children came together, two girls and a boy from the second bedroom, and Frajda offered more introductions. Gisja and Hesia, who could pass as twins with their cherub faces and dark eyes, if not for the couple inches of difference in height. Hewel, probably Krys' age but twice as stocky, hung from his matka's skirts until she asked Cyna to take him to the outhouse and then dress him for the day.

The kitchen was soon filled with chatter and giggles as children came and went from dressing and their chores. Cyna helped her mother with breakfast while the younger girls entertained the littlest two boys with spoons and blocks on the floor. When Zoita returned, she made herself useful starting a fire in the stove and mixing batter. Nadia felt helpless, but she had not been raised into this life. Thankfully, Arek gave her an excuse to sit and soak up everything surrounding her.

The home was small and simple—especially compared to the grand Roenne manor, but Nadia would have happily given that up for siblings who nudged her and whispered in her ear, bringing her to laughter. For a mother who did not hesitate to give praise or an arm around her shoulders.

Nadia looked around. Something was missing from such perfection. "Where is your husband?"

Frajda looked up from the stack of plates she had set on the table and swatted at a strand of hair that had escaped her bun. "Ira had an accident about a year ago. He never recovered." Though she spoke in vague terms, something in her eyes declared that she knew each day that had passed and each minute too.

"I'm sorry." Nadia's heart had learned the pain of loss, but perhaps the other woman's pain was deeper. And what a burden to be left with. Seven children and the managing of this farm. Yet Frajda appeared happy and optimistic despite it all.

Despite the war crawling in their direction.

Nadia opened her mouth to ask her what she knew of the invasion and the bombing of Warsaw—even now the low rumble sounded like thunder in the south. High-pitched giggling erupted from the youngest two boys, their sisters attacking them with wiggling fingers. Nadia pressed her lips together, her gaze shifting to Krys, who sat so still, as though made of stone, yet eyes yearning to engage in such frivolity, to remember how to not be afraid.

David stepped into the house, and all eyes turned to him. He simply pressed his mouth into a tight smile and shifted a chair beside Krys, who quickly abandoned her chair for his lap. Bieta followed suit, nestling against him.

Stepping into an embrace.

Nadia redirected her attention so that David would not notice the red likely accompanying the heat creeping upward through her face at the thought of their conversation—and how tightly she had clung to his side. How much she had wished he would kiss her again.

Soon conversation faded into hurried eating. Tension radiated from David, reminding her of the need to continue their journey toward Lithuania. He finished first and set the girls back on the chair, a kiss pressed onto each head before he began packing their few belongings back into the cart. Frajda followed him with a collection of blankets, diapers, and a bottle of milk.

Nadia watched from the house, relief and gratitude weakening her resolve to walk away with only a thank-you. A new urgency grew within her—to save this family, this love and laughter she so envied. She handed Arek to Zoita and made her way to their hostess.

"I must speak with you." Nadia slipped her arm through Frajda's and led her toward the barn and whatever seclusion it would offer. "I cannot leave here without—"

"You needn't say anything. I will take him and love him as my own. He will be raised in his faith. I was about to wean Efraim, so there will be plenty of milk for another."

"What? No." The protest escaped Nadia before the logic settled in.

"Oh." Red infused the woman's face. "I just assumed, because he was not your own and you aren't even Jewish. You have no husband." She glanced back to the cart and the gathering. "Unless you and your American have plans."

"There is nothing between us." It almost felt a lie after the intimacy of that morning and the kiss they had shared not quite a week earlier. "But I promised his mother I would care for him."

"Would not leaving him here fulfill that promise? He would be cared for and loved and have a family."

Exactly what any mother would want for her child under normal circumstances. "It will not be safe here. The Germans are already at Warsaw. They have been bombing the city for almost two weeks, shooting at civilians and soldiers alike. They will be here in a matter of days. You cannot remain here with your children with no protection. You will not be safe. Especially since—" Nadia bit her tongue. The woman had already lost all color.

"We have heard them in the distance, but I couldn't be certain what was happening. We are not so close to our neighbors—they look down on us because. . ." She shrugged, her head shaking.

"Because you are Jewish?"

Her jaw tightened, and she folded her arms across her stomach.

"That is why you must listen to me. David is certain the Germans have plans against your people. They already hate Poles, but it may be worse for your family."

"A woman and children?"

"Your oldest son is hardly a child anymore."

Frajda hugged herself as though suddenly chilled. "What can I do? Everything we have, our needs for daily life, are here. This farm is everything to us and all we have left of my Ira. Nie, we will stay here and trust to not gain any attention. We are a small farm far from other settlements. Warsaw is their focus. The cities," she said with more confidence. Or perhaps she simply tried to convince herself. "All will be well."

"You could come with us." Nadia laid a hand on Frajda's arm, needing her to truly listen. "We were supposed to meet a plane before our radio was destroyed, but we will make our way to Lithuania. I have family there who can help us reach England."

"England! I have nothing there. No one." Frajda looked more panicked than convinced. "I cannot drag seven children by foot to Lithuania, never mind start a new life in a land so foreign as England. We do not even speak English."

"But you would be alive. Your children would be safe!"

Frajda shook her head. "I thank you for trying to help us, but we are better off here, in our home."

The fight slipped away, leaving only a sense of dread for what awaited this perfect family. "Very well." Nadia started back toward the cart. The morning was almost spent, and they needed more miles between them and Warsaw.

"*Czekać.* The radio. What kind of radio do you need?"

Nadia glanced back. "One strong enough to talk to someone in London."

"My husband has a radio, but I don't know how well it works. He made it himself, a hobby of sorts." She motioned for Nadia to follow before disappearing into the barn.

"David!" Nadia caught his attention before following. His footsteps pounded after her, and he reached them at the foot of a ladder to the loft. Nadia waved for him to lead the way. There was a small pile of new hay, and at the far end, under a small window stood a makeshift desk with equipment on top. A wire ran up through the roof.

"You have electricity here?"

Frajda's laugh was tinged with longing. "My Ira insisted on it when we had the line put to the house. This was his space, somewhere to get away from the noise of the children, to escape for a few minutes. It should all still work."

David maneuvered past and sat on the handmade chair, his hands not quite steady as he set up the radio and dusted off the receiver. A moment later, static buzzed in their ears. Nadia held her breath as more adjustments were made and he began his callout for the *Times*.

"Can you hear me?"

The static sharpened, then faded. "Yes. Who is this?"

David glanced back at Nadia, a grin spreading across his face. "This is David Reid. I need to speak with Thomas Kent."

"He's not in the office at this time."

"No. I need information from him. It can't wait. Lives depend on it."

"Reid, you said?"

"Yes. Is there anyone else who might know—"

"Hold." The voice disappeared, and the static grew louder, scratching against Nadia's nerves.

"We don't have time for this," David grumbled, voicing Nadia's thoughts. They had less than twenty hours before the rendezvous and still no idea how far or in what direction they needed to go.

"Mister Reid, are you there?" A new voice cut through the buzz in their ears.

David jerked the handset back to his mouth. "Yes. Yes, I'm here."

"Mister Kent left a message when he was unable to reach you earlier." The man began listing groupings of numbers and degrees of longitude and latitude, and David scrambled to grab a nearby paper and pencil with blunt lead. "You already have the time?"

"Yes, but another day would help. I'm not sure we can make it so far."

"I'm afraid the arrangements cannot be changed. Even the slightest. If you cannot make the rendezvous in time, we would rather not go through the expense."

Nadia hugged herself, a sudden chill catching her off guard. There was something about the man's voice, as though he had no care for the lives at stake, the children's lives.

"We'll be there." David's tone was firm. He clicked off the radio and dropped the handset. A rumble in the distance deepened the chill. David turned, grim-faced. "I need a map."

Nadia quickly translated, and Frajda stepped past and began shuffling through the desk's drawers. David grabbed a folded sheet from her hand and spread it out beside the radio. "Where are we?"

Nadia moved to his other side to better see his finger slip down a line of longitude. His other hand traced latitude until he'd pinpointed a location between two villages—to the west. Toward the Germans' advance.

≡ CHAPTER 21 ≡

Again the sun dipped below the horizon, a stunning array of pinks and blues against a patchwork of clouds, as though Mother Nature had no concern for their plight or the plight of so many Poles. David couldn't help but wonder how many had died today and why the skies weren't painted red or black instead. He leaned forward, his grip on the cart painful after hours of dragging the thing up hills and over rough patches of road. But rest was far from his mind. He'd rest in London when these children and Nadia were safe. Because one thing he was certain of—the death count was at its beginning. He didn't want to imagine what the future held for this land.

The *tat-tat* of machine gun fire slowed his steps.

"No plane," Nadia whispered beside him.

He nodded. They knew the sound well enough, but before there had always been planes overhead. Now the skies were silent. "Ground troops." He searched the western horizon, but little was visible thanks to the glow of the sun. Only a chimney of smoke rose from over what appeared to be a village. As the skies darkened, a glow became more evident. From the lights or the houses? No, one area seemed brighter and covered a larger space than any lamp. Or even a bonfire.

"We should stop." Nadia set her hand on his arm, drawing his gaze. She glanced to the children nestled together in the cart. The girls watched them, probably curious about why they had paused.

"We can't afford to stop."

She turned away from the children and lowered her voice. "What if the meeting place is in the middle of the German troops?"

"I've been worrying the same thing every step of the way here. And it looks like that might be a possibility. But we're so close. Tomorrow morning we might be on our way away from here, and the children will be safe. The other option is hundreds of miles of uncertainty."

"But maybe fewer Germans," Nadia murmured.

"Yeah." David blew out his breath. At least it would be dark soon. If they traveled quietly, they would probably see the Germans long before they were seen. But what if he was wrong and he led them to their deaths? He'd been mistaken before. "It's your call. Skirt the village and continue carefully to the rendezvous? Or turn around and try a different route?"

A groan rose in her throat. "It's not fair to put it on me. I might choose poorly."

"Better you than me," he quipped.

She shoved her elbow into his ribs. "Maybe we should vote."

He offered a stiff shrug, not wanting to commit. "You speak with Zoita and tell me what you decide."

Nadia stepped away without another word. She slipped her arm through the older woman's and led her from the listening ears of the children. Their prolonged discussions sharpened the edge on his nerves. Now that he had put the decision in Nadia's hands, he wanted to argue for continuing their course. They were so close. If they could avoid the Germans—as a small group, how hard could it be?—and meet the plane, this nightmare could be over by the end of tomorrow. Safe in London twenty-four hours from now.

He tensed as the women returned. Nadia set her jaw, while Zoita's eyes held more uncertainty. Perhaps some fear.

"Which way do we head?" He tried not to sound resigned, holding his arguments at bay.

"West."

The air whooshed from his lungs. "Good." He couldn't completely contain his relief. Twenty-four hours to England. Any other option was too painful to contemplate. "Let's go."

He took up the handles of the cart and leaned forward. His leg and arm muscles ached from the miles already crossed. Exhaustion clawed at him, taunting with despair and whispers to pause for a little while and rest. There was no time for that. One more night of torture would be worth the reward of leaving Poland for good.

Headed west, they crawled through the evening, keeping distance between themselves and the village he'd identified on the map. As the sun set, the glow of the town rose from the darkness as though the flame of a candle in the distance. Periodically, gunfire or artillery broke through the otherwise peaceful evening. But really, the peacefulness was fiction, and David braced for whatever lay over each consecutive rise or around the next turn in their path. He wished he had time to scout ahead and make certain the way was clear, but there was no time. And less strength.

Nadia groaned behind him, disgust in the tone. His next inhale brought understanding. A stench. Smoke tinged with something horrible. Thankfully, the light wind swept it away. A moment later, he felt Nadia at his side. "Do you think they have set the village on fire?" she whispered.

David looked to the glow on the horizon. "Not the whole village, I don't think. At least not yet." But who knew if that was the fate of every town and village the Germans had swept over? Did anything remain of western Poland? And what of the people?

"I wish we knew."

"I know." But what choice did they have but to keep walking, to ignore all else?

Nadia's hand gripped above his elbow, and she leaned into his arm. "What's out there, hidden in the dark?"

An army. Hundreds of tanks. Death.

They continued walking, each step a labor and the night growing quieter with each passing hour. The heavy breathing of the children asleep in the cart and the creak of the axle were soon all he heard. Gradually the pressure on his arm grew heavier, making each step forward more difficult. He glanced at the woman whose head rested against his shoulder. Her eyes were closed, her steps dragging beside his own.

David allowed his feet to pause, and Nadia startled from her sleep. "I'm impressed," he whispered.

"Co? *Gdzie?*" Her eyelids fluttered, and she hid a yawn behind her hand—no longer on his arm.

"I don't think I've ever met anyone who could sleep while walking."

She pushed into him with her shoulder, what probably would have been an irritated nudge if she'd had any strength in her limbs. He lowered the cart and reached to steady her. Her whole body slumped against his.

"I have never been so exhausted. I would give anything for a bed."

"Soon. Soon we will be in England, and you can sleep for days."

"I will need to."

He steadied her on her feet and pulled the map from his pocket. He crouched down to shine the flashlight over the paper, shielding the light with his body so it would be less visible to anyone nearby. "If only I could figure out where we are, but it's so dark."

Nadia sank down beside him, her finger moving across the map. "We are past this village, no?"

"Yes."

"And this river?"

"Not yet, but we are probably close."

"We must be close. It will surely only take us another hour or so to reach the plane." She fingered the marked meeting place. "Might we miss it if we continue in the dark, half asleep?"

"I'm pretty sure you were all the way asleep." He couldn't help the chuckle that somehow found its way to his throat.

Her eyes narrowed, but she didn't argue. "Can we stop for even a short while?"

The need to make sure they made it in time sank under the logic of her request. If they pushed too far tonight, they might get turned around and have farther to go in the morning. If they slept till dawn, they could travel quicker and with more confidence.

"All right. Lie down and get some sleep. Heaven knows how long we have before Arek needs something."

Nadia moaned as she sank to the ground, her head finding David's knee. He adjusted to better serve as a pillow and leaned against the cart for support. He set the flashlight to hold the map in place and closed his eyes. They burned painfully for a few moments before relief finally came. His mind immediately slipped from location and time to the weight of the head on his leg and the silky hair woven between his fingers.

September 13, 1939

Nadia woke with a start and a sharp pain in her scalp. She lowered her head back to her makeshift pillow and eased David's fingers from her hair. A sigh slipped from his mouth, but he did not wake. His head leaned over his arm, braced against the side of the cart. She filled her lungs but remained in place, looking up at the man who had risked and sacrificed so much to save her. The dim glow of approaching dawn showed little detail, but she had already memorized everything about him. He had become her strength to keep trying, keep going. He had become her hope that they would succeed in their plight. Somehow, he had even managed to stir faith within her—or at least the desire to believe in a loving Father, a kind Savior, and a hope of more after life was stolen away.

David stirred, and she reluctantly pushed into a sitting position and stretched her arms. They protested with zinging pain along stiff muscles. Arek was often unsatisfied with riding in the cart, and her arms and shoulders had not yet become accustomed to the extra burden. He began a whimpering protest. Perhaps he was the cause of her waking.

An image of a body stretched out in the dirt drove the thought from her. Her dream—or nightmare—returned in flashes of terror, turning her stomach inside out. The bleeding body was a boy, one of Frajda's sons. Their house burned behind her. Panic shortened Nadia's breath. What had happened to the rest of the family?

"Nadia?" David's voice snatched at her racing thoughts, and she twisted to look at him. "Are you okay?"

"Of course." She started to stand, and David moved to assist.

"*Dzięki*," she whispered.

He nodded and found his feet, though his brow pinched with concern. "Just a bad dream."

Another nod, and a hard look at his watch. "It's already half past five. Can you feed him while we walk?" He straightened the satchel over his shoulder—so much a part of him how.

"Of course." She poured the last of the milk from the farm into the bottle and tucked it under her shirt to hopefully warm it a little while she changed Arek's wet diaper. Two clean ones remained from the stash Frajda had provided. If London was not in their near future, they would be dependent on the generosity of another farm.

We have to make it.

Nadia pulled Arek into her arms as the clicking of a shutter pulled her around. David hid behind his camera, only the hint of a smile visible. No, not quite a smile. The camera clicked again, and she forced a glare. "I am sure I look horrible. You are wasting your film."

"Not a waste." David lowered the camera momentarily and stepped to the edge of the cart. The shutter flashed as he captured the two girls, arms and legs twisted around each other, Krys' head on Bieta's chest. Still fast asleep.

"I can't believe how strong they have been. And so young." An ache rose in Nadia's chest. "I feel so weak by comparison." There was so much she wanted to complain about, so much to protest. She had been raised to be an elegant lady, not a peasant or nursemaid or governess or pilgrim. If she had gone with her mother, she would have slept under downy quilts last night in her grandparents' grand home. Her stomach would be filled, with every craving satisfied—not grumbling and pinching at the slightest thought of the half loaf they had saved.

But what would have become of these three children?

What would become of those they left behind?

"I'll be back in a minute," David said, his camera again tucked into the bag. He started out toward a thicket, and she turned her body fully away to allow him complete privacy. Arek, however, had soiled his diaper, and Nadia cringed at the smell rising from his pants. No wonder her mother had adopted a hands-off approach to parenting. While Nadia understood why a lady would not wish to inflict her sensitivities to diaper changing, nothing compared to the joy of holding a baby close, soothing his fears and discomforts.

Joy? Again, the thought of happiness was so out of place amid so much torment.

"Must we wake the children?" Zoita asked in a soft voice, stepping near. Her hand settled on Nadia's shoulder while she offered a smile to the babe.

"Not yet. It will be another long day." But hopefully the last. Nadia hurried with Arek to keep his protesting to a minimum—though it seemed to have little effect on the exhausted girls. The milk was not quite warm but not as cool by the time she slipped the nipple into the baby's mouth. Arek's protests merged into grunts and hungry smacks against the rubber. She cradled him close and brushed his fuzzy hair on the top of his head. Oh, what a handsome boy. But what would his life be like once they reached London? She had not allowed herself to truly consider until now, but they were so close. Hope bubbled up within her.

"Gdzie, Pan David?"

Nadia looked at Zoita and her look of concern. "He stepped into the bushes for a moment."

"But he is not yet returned?"

Nadia stole a quick glance to where he had disappeared. Arek had almost finished his breakfast. Zoita was right. David had been gone longer than usual. Longer than he should. Unless something was wrong with him. It was not as though she could go hunting for him.

She quickly shifted her thoughts back to matters at hand. "I am sure he will return soon. Let us prepare something to have ready for when the children awake." The sun was almost breaching the horizon. David would want to hurry when he returned.

If he returns.

The thought startled her, and she shoved it away. Of course David would return. He had only slipped away for a few minutes. There was no sign of Germans nearby. Most of the world still slept, the sky dim as the sun warmed the colors along the horizon.

Footsteps behind her relaxed her shoulders. Finally.

She turned and jerked, startling Arek from his bottle. He whimpered in protest, and Nadia found the presence of mind to replace the rubber nipple in his mouth before finding her voice. "David?"

He gave a tight smile—nothing was happy in his expression. In fact, he looked an odd sort of ashen gray as he led a young woman, perhaps more girl than woman, holding a toddler of two or three.

"Where did they come from?"

"The village." His voice was not quite steady. His hand trembled as he set it on the girl's arm and directed her toward the cart. Nadia started to ask more, but he shook his head. "Not now." He glanced to the cart and the wide eyes peering over the side. Krys and Bieta took in the newcomers with the open curiosity Nadia shared.

David gripped Nadia's hand as he came alongside her. "We need to leave."

She managed a nod and hurried to gather the blanket she had used for Arek. Bieta took the baby eagerly, her eyes still on the other girl and her young brother. Nadia offered to take the toddler from the girl, but her head trembled with a shake, and she clung tighter to the boy who protested at his sister's hold.

"She won't hurt you." David spoke in Polish, though with a heavy accent.

Nadia set her hands on the girl's arms and waited until she raised her gaze. "We will help you. And keep you safe."

A tremor moved through the girl's body as she fell forward into Nadia's arms, as though her legs had suddenly given up. The trembling turned to sobs and pained murmurs, with an accent of her own. Yiddish. The girl was Jewish. Nadia looked to David for answers but was again met by the subtle shake of his head, as though whatever happened was too horrible to voice.

⹐CHAPTER 22⹑

David quickened the pace with yet another glance at his watch. Thirty-five minutes. But they were close. They had to be. He had never been so determined to leave Poland—and that was saying a lot. He replayed the girl's words over in his head, hoping to find that he had misunderstood.

Nadia's arm brushed his as she came alongside. "What are you hiding? What did she tell you?"

He glanced back at the young woman still clinging to her little brother, not willing to be parted from him, and shook his head.

"No one else will understand if we are speaking in English." Nadia huffed a breath. "Did you even understand her correctly?"

"I understood enough. Too much. I understand better than I speak."

She sighed. "I can understand that."

"I suppose so. You speak a dozen languages."

"Only half a dozen," she murmured beside him, hitching Arek higher against her shoulder. Somehow he had already succumbed to the steady pace and slipped back asleep. "But you are correct—there are those I understand much better than I speak."

"Like which?" A much safer conversation and a distraction from his own thoughts.

"Italian. Even French to a certain extent." She glared at him. "But that is not what we are discussing. I need to know."

"No, you don't."

"David!" Despite the frustration in her voice, her hand slipped around his arm and gave a gentle squeeze. He met her gaze and felt his defenses falter. But oh, how he wanted to protect her. "What happened to her family?"

"Nazis." He wanted to spit to clear the bitterness from his mouth. "Hitler's *Mien Kampf* enacted upon the world's supposed nemesis but with cruelty I never imagined possible. Not in our modern era. People should know better. It's not the Dark Ages. I don't get it." Pain spiked through his gut, making him want to hurl. If there was anything in his stomach, he may have.

"The story of Poland," she whispered beside him.

"What?"

"Poland. In the last two hundred years, we have only been truly independent for twenty. Invasion. War. Our borders constantly changing, being rewritten. My father's true pride is the fact that somehow our family remained intact, even kept possession of some of our ancestral lands despite it all."

Until now. She broke off speaking, but his mind finished her thought.

"What did they do in that village?"

He wanted to groan. He'd hoped she had forgotten. The trees thickened ahead, and he no longer felt safe following the road. They had made it this far. He lowered the cart's handles to the ground and turned to help Krys out. Bieta already walked alongside. Their eyes widened.

"We have arrived?" Bieta questioned.

"Almost," Nadia answered for him. She looked to him as though to test her understanding. "We will go on foot from here? Leave the cart?"

"Tak." He checked the map to make sure. Through these trees and across a stream, and they should be there. Just in time. Krys hugged his neck, and he held her small body against him, then took Bieta's hand and turned into the thicket.

Nadia stayed at his side. The girl and her brother close behind. Zoita and her son bringing up the rear.

"You were saying?"

There would be no avoiding it. "They ordered every Jew and some of their neighbors into the synagogue." He lowered his voice, though no one else should understand his words. He held tighter to his girls.

All color drained from Nadia's face. "They did not. . .They did not shoot them?"

"No."

The furrow of puzzling through his riddles smoothed as her eyes widened. Her feet faltered. Her voice barely rose above a whisper. "The fires."

"We need to keep walking." He nudged her forward with his shoulder. "We need to get these children away from here."

Nadia pressed her mouth to Arek's head. "How did they escape?"

"I don't know. I don't know if she'll even be ready to talk about it for a while." *If ever.* And it was suddenly hard to picture all those men, women, and children slipping from their lives into God's waiting arms. But oh, how he tried. He had to believe that God was still in control, that He had purposes, reasons, goodness, and the power to save.

They walked in silence for a few more minutes before a rumbling sound filtered through the trees. David pushed into a jog. The clearing was just ahead. He could see the thinning trees. And just beyond—

"Stop. Przestań! Quickly." David hit his knees with enough force to bruise, but he hardly felt it. He set Krys on the ground and pressed a finger to her lips. He squeezed Bieta's hand and looked to Nadia. "Keep everyone quiet. I'll be right back."

"David." She peered past him, trying to see beyond the summer-laden branches.

"Germans," he whispered, the word shattering any hope he'd clung to. He would have to find a way to signal the plane to leave without them. He slipped away from the small group. Three women and five children. How would he keep them safe long enough to escape the country? The weight of the task pressed over him as he crept toward the enemy.

A fallen log near the edge of the grove added some cover, and he crouched behind. A road ran perpendicular to his position, with the stream just beyond and an open field to the left—the rendezvous. He'd leap for joy if not for a lone jeep parked farther up the road and the three German soldiers headed in his direction.

David slunk back into the trees, keeping low and moving slowly. The Germans couldn't have their coordinates or they would be parked closer to the field. Unless they purposefully laid a trap. No, how would they know the timing? It had to be a coincidence. Either way, he had to figure out how to warn the plane away. . .or get rid of the Germans.

Except they were armed, and he only had a simple revolver with a couple shots left.

Nadia crouched with Arek held tight, Bieta and Krys pressed to her sides. Zoita and her son sat just beyond, eyes expectant. The young woman and her little brother huddled together, rocking, trembling. Faces still stained with soot.

Warmth slipped into his hand, and he looked to Nadia, her large eyes swirling with fear and questioning. Her lips pursed as though to mask the depth of that fear.

"There aren't many," he heard himself whisper. "I need you to wait. In ten minutes, if everything is clear, get yourselves across the road to the open field." He pointed in the direction they needed to go while his brain shuffled through every scenario. How easily things could go south. How easy it was to fail.

Nadia shook her head. "No," she mouthed.

He leaned his head against hers, temple to temple, and pressed his mouth against her ear. "I will be fine as long as I know you are safe," he breathed. "I need you to be safe."

She turned her head, and the warmth of her lips moved over his for the briefest moment before she drew away and peered up.

All he could offer was a half smile. If that. He might never see her again. He'd probably never know if they made it.

"Please," her eyes filled. "We can make it to the border."

"No, we can't. Not with the children. It's too far. Too much is at risk." He pulled his camera bag from over his head and hooked it over Nadia's neck. "Give the film to Mr. Kent like we agreed. Maybe it'll make a difference." David could only pray that it would—that someone would come to Poland's aid. He brushed his hand over Krys' hair and managed a smile for Bieta. His moment for redemption had come. He'd not fail this time.

Though he wasn't sure how to succeed either.

The regret of never truly kissing Nadia nagged his thoughts—the last thing that should be on his mind, but a man about to face death should be granted some allowance, shouldn't he? David turned back to her and sank his fingers into her hair. Her lips met his halfway with a force he'd not expected but eagerly returned. There was no time to tell her how hard he'd fallen for her, how much he admired her, wanted her, loved her. No time to thank her for listening to him ramble about things he didn't quite understand or tell her how much she'd helped him find himself. No words to express this twisting sensation in his heart and how much he didn't want to die, if only because he wanted to kiss her like this again someday. But if he did die today, at least he'd go without regrets. He'd done what he could. The rest would be up to God.

The murmur of German voices pulled them apart.

A too brief meeting of their gazes. A squeeze of her hand. Their silent goodbye.

Trying his best to come up with a plan and not get lost in remembering Nadia's kiss, David made his way along the road to where the German jeep sat empty. Easy enough to get in and drive away, but he needed the Germans to go with him. A distraction would be a start. Filling his lungs, hopefully not for the last time, David straightened and walked toward the jeep.

I have no idea what I'm doing, Lord. But please help it work.

With each step, he waited for a shot to ring out. These were the ones dropping bombs on civilians, opening machine gun fire on families, burning churches filled with worshippers.

A shout rang out in German, and the pounding of boots headed his direction—away from Nadia and the others. David stretched his hands over his head.

A shot rang near his ear, and he dropped low, thankfully behind cover of the jeep.

"Please! I am American." It would probably help more if he could yell it in German, but that was a lot worse than his Polish. "American!"

Boots circled the jeep and rifles pinned him to the ground. "*Amerikaner?*"

"*Ja, ja.*" At least he knew that word. He had somehow ended up on his back, staring up the polished barrels of two rifles. Splotches appeared before his eyes, and he had to remind himself to take a breath.

"A spy?" one of the soldiers questioned, his English heavy but understandable.

Hallelujah!

"*Nien*. A student. I am a photographer." The closer he kept to the truth, the easier the sell.

The one seemed to translate for the other, who asked another question. A translation was provided. "Where is your camera?"

"I traded it for food and transportation—though not as far as I thought apparently. I'm trying to go home." David pushed to his knees, hands still raised. "We are not enemies—our countries are not at war."

The Germans seemed to discuss that, allowing David time to find his feet.

"Please take me to your commander. I came from Warsaw. Maybe I have information that might help." Though not likely anything they didn't already know even if they hadn't overrun the city.

They spoke back and forth while patting down his clothes for any weapon he might be hiding. "Where are your papers? Your visa?"

"I. . ." A curse slipped from his mouth before he could stop it—not the best move when needing God on your side. His identification had been the last thing on his mind when he'd handed over his camera bag. All he could think of was the images he'd captured and how badly they needed to be seen. "Stolen," he muttered, curbing his tongue this time. "I can explain more to your commander. Is your army far?" Not that he wanted to throw himself into an anthill swarming with Nazis, but self-preservation was not his goal. What other German words did he know? "*Bitte.*" Hopefully he'd pronounced *please* correctly.

He was pushed into the back of the jeep, and the others climbed in, only one gun trained on him since he was unarmed, the pistol also tucked safely away in the camera bag. He wished he could consider it an improvement to his situation, but as the engine roared to life, he braced himself for leaving the safety of the frying pan. What inferno awaited him?

☰CHAPTER 23☰

Oh, please, keep him alive. Nadia wasn't sure if it was a mantra or a prayer or a little of both, but she couldn't help the repeated plea from silently bleeding from her heart. She had never felt like this for anyone—other than Tata. Yet her feelings for David were decidedly different than the ones she had for her father, the kiss they had shared still burning on her lips and in her chest. *Oh, please, keep him alive.*

Ten minutes. Ten minutes had passed and there was no sign of more Germans. Nadia squeezed Bieta's hand, trying to give her a reassuring look before bracing Arek and finding her feet. Her legs protested at first, numb after crouching for so long. She looked to Zoita, whose eyes glistened. The older woman wiped at her cheeks, and Nadia swallowed hard against another surge of emotion. *Oh, please, keep him alive.*

"We need to go."

Zoita nodded and set a hand on her son's back, encouraging him to move. Even the youth's eyes were large, as though still reconciling with what he had just seen—David freely giving himself over to the enemy. For them. There were no tears in the younger woman's eyes. She knelt in silence, a slight sway betraying emotions too strong to be fully expressed. Zoita encouraged her forward.

A soft rumble was heard overhead. A plane.

Uncertainty twinged Nadia's nerves, igniting them. Was it their salvation or the enemy ready to cut them down as soon as they stepped onto the road or open field? She moved toward the edge of the treed area, eyes raised to the skies. If only David were still here to move forward with decisiveness and a better understanding of aircraft than her.

"Wait here," she whispered to those who followed her, whose lives were suddenly fully in her hands. The weight settled onto her shoulders—was this what David had felt? Poor man.

Please, keep him alive.

Keep us alive too.

The rumble grew louder, the plane nearing. She glanced back at her small party. "I'll go across and make sure all is safe."

Krys and Bieta both cinched themselves to her sides, and even Zoita took a step forward.

"I'll be right back," she tried to assure them.

The plane was almost over them now, and she spun to the field. Would the pilot even land if no one was there? Or would he assume they had not arrived in time? He would not stay long with Germans so close.

She felt herself duck, curling her body over Arek, the popping of machine guns replaying in her mind. But there was no other sound than the engine as it changed pitches and the plane dropped lower, swinging a circle toward the open field. It had to be the British.

"Come!" She rushed forward, not allowing herself to consider any dangers that might still lurk nearby. Over the road and through the field, tall grass grabbed at her ankles. The small plane was rolling to a stop. They had made it in time. They would soon be safe. Why, then, did her stomach twist and her heart pound so painfully?

The pilot appeared at the side of the plane, pulling the hatch-like door inside. Relief showed on his face, and he waved them forward. "Lady Roenne?" He looked past her. "Where is Reid?"

"The Germans." She gulped for a breath. "He did not make it." She yanked the camera bag from around her neck and thrust it up to the pilot. "Here is the film he promised the *Times.*"

The man took the bag but didn't say anything. He seemed hesitant. Perhaps trying to process what she had told him. After a moment, he seemed to come to his senses and extended a hand. "Let's get you all loaded and be on our way."

Nadia handed him the crying baby, not what he had expected from the look on his face. But he retained hold while Nadia boosted Bieta inside. Thankfully, the girl had the presence of mind to relieve the pilot of the baby, though probably more for Arek's sake than the man's. Krys went in next, followed by Aleksy and Zoita, who hurried to settle the children into place. The young woman hesitated several feet back, her brother clasped to her.

"It will be all right," Nadia said gently, trying not to picture what they had escaped. "You will be safe."

But instead of stepping forward, the girl glanced behind, probably thinking of those they would never see again. Nadia couldn't help but think of the same—for some reason, after David, Frajda and her children were foremost in her thoughts. What would become of them once the Germans made it to their farm? Images from her nightmare flashed across her mind. Along with the sickening sensation, the whisper to her thoughts, that no one in that family would survive the Germans.

"Let's go!" the pilot hollered, and Nadia realized everyone was loaded and waiting for her. It was time to leave Poland.

Her feet remained planted on the ground. She could not leave. Even while looking into the faces of the children who owned her heart. Zoita cradled Arek. She would watch over the girls.

"Zoita, promise me you will keep the children safe."

The woman's eyes stretched wide, but there was a slightest nod.

Nadia switched to English, her focus on the pilot. "I need a paper and something to write with. Quickly!"

"What? There's no time for that. We need to leave."

"Not yet. The photographs. You have the film. They need to be seen."

"What are you doing?" the pilot demanded. "You can't stay here."

"There are people I cannot leave behind." Even if doing so felt like a betrayal of David's efforts to keep her safe. And Tata's final wishes. Neither of them would have to live with what she knew in her heart. She did not know how she knew, but the feeling refused to leave.

And if you die in the process? a silent voice pestered.

There was no time to consider that. She grabbed David's satchel and yanked out the map, a notebook, and pencil. She scribbled a letter for her father's friend. "Take this note to the Earl of Selborne. He will take care of my friends." Nadia cast one last glance at the children and her beloved Arek, and her heart ripped open a little. How would he fare without her? Would he even know the difference of who held his bottle and cuddled him close? If anything happened to her, he would forget her quickly. All the children would. Yet she would carry them in her heart beyond this life. "Thank you for coming for them."

Nadia slid to the ground and jogged away from the plane—again. What was wrong with her? She was supposed to be in London watching all of this unfold at a distance. Not in the middle of it. But somehow it was not about her anymore—not like how her whole life had been up to this point. Maybe it was losing her parents. Maybe it was witnessing the devastation the Nazis had brought. Maybe it was David's faith and courage—that he was even willing to give his life for his friends. Somehow, that was one of the few verses she remembered from years of dutiful attendance at church.

The roar of an engine turned her. The plane jostled over the field, picking up speed until it could lift from the ground and climb steadily toward the clouds. She clamped her jaw against tears, but they slipped down her face. Her legs lost their strength, and she sank into the grass. As her knees struck the ground, the floodgates opened, a sob in her throat. The pain she'd been holding on to so tightly crashed against her resolve with a force she'd never known—could not restrain. The past two weeks rolled through her mind with mocking clarity.

Try to forget me, her memories taunted. Her father bleeding out onto the marble floor. Her mother fleeing with the Nazi officer. The race to Warsaw in the middle of the night. The first plane taking flight while she and David, a stranger to her, remained on the ground. The bombs that fell soon after, the fear like none she'd never experienced before, David's arms offering comfort. Death on the streets of Warsaw and in the maternity hospital. Hiding in cellars, David's constant presence like a fortifying stone, his embrace in a hiding place—as platonic as she had once considered it. Until they had kissed.

Now he was gone with his faith.

Everyone was gone.

This was what it felt like to be truly alone.

Alone with only memories and pain.

CHAPTER 24

The roar of a plane behind them turned the German soldiers toward the small dark speck lowering out of sight. "Vat plane is that?" one demanded.

"How would I know?" It took every ounce of willpower for David to keep his face passive. "Probably one of yours."

The jeep jerked to a stop, and the soldiers argued among themselves, probably about whether to go back or continue on.

David forced his jaw to relax while lifting a silent prayer toward the heavens. He hadn't stopped his silent pleas for Nadia and the children since he'd been loaded into the back of the jeep, the young soldier's rifle aimed at his heart. Thankfully, the soldier no longer rested his finger against the trigger—especially considering how rutted this road was.

The jeep lurched forward, continuing in a southeasterly direction. Back toward Warsaw.

David thought he was done with that city. He sure felt done with it.

But at least they were still headed away from the plane, and at least he was still alive. Maybe he would survive this after all.

Doubts settled into the pit of his stomach as they came around a corner and over a rise. At first, he saw just a few men and vehicles rolling slowly southward. Gradually his vision expanded to the rows and rows of not just soldiers but the tanks that led the way, setting the pace. Thousands. Thousands of Nazis. The same who had burned villages and shot those trying to escape. A grotesque machine of death and pain.

He wished he had his camera.

The German driving the jeep seemed to have a destination in mind, winding through the army, past soldiers on foot and a convoy of eight or nine trucks arriving from due east. The jeep jostled to a stop near a cluster of officers gathered off to the side, where the first of the trucks had stopped, probably to receive further instruction or be unloaded. One of the soldiers jumped from the jeep and jogged to where an older officer stood watching, making comments to the lower officer on his right. After a few words, the officer and all near him turned to where David remained sitting. He managed a tight smile, but all he could think of was the death they had left in their wake. Of Bieta and Krys' family shot down in cold blood because of orders men like these had given. Of that young woman and her little brother barely escaping the horrible death inflicted on their friends and family.

Several uniformed men, including officers, started toward the jeep, and David was ordered by his guard to climb out. He tried to keep his stance casual, to convince them he was a passive civilian and not their enemy—though they were his.

"*Amerikaner?*" the senior officer asked, eyeing him up and down. Clean-shaven, nothing hid the man's leathery skin and deep-set lines. He had spent most of his life frowning. Probably a lifelong soldier, old enough to have commanded in the Great War as well. He spoke rapidly and sternly in German, and David didn't even try to guess what was being said. His mind buzzed with exhaustion and something far too recognizable as fear. One word and he could be shot. Or hurt in any way they desired. Helplessness was not a new sensation but one he'd always despised.

The soldiers who had taken him fired back with quick answers, likely explaining his lack of identification and reasons for being in Poland in the first place. At one point, the officers laughed, not a pleasant sound. Mocking. Irritated. The older officer glanced at the trucks, the first one now empty and looping around toward the west, and gave quick orders. The other men shared glances but sounded affirmative in their replies.

When the officers turned to leave, one of the soldiers from the jeep took David's arm and directed him forward—the one who spoke some English.

"What'd they say?" David fell into step with him.

"They not vant trouble dealing vith you. Vill send to Germany on trucks."

"Why can't I just go? I'll find my own way out of Poland."

"Yet you have no papers, no proof you are vat you say. I do not know if this concerns them, but *I* do not trust you." He nodded toward the second truck being unloaded. "Berlin vill decide."

September 14, 1939

The morning sun crept steadily higher but offered little warmth yet. Nadia hugged herself against the deep chill that had settled into her bones during the night. Or maybe a lack of food and rest over the past twenty-four hours left her depleted. Knowing the Germans were so near, she had tried to travel as far as possible during the night, pausing only for an hour or so when she could no longer walk straight. She hid in a ditch and allowed herself to succumb to a fitful sleep.

Relief weakened her limbs at the sight of the farmhouse in the soft glow of morning. She attempted to quicken her pace, but her legs refused. The cow stood watching from the paddock beside the barn, and a loneliness for Arek tugged at Nadia's heart. She held on to the hope that he was safely in England with the others, with a full stomach and clean diaper. Oh, how he had needed a bath.

Oh, how she needed a bath! Her mother would have a fit if she could see—and smell—her now. Acutely self-conscious as she approached the door, Nadia pulled her hair free from the ribbon she had secured it with, and combed fingers through her tangled tresses. What a disaster. She finally tied her hair at the nape of her neck and tucked her blouse back into her skirt. Then raised her fist to the door. She should not feel so uncertain; she was the daughter of Baron Roenne.

One of the young girls, Gisja, opened the door and grinned, then shouted to her mother to come. No, Nadia was not uncertain about herself but of her ability to convince Frajda and her family to leave everything to follow her to a foreign country.

"Lady Nadia? What has happened?" Frajda's eyes widened. "Did you not make it in time?" She jerked to the side to look past. "Where are

159

the others, the children?"

"They are safe. They should be safely in England by now." Nadia stepped in and closed the door, leaning against it for support. "Except for David. The Germans took him." Voicing it solidified the reality, and her vision swam.

Frajda's hand covered her mouth. "Nie."

The door was no longer sufficient to the task of holding Nadia upright, so she slipped onto the closest chair at the table.

Shocked silence settled into the room, no one else moving from their places near the doorway.

"He was alive last I saw him," Nadia whispered, her throat scratchy and tight. She had no proof that was still true. After all the death the Germans had inflicted over the past couple of weeks, it was easier to imagine them offloading him and putting a bullet in his head. She clamped her eyes closed to keep her tears in place and forced herself to imagine otherwise. David had to be alive. She needed him to be.

"You look exhausted." The compassion in Frajda's voice poked at Nadia's resolve to remain in control of her emotions. The other woman crossed the kitchen and returned with a glass of water and a thick slice of bread, which she placed in front of Nadia. "Why did you not leave with the others?"

Nadia took a long drink before answering. How best to broach the reason for her return? She could not hold back if she were to convince Frajda to come with her. "I could not leave Poland with your family on my conscience."

The woman lowered into the chair across from her, shoulders drawn back with resolve. "We will be well enough off. All will be well."

Nadia's head shook on its own accord. "Nie. Nothing is well out there. You do not understand. The Germans have already. . ." She glanced to the children who had gathered around to listen.

Frajda jerked to her feet and shooed them from the house, placing the older ones in charge of the younger while assigning tasks for each to do. When the door finally closed and the house settled into silence, Frajda returned to her chair.

Nadia did not wait for her to speak. "Your family will not survive what is coming. Do not ask me how I know, but I do. I have never felt anything so strongly—with more conviction. The feeling was so overwhelming, I could not climb onto that plane and leave you and your children to that fate." Tears again clouded her vision and trickled free when she attempted to blink them back. She brushed them away, hating how weak they made her feel. She had been taught to control her emotions, to not show weakness. Perhaps it was the exhaustion. "You must come with me. We will make our way to Lithuania and then to England. When the war is over, you can come home. I will do everything in my power to help you restore your farm."

Frajda pressed a palm to her forehead and murmured something in Yiddish. Perhaps a prayer? "Wars come and go like the seasons. Perhaps we have not known it in our lives, but look at our history and the stories our parents and grandparents tell."

Nadia well knew Poland's history and her own family's precarious position in it. How many times had her family fled in centuries past or struck bargains with the invading force to allow them some degree of privilege and safety? Few of Polish aristocracy had remained intact through it all. Her family would now join them in memory only. A note in history and little more.

"How can we turn our backs on our livelihood and life?"

Had her father felt the same? Despite arranging for her departure from Poland, he had intended to stay.

And now he was dead.

Nadia looked at the woman across from her. Laughter and happy screams filtered through the walls of the small home, one that knew so much love. In a flash of thought, she pictured the door barred, walls engulfed in flame, the bodies of the two older boys bloody out on the dry ground just outside. She shook the image from her head, but the impression remained etched into her. "It is different this time. There is an evil the Nazis bring with them." She straightened, meeting the woman's hesitant gaze. She would sit here and tell every horrible thing she had heard and seen, every rumor of the atrocities in Germany, until Frajda agreed to pack up what they could carry and flee with her. Nadia would not leave without them.

⚏ CHAPTER 25 ⚏

September 16, 1939

David fell to his knees, his short breaths not enough to feed his lungs, but a sharp pain in his ribs kept them from expanding. The sharp toe of a boot rolled him to his side, and all breath was lost.

"You keep saying, but you have no vay to prove you are not spy for British."

David clamped his teeth against the pain as he pushed back to his knees and tried to meet the officer's steely gaze. After being loaded onto an empty supply truck returning to Germany, David had ended up in a holding cell not far from Berlin, from what he understood. "I don't sound British."

"You think all our spies *sound* German?" The tormentor was dressed in a crisp gray uniform. David had learned to recognize the Schutzstaffel, or SS, from the twin silver markings that looked more like lightning bolts than two *S*'s. "Vhy vere you in Poland? Vat information have you hoped to gain?"

"None." David closed his eyes. His head hurt even worse than his ribs, and his nose was likely broken. A day of bouncing in the back of a truck, hands shackled, and then two days of no food while isolated in a cold cell had preceded this *chat*. Three days of nothing but thoughts of Nadia and the kids. Had they made it away? Were they in England and safe? Would he ever see them again? When the discomfort and unknown became too much, he'd focus on Nadia's kiss and what it did to him. He remembered the smoothness of her cheek and the tingling of his lips that had been slow to fade. The mist in her eyes. The sound of his name on her lips.

A blow to David's face sent him reeling, and he tried to catch himself for the little good it did, but he had learned the danger of staying on the ground. "I am American. Our countries are not at war." He'd repeated it enough times but somehow still hoped it would sink in past the skull-crested caps the SS wore. He had the sinking feeling the man didn't care who he interrogated or what answers were given, only the sport it provided.

Because what could be better *sport* than pummeling another man into oblivion?

The interview halted mercifully at the opening of the door to the small, cell-like room, and David again tried to catch his breath and ease the burning in his lungs. Two more soldiers entered, but their uniforms were different. Black and looming over him like storm clouds. One stood by, watching him with interest, arms across his chest, while the other came alongside the SS officer and spoke quickly. The conversation ricocheted back and forth between the two men while David's concentration drifted. It wasn't as though he understood more than a word or two anyway. He turned inward, mentally tallying each breath while trying to find a position that eased some of the pain.

At least he was still alive. For now. Would his family ever learn of his death, or would the Nazis simply hide the fact by burying his body in an unknown grave? Would he simply disappear without a trace? With the war in Poland, his parents would eventually be forced to assume he'd not survived. He'd like to think they would be better off, though he knew it would break his mother's heart.

Wasn't that his specialty?

He should have asked Nadia to contact his family, tell them what happened. Then they wouldn't be left to wonder.

Boots making their retreat against the stone floor brought David's head up. The tormentor closed the door in his wake, and relief washed through David. Perhaps it was only a reprieve from the interrogation, but he would take it. He sank onto his side on the floor and closed his eyes, though not unaware of the two still hovering over him, their conversation casual—hints of amusement—but not at all understandable.

David tuned them out and tried to imagine seeing Nadia again in London, though he'd given up believing he'd make it there alive. He pictured a smile blooming on her face at the sight of him, her pace quickening to him. Would she weep with relief or throw herself into his arms and hold tight? He dreamed of a kiss like the one they had already shared, only they wouldn't rush this one. He would hold her and tell her it had been the thought of her that had kept him going. He would wipe away her tears of joy with his thumb and kiss her again.

"*Aufstehen!*"

David jerked at the command—one he'd heard before. He pushed himself onto his hands and knees and, teeth gritted, maneuvered to his feet. His legs barely held him, and the agony in his side suggested a broken rib. Blotches swam across his vision, threatening to steal it completely, but he was aware of the door opening before him.

"*Wandern!*"

A shove from behind caused David to stumble. He tried to catch himself, but hot agony exploded through his torso. Blackness flashed across his vision, dragging him down.

———≈———

Nadia stood with a toddler on her hip, a bounce the only thing keeping Efraim from shrieking for his mother, who bustled out of the farmhouse with yet another bundle of clothes and bedding to load into the wagon. This was taking too long, and nervous energy aided in keeping the child hushed.

"We must be on our way before noon," Nadia mumbled loud enough for Frajda to hear the frustration. This had taken too long. The Nazis could not be far off.

Frajda kept her eyes diverted and hurried back into the house for another load of who knew what. Did she not realize they would be unable to take their whole household? It simply would not fit in the small wagon with seven kids.

Nadia bit back further comment. At least she had agreed to come. After pressuring the woman for most of a day, Frajda had finally managed a nod and told her children to begin their preparations. After most of yesterday spent visiting neighbors to sell the livestock for a small fraction of what they were worth, they finally started loading the wagon and could begin their journey. Every minute spent lingering gnawed on Nadia's nerves as she watched the road for the first sign of the Germans.

This time when Frajda returned, Nadia helped her load her bundle then gripped her arm to keep her from returning to the house. "We need to leave. Now."

"But. . ." Frajda's eyes slipped closed, and then she nodded. "Children. Into the wagon. It is time we go."

Somber-faced youth toted their younger siblings and loaded them into the back among the bundles and crates of possessions. Binjamin took the reins, and Nadia climbed onto the seat beside him. She had never sat on a wagon this old and hoped it would hold together. While she had enjoyed buggy rides in the past for pleasure alone, she already missed the convenience of an automobile.

Frajda slipped into the house one last time, lingering at the door as she closed it. She kept her gaze lowered when she finally settled into the back with the younger children. Maybe when they were far from here and safe, Nadia would find it within her to forgive the woman's hesitancy.

But first they would travel directly east for several miles to collect Frajda's in-laws. Nadia only hoped they were quicker to come and not already behind German lines.

The wagon rolled far too slowly over the rutted road. Nadia had not thought the road so bad, but the wagon's springs were stiff, and every stone or pothole jolted through her spine. She would not likely sleep again until they reached Lithuania, but she allowed her eyes to close for a moment. There she found David, and her chest constricted around her heart, making the ache sting. After witnessing her parents' relationship, she had not imagined such deep feelings for a man. So many of the marriages she had witnessed over the years had suggested tolerance and sometimes respect. Not love. Love seemed only for novels.

Love?

Heat rushed through her. Was this love she felt? For an American, no less? No. He was simply David, the man who had resolved to keep her safe. A man with courage and faith that moved her to want to follow and believe. A man whose subtle smile buoyed her strength and spirits.

Whose eyes had seen beyond the walls she had tried to place between them. Whose kiss had melted every last barrier around her heart.

"Please keep him safe, God." *I want to see him again.* Among other things.

"What was that?" Binjamin asked from beside her.

"Nothing." She focused on her hands, running her fingers over her coarse palms. A heavy lotion would help a little, but she hardly cared now.

"You are thinking about your friend? The one the Germans captured?"

She released a breath and nodded.

"Do you think they killed him?"

"I pray they have not."

The young man nodded. "I will pray for your friend as well."

"Dziękuję." She studied the young man for a moment, trying to forget the image of him from her dream, but it had been so clear. She searched his face for features that might make his heritage obvious, but as with David, they were subtle. What if a German recognized David's Jewish ancestry? Would they treat him differently than if they believed him to be simply American? The tightness between her shoulders intensified, increasing the pulsating ache between her temples.

"Matka said you lived in a large house, not like ours. Did you have an automobile?"

Nadia nodded, clinging to the distraction. "My father had several. Beautiful cars." They hit a rut, and Nadia gripped the side of the seat. "And comfortable."

"I rode in a truck once." The young man beamed with pride. "I caught a ride with one of the neighboring farmers. Usually they didn't want much to do with us, but I was caught in the snow."

"A relief to climb into a warm cab, I imagine."

His face fell and his eyes darted away. Nadia's stomach dropped.

"At least the way home was quicker," she remedied.

"Tak."

"I think there will be opportunity in Lithuania or England. You will see." She would do her best to make it happen.

"You are confident they will want us there?" He lowered his voice, tipping toward her. "I overheard what you told my mother about the Germans and their hate for Jews. I listened at the door. Perhaps we will be disliked wherever we go."

"No," she said quickly, before even considering an argument. "Perhaps there are those who will not like us because we are Polish or because you are Jewish, but not everyone is like that."

"You are not like that."

"No, I believe all people deserve to be treated fairly."

"Even Germans?"

Oh, what a question! She wanted to hate them, but she was one of them in a small way. Her mother. Yes, Nadia wanted to hate her, but did she? Grandparents and cousins. She had never been close, but neither did she believe them evil. "I hate Nazis and Germans who are hurting our people, but I think we must be careful how we judge individuals."

He seemed to consider that. The road turned, and they lowered into a small, treed valley and toward a bridge over a stream. "I liked your friend. The American. He was kind."

"Yes. David is a kind man. And his mother is Jewish. His grandparents were Poles."

His eyes widened and a smile tipped up the corner of his mouth. "No wonder I liked him."

Nadia chuckled and offered another prayer for David's safety. If only she could trust him to God's hands.

They rose on the other side of the valley and from the trees. The wagon jerked to a stop the same instant Nadia registered the green trucks parked along the side of the road ahead and the Germans blending in far too well with their background. A group of no more than a hundred or so, but more than her small group had any hope of fleeing or slipping past. A handful of soldiers raised their rifles and jogged toward them. Nadia's heart stalled in her chest. She had led this family to their deaths.

⟩CHAPTER 26⟨

David squinted up at the ceiling with the eye that wasn't swollen shut. Each breath ached, but he'd figured out a rhythm to keep the pain from deepening. The four tight walls closed in around him, while his mind struggled to escape his conditions. Nadia was the easiest to focus on, but with each hour a sinking sensation met him when he turned his thoughts to her. Had she made it out of Poland? Had the plane arrived safely in England? What if something had gone wrong? Would he ever know?

Prayers slipped constantly through him, though he never voiced them.

He shifted, and a groan vibrated his chest. He still wasn't sure how to pray for himself. Did that not make him a hypocrite? Ignoring God for years and then suddenly plying Him with demands?

Above David, a small spider crept along the ceiling, tiny legs clinging to the rough plaster. The lucky fellow probably had no idea what life existed beyond this room. That somewhere out there a man lived in luxury while setting the world to war, slaughtering hundreds, perhaps thousands. Soldiers marched. Tanks rolled out of factories and on to destroy livelihoods and homes. Men and women attempted to figure out what was happening in the world around them. Children played.

Bieta and Krys should be on their family's farm in Poland, playing with dolls or tossing stones into a creek, innocent and carefree.

Arek should be looking into the face of his mother while his father leaned over, beaming with pride over his firstborn son.

Aleksy should be in school, kicking a ball around the streets of Warsaw with his friends.

Lady Nadezhda should be enjoying her parties and the company of her father.

David should be home making something of his life. Not wasting it running from himself and his family.

The whine of hinges made David wince, and he cocked his head enough to see who entered. An officer, but not the SS. It was too soon to feel relief, judging from the black of the man's uniform. David had heard about the Gestapo.

"You are David Reid, the American?"

The man's English was impressive—the best David had heard so far, and he pushed into a sitting position. He gasped at the spike of pain in his side but managed to prop himself upright. "And you?" His voice rasped, and he tried to swallow, but his throat was dry, and it scratched at the motion.

The man gave a quick order to a guard at his side, and the man jumped to obey, bringing a cup of water to David. The warm liquid left much to be desired but washed away some of the discomfort and sour taste in his mouth. With another order, the guard left, the door closing behind him.

"It is better for you not to know my name," the officer stated. "But I am sorry for your treatment here."

"Are you?" David didn't realize he'd spoken the question until the man tightened a smile at him.

"We are not at war with the United States of America, and I would prefer to keep it that way."

"I'm pretty sure I have little influence one way or another."

He chuckled, low and throaty. "I do not imagine so. A student of photography studying in Poland." The officer shook his head, but his eyes remained on David. "Perhaps you would have been wiser choosing one of Germany's fine universities."

"Probably a wiser choice." David slid the words between his teeth. The man had to know how repulsive the idea was to him at this point. "What now?"

"You will soon be freed."

"Will I?" Or did they plan to shoot him as soon as he stepped outside the building? After the treatment of the last couple days, he found it hard to believe they planned to set him free into the streets of Berlin.

"Ja, of course. My men will see you delivered to wherever you wish to go."

David pushed up a little higher while trying to contain the wince as pain spiked through his torso. "How about England? I think it well past time I arrange for passage back to the United States."

"Unfortunately, as you must be aware, both England and France have declared war against us, making that a difficult request."

Black splotches danced in David's vision. "Maybe I'll settle for a hospital for now." A wave of nausea lowered him back to the cot.

The man answered in German, but it took a moment for David to register that he was no longer a part of the conversation. Just as well. It was all he could do to keep his vision clear and his stomach from heaving. No, England was not to be—at least not anytime soon. Medical attention might be all he could ask for if the Gestapo officer truly didn't intend to simply make him disappear.

———≈———

"Say nothing unless you have no choice," Nadia ordered. "Wait for me." She slid to the ground and rushed toward the Germans, arms waving above her head. She forced a wide smile to her lips and joy into her voice. She had spent most of her life learning to hide her true emotions. If there was ever such a need, it was now.

"*Wunderbar!*" she sang out in German. "You have come!"

The soldiers slowed their advance.

"I have prayed, and now you have given us hope!"

Their weapons lowered. "Who are you?" one of the soldiers questioned.

Nadia threw her arms around his neck and pressed her lips against his cheek. "My family is German. When we heard of the invasion, we wished to return to the fatherland, but the apartment with everything we owned was destroyed by the bombers." The words fell from her mouth as quick as she could think them. "But now we are finally safe! And soon we will be again in our dear Germany."

She slipped from the soldier's ready embrace and smiled sweetly at him, not allowing time for her stomach to roil before turning to the one with the insignia of a *leutnant*. She beamed up at him. "My grandparents have a grand estate near Dresden."

He glanced to the soldier beside him. "You are from Dresden."

Nadia again shifted her attention and stretched her smile wider. "Perhaps you have heard of Herr Schröder?"

A flicker of recognition crossed the young man's face. But of course. *Granfatehr* owned businesses all over Germany. His name was well-known. Especially since he had thrown his support behind the Nazi Party.

She looked back at the leutnant, the oldest of the men but by only a few years. He couldn't be older than thirty. "Have you ever been to Pirna, along the river?"

"I have not," the officer said stiffly, his gaze shifting to the wagon and the family waiting there.

"You are from?" There had to be something to bring down his guard. The others already stood around her like lovesick puppies. Thankfully, she had taken the time to bathe and comb her hair while waiting for Frajda. She'd seen the darkness that hung under her eyes, and her cheeks were more sunken than before, but it was not as though there were many German girls around to compare her to.

"Leipzig."

"So not very far at all. A beautiful city. I attended a party once at the Gohlis Palace. I quickly fell in love with the Saxon baroque architecture of its wings." Nadia still wasn't reaching him. "But the building I love best is St. Nicholas Church. The windows, roof peeks, stately tower."

His eyes softened. "Ja. I was married in that church."

She felt her own reserve ease. "And you have children now?"

"Three." The hint of a smile. "The last born one month ago."

"I am sorry you are not there, then. With your family." And she meant it. She cast a glance at the other youthful faces. None of these men should be here.

He provided a subtle nod. "But this is where my duty calls me."

Silence fell between them, as though no one was sure how to proceed. Then the officer cleared his throat. "You intend to return to Dresden in that cart?"

Nadia shrugged while feigning a wince. "I do not wish it, but other options have fled. We had a car, but unfortunately a wall fell on it."

It was the leutnant's turn to wince. "I have heard reports on the bombings and their effectiveness. It is good you are far from Warsaw now."

"I agree completely, but I will not feel truly safe until I am home."

He gave a tight smile and looked back to where the trucks and jeeps waited with the rest of the soldiers and probably higher-ranking officers. "Let me speak with Major Köhler. I will return."

Nadia watched him go, then glanced back to make sure Frajda and the children were safely in their wagon. Several soldiers remained at her side, standing with their rifles relaxed on their arms while they stared far too openly at her. Probably just admiring a Germanic maiden, but she felt as though they were looking for the slightest mistake that would bring their rifles back into play.

Minutes ticked by in her head, seconds piled on seconds. Life and death balanced in the center. She managed a few shy smiles at those nearest, including the one she had kissed. He still wore a wash of red in his cheeks, made brighter as one of his companions nudged him.

"You probably all have girls back home waiting for you."

"Not as pretty as you, though," said one in his midtwenties. She could imagine him quite the charmer with his deep blue eyes and hair blonder than hers.

"I wish I had on something more flattering." She brushed her hand down her skirt. "I am afraid I must look quite droll right now."

"We're used to roughing it," he replied, his eyes taking a tour of the whole of her. She felt her own blush rush to her cheeks, something she usually held more control over. But never had she felt more exposed. This was not a ballroom or parlor where she flirted with young gentlemen who acted well because of the expectations of the audience surrounding them. She was alone in the middle of a swarm of men who had been away from their girlfriends, wives, and even mothers for too long.

She raised her chin. As long as it was light of day and they were within sight of their superiors, she was probably safe enough. "I do not think I will ever be used to such conditions."

The man was about to say something more but clamped his mouth closed at the return of the leutnant. The officer wore a smile. "We will be able to assist you, Fräulein. One of the supply trucks will be returning to Germany shortly. The major has agreed you and your family may ride as far as the depot in Szczecin. It should be easy to find a train home from there."

Nadia's chest refused breath, but she grinned broadly. "*Danke,* Leutnant! That is perfect."

Now what, God?

≣CHAPTER 27≣

The rocking of the truck offered no lulling effect for the nerves and muscles bunched tight in Nadia's shoulders, spiking pain into her head. They had been driving most of an hour now, due west, on their way *back* to Germany. She rode in the cab of the truck with the driver but had suggested Frajda and the children ride in the back so they could rest. Some of their possessions had been loaded, and miraculously, Frajda and the boys had managed with answering ja, nien, or employing a simple nod. Nadia had done all the speaking and explaining of why they had no papers to prove their identities—lost when their apartment had burned—or why her cousins looked nothing like her—traits from her father's side, obviously. She sensed suspicion from some of the men but had somehow won the trust of Leutnant Braun, and he hurried them on their way.

Another rut jarred David's revolver against her spine. She hesitated to use it. Firstly, because she never had shot a gun before. Secondly, because the soldier driving the truck would likely have no such hesitation using the pistol at his side.

Germany.

If it were only her, she could continue to her grandparents' estate and no one would question her. She had inherited enough of her mother's features and spoke German as well as she spoke Polish. But with a family of Jewish Poles in tow? They simply could not reach Germany. Once there, how would they ever manage to leave—especially since they had only their Polish paperwork?

No, entering Germany was not an option. But they were in a lone truck, traveling with one driver. Since he weighed twice what she did, overpowering him was not an option.

Now what, God?

She told herself she was merely testing to see if God was anything like David believed, but in reality, she was at a loss, and He was her only resource.

A knocking came from behind them. The driver did not even glance.

"I am sorry, but perhaps one of the children must relieve themselves or has grown ill." Nadia tried to add a pleading to her voice. She had to convince him to pull over the truck.

"We haven't the time."

The knocking grew louder.

"Though I do not imagine your superiors want a mess in the back of their truck."

"It can be washed out."

What was wrong with this man? His jaw clenched as he stared down the road. The knocking continued, not letting up. "I am sorry, sir. You have been so patient, and we are so grateful for this ride, but please, let me see what they need."

He cursed, but the knocking must have grown equally annoying to him. He shoved his foot onto the brake. Nadia opened her door to jump to the ground, but the soldier beat her to it and started around the back of the truck, heavy boots stomping out his anger. She glanced to the rifle that hung behind her head.

You have no choice.

She grabbed the gun and jumped to the ground, pulse racing. She hurried to the back of the truck, unsure of what to do with the rifle until she heard a thud. The German rolled to her side of the truck, Binjamin clinging to his back, trying to get a hold around his neck. She brought the gun to her shoulder.

"Stop!"

The soldier's face jerked in her direction, his gaze widening as it met the rifle. He opened the hand gripping Binjamin's hair, palm wide as it turned to her.

"Quickly, take his gun."

The boy reacted, untangling himself and yanking the pistol from its holster.

Nadia kept her aim, whether or not either of the guns were loaded, they seemed to subdue the man. He lay glaring up at her. But now what?

Binjamin pressed the pistol to the German's head, the tension in his jaw visible.

"Do not do it, Binjamin," she said in Polish.

The boy didn't look up. "After everything these creatures have done to our people? Where is the justice?"

Nadia's chest clenched. Yes, the Germans deserved punishment for their crimes against her father, against the people massacred in Warsaw and in so many villages. The truck would be theirs. They would arrive in Lithuania within a couple of days.

"Bitte." The hate had slipped from the soldier's eyes, leaving only panic. Fear.

"We must kill him." Binjamin sounded like he was trying to convince himself as well as her.

"Nie." Strength fled, but Nadia managed to keep her weapon aimed. "He is a driver. He has not killed anyone." *Probably* not. Either way, Nadia did not want to be responsible for doling out God's justice. She did not want blood on her hands. Or on the hands of the young man across from her. "We will leave him here. Unarmed."

Binjamin's hand shook, and a second raised to support it. "We're at war."

"Tak. But we do not need to add to the death count."

Frajda appeared behind him. She set a hand on his shoulder and whispered something. A tear slipped down the boy's cheek, and he nodded. Slowly, he drew back.

"Everyone needs to get back into the truck." Nadia said in Polish before switching to German. "You, stand, and keep your hands near your head."

The soldier moved slowly. The anger was returning now, his gaze narrowing at her. "You are betraying your fatherland, your people?"

"Nien. This is my land. I am Polish."

He swore and made a step toward her, but Binjamin pressed the gun to his back.

"He will not hesitate to pull that trigger," Nadia reminded the soldier. "Now start walking away from the truck." She motioned in the direction required.

Since Binjamin had his gun trained on the German as he started to move, Nadia ordered Frajda to make sure all the children were in the truck, and then headed toward the cab. The truck had been left running, so all she had to do was make sure she was able to drive it.

Nadia set the rifle on the bench seat and leaned into the cab. A simple stick shift on the floor. While she did not share her father's obsession with cars, she had demanded to learn how to drive. With several gas cans strapped on the side of the truck, there was no reason they could not make it out of Poland.

A yelp of surprise was followed by a thud. Nadia spun and dropped from the truck before she realized she had left the rifle behind. Somehow the German had managed to overpower Binjamin. The crack of the pistol's discharge. The boy dropped. Nadia grabbed for David's revolver and swung it upward. It jerked in her hands, a round of ammunition, then a second and a third exploding from the barrel. The German was half-turned, his eyes widened as though shocked. Or was it pain? He fell sideways and slumped facedown.

Frajda's scream jerked Nadia's attention back to Binjamin, and her dream flashed through her mind. He lay in his blood. His mother fell on her knees beside him, wadding her shawl over his wound. Nadia could not loosen her grip on the revolver, her feet frozen in place, her mind trying to grasp what had happened. What had she done? She looked to the German and the three holes in his uniform leaching scarlet. He did not move.

She had to know.

Nadia forced her legs to heed her demand and stepped to the man. She nudged his shoulder with her boot. No groan. Nothing. She lowered the revolver and pushed him over onto his back. Not an easy feat with how large he was. His body sagged. His eyes stared blankly. Just as Tata's had.

Nadia's stomach roiled, and she clenched her teeth against the bile rising in her throat. She only made it a couple of feet before she heaved, emptying her stomach into the low grass. But she had no time for this. While the German was no longer a threat, Binjamin moaned under his mother's ministrations. They needed to do what they could to keep him alive until they found help.

A medical kit sat behind the seat in the truck, and Nadia traded the revolver for the large case. She had it pried open by the time she reached Binjamin's side and glanced only briefly at his tearstained face before focusing on the wound. Frajda seemed to have staunched the flow of blood, but Nadia remembered David's care with Bieta's injury. She braced a hand on the wound while rolling him up enough to see his back and the lack of exit. The bullet would have to be removed. But that was far above her abilities. All they could do for now was to keep pressure on his wound and get him into the truck.

He cried out as she lowered him back down, and she searched the med kit for something to dull the pain. Thankfully, the Germans were well supplied, and within a few minutes they had managed to get Binjamin into the back of the truck, blankets and bundles of clothes propped around him to make him as comfortable as possible. Nadia tried not to look at the dead German as she climbed into the cab of the truck. There was no time to do anything for him. Not with a boy's life on the line—no, not just his. Everyone in this truck was at risk. She would not be able to talk her way past any more Germans.

Unless. . .

Nadia quickly searched and found a spare uniform, though much too large for her. A few tucks and a roll of the sleeves helped but would only disguise her from a distance. If the truck was made to stop, the Germans would immediately see the truth. She twisted her hair onto her head and pressed a cap into place, tossing a prayer heavenward that she would not be compelled to stop.

⊒CHAPTER 28⊒

Not quite midnight—a day that seemed never to end. Nadia's arms and shoulders ached from her grip on the steering wheel as she peered through the windshield at what little of the road the headlights illuminated. According to the map, she was headed northwest. They had recently passed through a village, and Nadia had been tempted to stop and find help for Binjamin, but rubble and several burnt-out houses suggested the Germans controlled the area.

Ahead, a light flickered, and Nadia slowed the truck. No. The light was steady enough. It was a hedge of trees that caused the effect. She turned off the truck's lamps and purred slowly forward. She could see clearer now as she came through the trees and a house appeared ahead. Perhaps a farm would be worth the risk for Binjamin's sake.

Nadia turned off the road, but only far enough to remove the truck from the sight of any passersby, then killed the engine. She climbed to the ground and slipped out of the German coat and hat.

"What has happened?" Frajda asked when Nadia poked her head in the back.

"There is a house here. Perhaps they can help." She shone a torch on Binjamin, whose eyes remained closed. "How is he?"

"Not well." Frajda wiped a hand down her face. "I don't know what else to do."

"I will be back." Hopefully with someone who had more knowledge of wounds than she. Nadia jogged through the quiet yard. Almost too quiet. No dog greeted her. No farm animals were visible. But maybe only because of the lateness. She climbed the several steps and laid her fist to the door with a gentle knock.

Silence. The low light in the window flickered and went out.

Nadia's pulse sped and all sleepiness fled. She pressed her ear to the door and listened to the murmur of voices. Someone was angry. Another just wanted everyone to be quiet.

Nadia knocked again. "Please, we need help."

More arguing. Surely they did not think her a German. Nazis would not wait on ceremony, and the door would already be off its hinges.

The door opened a crack and a man peered out at her. "Who are you?"

"I have a wounded boy with me. We need help removing the bullet."

A murmur from behind the man was followed by a woman pulling the door wider. "Don't make them stand out in the dark, Leon." An older woman with white streaking her hair lifted a candle to better see Nadia's face. "Someone has been wounded, you say?"

"Yes. Can you help him? Is there a doctor who can be sent for?"

She shook her head vehemently. "Not near enough to make it safely. Bring the boy in, and we'll see what can be done." She swatted at the man beside her. "Hurry and help her."

Without another word, they turned into the darkness, and Nadia led the way to the truck. The man pulled up short at the sight of it. "That is one of the German's trucks."

"Yes. We managed to. . .seize it from them. Though please do not ask me how." Nadia climbed in and quickly explained to Frajda that they would pause here for a few hours. Hopefully no longer. She itched to be on the road again, putting distance between her and the body she had left in the dirt. Images accompanied her thoughts, and her stomach turned. Nadia tried to focus on helping the children from the truck so they could stretch their legs and relieve themselves. Then she cradled half of Binjamin's torso, with his mother lifting beside her and the stranger guiding his legs.

The boy screamed out at the first movement, and Nadia looked to the man. "Is there any way we can bring the hot water and what is needed here so he does not need to be moved? We will be leaving again as soon as we are able."

The man grunted what sounded like acknowledgment and lowered the boy's legs before disappearing into the night. Nadia and Frajda remained, situating Binjamin in his place and peeling away the bandage. Nadia made a quick list of the things they would need. Alcohol to clean the wound, as not much remained in the med kit, and something long and sharp to dig for the bullet. Clean cloths. Light. Her mind spun as she headed back to the house. Two women met her just outside.

The older one offered a sympathetic smile, her arms laden. "I am a midwife. Perhaps not the person you would usually call for such injuries, but I have tended much over my years."

Nadia summoned a breath and a thanks, then guided them to the truck. The second woman held a lamp high but seemed content to stand aside and avert her eyes.

"Someone must hold his arms," the older woman instructed. She dug through the German medical kit and seemed pleased with her findings. She doused everything in alcohol and cleaned the area surrounding the wound. Nadia would have felt better about the low flow of blood leaking from the closed skin if they didn't have to reopen it.

"Don't let him move," the woman said gently. Her head tipped forward with a mumbled prayer.

Nadia slid her fingers through Binjamin's and gripped tight.

The youth screamed, and her whole body jerked forward, as did Frajda's on the side opposite. They scrambled to regain their grips, but the young man was incredibly strong in his agony. Nadia pinned his wrist with her leg, sitting directly above and pressing down on his shoulder, the only way to keep him still. Tears leaked down her cheeks. She should not have let her guard down around the German. She should have kept Binjamin safe.

His scream was muffled by a wad of cloth the midwife had pressed into his mouth. Nadia bit down on her lip to keep her own sobs at bay. And then abruptly, the fight slipped away, and his body sagged. Nadia's attention snapped to the midwife and the blood. Oh, so much blood. Dark blotches threatened to unseat her. "Is he. . .?" She could not say it.

"Unconscious." The reassurance fell flat. How long before he slipped further?

Nadia loosened her hold but clamped her eyes closed, a prayer coming to her lips. She had found herself praying more this past week than during her whole life before. Was it the invasion? Or David?

She added him to her pleas, not stopping until the midwife sputtered a laugh of relief. Something hard clanked against the floor of the truck.

"Thank You, God."

The work of staunching the flow of blood and adding thick bandaging didn't take nearly as long as it felt. Soon the women were returning to the house, the lantern waving farewell. Nadia remained in place on the floor beside Binjamin and his mother, watching the steady rise and fall of his chest for a few minutes before relaxing against the side of a crate and allowing her eyes to close again, but this time in rest. A short reprieve before she collected the children and whoever else wanted to risk their lives with her. She could only pray they had better success in their journey tomorrow, pray that Binjamin would be able to start healing now, pray that they would be able to avoid the Germans, pray that she could stay awake through the night. Pray that they would make it out of Poland. . .and that when she did, David would somehow be waiting for her—that she would see him again.

September 17, 1939

David tried not to breathe too deeply, but standing in one place for most of an hour had done nothing for his aching ribs. Thankfully, a doctor had declared them only bruised, not broken. David questioned the definition. They might not be in pieces or at risk of puncturing his lungs, but he was pretty sure at least one had been cracked.

The rumble of a car brought his head up. When the black sedan rolled to a stop in front of the designated store, a bakery with the scent of fresh bread wafting down the street, David started out from his hiding place.

He had been moved to the apartment above the day before and told to wait and watch for his getaway from Germany. With the look of the parked car waiting for him, a beautiful Horch, he almost felt like a bank robber or Chicago gangster. His walk felt too slow to be casual, but he didn't want to draw any attention. The line at the bakery had been forming over the past hour, and the proprietor had just opened the doors to let the first inside.

A young woman smiled at him as she moved past. Hopefully she didn't look closely enough to see the yellow and blue hue that remained around one eye or the cuts near his ear and beside his mouth, making him look like a prizefighter after a match. He tipped his head politely with hopes of obscuring her view. The back door of the car opened, and a man in a brown suit waved him inside.

"Schnell," the man said tersely. *Quickly* was one German word David had picked up since his arrival in this country. He found his seat and closed the door. As the car jerked forward, David took a moment to allow the pain to subside.

A parcel wrapped in brown paper was set on his lap, along with a folder.

The German motioned for David to open the folder. Inside was a set of documents in German, a train ticket, a loose paper that appeared to be a letter, and money. He unfolded the letter.

> *I must be careful about my movements and any ties to you, as I am always watched, always under suspicion by those under me. These men will deliver you to a train station. Speak to no one and do not mention my involvement. The one thing I ask is for you to mail this parcel once you reach England.*
>
> *My thanks.*

David read the note several times, though the instructions were simple enough. The mystery behind it all was the most curious, but he would not question it if he was able to reach England in one piece.

No one spoke for the entirety of the car ride that took them out of the city and through a long stretch of green countryside, hints of autumn speckling the trees. Shortly after entering a smaller town, the car pulled into the train station only minutes before the train itself squealed its arrival. David's confidence grew as the timing and planning became more evident with each step.

The man beside him waved to the door, and David nodded his understanding. He climbed out and started toward the train, the ticket already in hand, parcel tucked under his left arm and away from his sore ribs. He worked his way through the flow of passengers disembarking and hurrying aboard. No one seemed to regard him, and he soon lowered onto a seat and placed the parcel back on his lap. It had a decent weight to it, like a book perhaps. For all he knew, he was being used to transport German military secrets. Except the address was in the United States. Michigan. Not the destination he would guess for government secrets.

"*Ist hier noch frei?*"

David looked up at the woman standing in the aisle and gave a tight smile. She was probably asking about the seat across from him. He waved her to it so she wouldn't become suspicious at being ignored. That seemed to appease her, and she dropped into the seat. A second woman who was older—probably her grandmother—followed. The grandmother gave a curious, or perhaps suspicious, look, and the younger woman started talking again. David tipped his head back against the seat and pulled his hat over his face. Better they think him exhausted or rude than American.

By the time the train rolled forward, the woman had given up on conversation and contented herself with reading. Heaven be praised. David dozed on and off for what felt like hours, not removing his hat from his face. The women removed themselves at some point during the ride and were replaced by an older man with one arm. An accident in his trade or an injury from the Great War? Was there a chance this current war could become so big? Would America intervene as they had the last time Germany had overstepped?

The thought settled into his stomach like a shovelful of sand and left the same dry feeling in his mouth. The war with Poland already involved France, England, and most of her commonwealth, including Canada, Australia, and India—though they hadn't come to a grand rescue yet. Poland was already on the verge of crumbling. What next? How far would the Nazis spread their poison?

David set a hand gingerly on his ribs at the thought but quickly decided against it as the motion brought the older man's head up. The man said something. A question. *Swell.* David shook his head and tipped it forward this time, hat pulled low. His neck was still kinked from his last snooze, and sleep was far from his mind. What he wouldn't give for a newspaper to hide behind.

Thankfully, two or so hours later, the old fellow left one on his seat when he abandoned it at a station. Perfect timing as two Germans in uniforms started up the row minutes later. The train stood still. David watched from behind the paper as they paused at each bench. People already had their papers ready, and David reached for the documents he had been supplied. Hopefully they were what was required. He tried to act casual, feigning interest in an article as he spared a hand to provide his documents. A moment later, the papers were returned to him and the soldiers continued on. He breathed deep with instant regret. Hopefully, he was almost at his destination, because the pain in his chest continued to increase. Still, the train remained in place.

Time scratched against David's nerves like nails on a blackboard. He gritted his teeth, but soon his jaw ached too. Finally, he caught sight of the same soldiers on the platform outside his window. A minute later, the train jerked, rolled, and pulled forward.

The sun was setting off to his right behind tree-covered hills. A full day of travel left him barely upright and his head swirling, but he could make out well enough what was written on a sign beside the tracks. *Switzerland*. The train was leaving Germany. As far as ever from England, but a sense of safety and hope filled his chest with his next guarded breath. He stole a look at the money he had been provided and allowed for a smile. He hadn't been given German marks as he assumed, but Swiss francs.

"She'll be waiting," David whispered to himself, his first words spoken today. The first English words he'd heard in days. Nadia would be waiting in London for him.

⁝CHAPTER 29⁝

"Much farther?" Frajda questioned. Binjamin's head rested on her knee while the toddler cuddled in at her side. The young man remained pale and asleep, but he was still alive. For now.

Nadia shook her head, the weight of the young man's life heavy on her shoulders—all their lives. Two more families had joined them in their flight, bringing their numbers above twenty. And it was up to her to see them safely out of Poland. "We must be close." The sun lowered toward the horizon at their backs, and she cringed at the thought of another night of dark roads and keeping her eyes propped open. "Best we start moving again."

The woman gave a weary nod, and Nadia turned to the others, who had disembarked for a few minutes to stretch their legs. Leon, the man they had met at the farmhouse, poured the last of the petrol into the tank before returning the empty can to the side of the truck. He met her gaze with his darker one, the same question written there. Would it be enough?

"I will sit in the cab." Leon followed her to the front of the truck. "We are past the risk of being stopped by the Germans."

Nadia tucked loose strands of blond back under her cap. "We cannot be sure. Not something I want to risk."

"And you think they would mistake you for a soldier?" he scoffed. Though probably no older than her, he brought along a wife and three young children. Perhaps he was right and she needed to relinquish her control, the uniform (it would fit him better than her), the truck (except he had no experience driving), the guns (would he hold his head in a crisis)? Nie. She did not trust him enough.

Nadia kept her voice even and held his gaze, just as Tata did in arguments. "I plan to finish what I started. It is your choice to come or remain here." She climbed into the driver's seat and slapped the door closed. The window remained open due to the warmth of the day. "You can help by making sure everyone loads up and is ready to leave."

She watched him sulk away in the mirror, then turned her attention to the revolver on the seat beside her. Only one shot remained, but next time she would not hesitate—not risk another life.

Someone knocked against the back of the cab, signaling they were ready to leave. She glanced in the mirror to make sure all her passengers had returned to the back, then revved the engine to life. After driving for most of an hour, the road cut to the south. A jeep appeared up ahead, and Nadia jerked her foot off the gas pedal. German trucks and men. Blocking the road.

"*Boże*, proszę, nie!" But it was too late to turn back. She tried to catch her reflection in the side window for the little good it did. She tucked a loose strand of hair up and set both hands to the steering wheel. "Please, God, please. Help us make it through." A dozen scenarios rushed through her mind, all ending horribly. A soldier waved for her to slow.

Her foot hovered over the gas pedal. If she rammed her way through, they might stand a chance. Maybe they would only think she was in a hurry and not pursue. But if they did? If they opened fire with the machine gun mounted on the back of the nearest jeep?

"What do I do, God? What do I do?"

Her truck continued to slow, her foot still hovering. A second man, an officer, joined the first. He seemed familiar as she neared, still slowing. His blue eyes peered up at her, his brows bunching. Her pulse jammed. The officer. The same who had stolen her mother away—the one responsible for her father's death. . .would not be responsible for hers. She reached for the revolver.

He jerked the door open before she came to a stop, and recognition lit his face. "Move over." He shoved her aside. She lost her hold on the wheel but not the gun as she did as she was ordered. "I'll head him in the right direction," he told the soldier on the ground and then pressed his foot to the gas. The truck lurched forward. His jaw worked while he looked her over.

Nadia returned the scrutiny while keeping the revolver tucked under the side of her leg. She could not guess his game, but a little farther and she could threaten him to keep driving or shoot him and knock him out of her seat.

"What have you done, Nadezhda?"

She jerked at his use of her name. "How did you recognize me so easily?" Not that her disguise was that great, but the man had only seen her once. She was nothing to him.

"You have been on my mind a lot the last few weeks." He kept driving, continuing slowly east. "Among other things." He shook his head. "Perhaps God has been kind enough to grant me a second chance."

Anger spiked through her. "You should not be the one to mention God." She placed her finger over the trigger. She might not have it in her to shoot the man, but a little farther and she would force him out of the truck. "Where are you taking us?"

"Past the check stop. How did you get this truck? Do you know what they would have done to you if they realized you are not a real soldier?" He frowned at her. "What happened to the driver?"

The image invaded Nadia's thoughts before she could block it. "I would rather not say."

The officer seemed to read her silence and groaned. "He's dead? What have you done?" He looked at her sharply. "And why?" He glanced behind them, and his foot shifted to the brake. "Who is in the back of this truck? You are not alone, are you?"

She pulled the revolver from under her and aimed it at his chest. "Do not slow down."

He glanced from the road to her and then to the revolver. "You are headed for the Lithuanian border?"

"Your only concern is to drive."

"If only that were so." He set his jaw and sped the truck, but his eyes barely left her. "You should be glad to know your mother is safe with your grandparents."

Nadia kept her focus, determined not to let him distract her. "I do not care."

"She was very distressed to leave you behind. Tried to convince me to stay longer, to not leave without you. Told me things I refused to believe." His voice lowered, emotion playing with the words. "Until now."

"She was a fool to think I would leave with you after you murdered my father." She tightened her grip on the revolver.

The truck rocked as he pulled off the road and laid his foot to the brake. Something—or someone—thudded in the back. Nadia winced for their sakes but did not allow herself to lower her guard or the revolver.

"I was not the one who pulled the trigger." A muscle flexed in his straight jaw. "I hated him—I have hated him for more than two decades, but I am not responsible for his death."

"It was your man, your soldier who murdered him. So, ja, you are responsible. And I hate you for it. I hate my mother for leaving with you." *For abandoning me.* Acknowledgment spasmed within her chest, misting her vision.

"I do not blame you for hating me. But do not hate your mother. She loves you. Probably the only reason she told me. . ." He shook his head, but it seemed the fight had left him. His hands loosened their hold on the wheel as he looked over at her and the revolver still aimed at his chest. "I did not believe her," he said softly, as though speaking to himself. "Did not let myself. Not until I saw you again. How can I deny it now?"

"Deny what?"

He stiffened and shook his head. "I will walk back from here. If you continue along this road another mile before heading due north, you will avoid any other checkpoints. You should reach Lithuania before nightfall." He gave her a pointed look. "Do not continue to the east. The Soviets crossed those borders earlier today."

"The Soviets? Have they come to our aid?"

He shook his head.

Nadia did not lower the gun; the Soviets were the least of her worries. Nausea rolled within her. Or was it fear? Fear of what he might say. "What did my mother tell you?"

His blue eyes looked sad. His familiar gaze shifted from her to the gun and back again. Though probably only midforties, lines pinched the corners of his eyes. She knew those eyes.

"She said you were my daughter."

Nadia shook her head while bile climbed her throat. "Nie." He was lying. Mother had lied. And yet his blue eyes were the ones that stared back at her every time she looked in a mirror. She shoved the door open and almost fell out in an attempt to escape the realization, the German still watching her. The revolver fell to the grass just before she bent over and cast up the little she had eaten that day.

Footsteps rounded the truck toward her. She stepped away and whipped the sleeve of the uniform she wore across her mouth.

"I should not have told you. I had not planned to. Just to make sure you made it safely away."

Nadia backed away, unable to take her eyes off the man. "How? How could you be my father?" She had been born at the Rocnne Manor as Lady Nadezhda, named for her tata's grandmother. She was not the illegitimate offspring of a German officer.

"My parents owned a farm near your grandfather's country estate. I grew up with your mother and always loved her and wanted to marry her. She loved me too, but nothing I did or said could convince her to oppose her parents. One day she was gone. I waited for her return but later learned of her marriage to a wealthy baron. A man with everything I could never provide."

Nadia's heart stung for his pitiful story but more so for her part in it. Was that why Tata could never truly love her? And why Matka had never found happiness? Tears rolled free without permission. The German officer reached for her, but a movement in the corner of her eye caught her attention.

Leon crept toward the front of the truck. He watched them while crouching. His hand gripped David's revolver. His free hand motioned her out of the way while the other leveled the gun at the German.

Nadia froze in place, the image of the dead German soldier entangling her thoughts with vivid detail. But it was no longer that soldier she saw, but the face of this officer, his blue eyes staring up at her. Lifeless. His blood on her hands.

"Out of the way!" the Pole yelled, revolver unwavering.

The German began to turn, his blue eyes widening.

Nadia lunged at him, throwing her arms around his neck. "Do not shoot."

"Why are you protecting him?" Leon yelled.

"He is trying to help us." Nadia looked into the German's face, her father's face, now close enough to see the dark of whiskers recently shaved, the slope of his jaw, a mole near his ear. Nadia swallowed hard. She had inherited his ears too.

"They want us dead. What side are you on?"

What side? With both parents apparently German, she hardly knew who she was anymore. Nadia slipped her arms from her father's neck, but his fingers caught hers, keeping her from pulling away farther. "He is. . .a friend. Of my mother's. He will not hurt us." She peered into his face, unable to keep the question from her voice.

"You will have no trouble from me," the German murmured, and Nadia realized she did not even know his name—her own father's name. She knew nothing about him other than what he had disclosed in the past few minutes. Yet this was hardly the time for a long discussion. Frajda and others joined the man, looks of shock mingled with harder stares. Anger. Hate. These people had already suffered at the hands of the Germans, and here she stood, her hand still gripped in an officer's.

She pulled away but remained between her father and the gun still aimed. "We need to go."

"What about the German?" one of the women demanded.

Nadia glanced back and caught the subtle shake of the German's head.

"At least take his gun," Leon said.

"If I walk back to my lines without my revolver, they will know something is wrong."

"You could come with us," Nadia whispered, though she was not sure where the words came from. The idea was ludicrous. He was their enemy. Her enemy.

"There would be consequences for my brothers, my family."

Her family. Uncles and grandparents? Or did he also speak of a wife and children? Did she have half siblings? Questions swirled faster than she could process. "Then you had best be on your way."

He nodded but looked back to the revolver still trained on them.

Nadia stepped toward Leon, whose aim had not wavered. "Give me the gun, Leon."

"How can we trust you?" his wife voiced fears probably shared by all. She jostled their baby on her hip.

"You trusted me enough when you decided to join us." Nadia closed her eyes for a moment in an attempt to gather her thoughts, but they were too scattered, grasping at what she had just learned and the events unfolding, a bizarre echo. But this time she was not the one holding the revolver. Control of the situation slipped further away. She extended her hand. "Give me the gun."

"Not while the German is armed."

Everyone seemed to talk at once, arguing, shouting. The revolver waved in the air as Leon lunged to pass her. Nadia grabbed for it. Her ears rang from the crack her brain registered an instant before the piercing agony. The last bullet. Someone screamed. She did not think it was her, but her brain was too fuzzy to be sure. *Blood. Why was there so much blood everywhere?*

A woman screamed behind her, and Nadia raised her eyes to the German and the revolver he leveled past her. "Nie. No more. Bitte."

His hand wavered as he glanced at her. . .as she dropped to her knees. Her head continued to spin and her legs refused to hold her upright.

"Please go." Nadia's voice was losing strength as well. The pain in her shoulder throbbed in time with her heart. "I do not want anyone else to die."

She felt hands support her from behind, and pressure built over her wound. Agony speared through her and blackened her vision. She fought to remain conscious. Voices mumbled, but she could not quite understand them.

"Wait. . ." The word scratched her throat as she blinked back the darkness. She was somehow lying in the grass now, looking up at Frajda, who seemed distracted. Nadia searched the skies until she found the German, who lingered several paces away, brow furrowed with concern, gun lowered. "Before you go, I need to know. . .your name."

≡CHAPTER 30≡

October 1, 1939

Anticipation burned through David's blood, hurrying his steps through the cobbled streets. Strange how at home London felt even though he had never been to England before. Probably because the people around him spoke English—or at least a close approximation of his native tongue.

After days in Switzerland trying to find his bearings and then a long train ride to Paris, yet another train ride to the French coast, and a small boat across the channel, he wanted nothing more than to drop into a bed and not move for a month—well, nothing more except to see Nadia and the children again.

And so he made his way across the city to the London address of Lord Wintour, the Earl of Selborne. According to the folks David had asked, the earl also had a large estate near Kent, but he would be in London because of England's state of war. David stopped in front of the address he'd been provided. A large, three-story home, though only separate from the similar houses flanking it by a few feet. He jogged up the stairs and hammered on the door. No more waiting. He needed to know.

A tall gentleman in a black suit opened the door and eyed David up and down.

"Hi, I'm looking for Wintour."

He looked at the parcel in David's hands. "If that is for *Lord* Wintour, I will see he receives it."

David stuffed the parcel under his arm. "No. I need to speak with him in person."

"Lord Wintour is unavailable to callers. You may leave a card if you wish."

Understanding ignited. The butler. David straightened his worn tweed jacket that was in dire need of wash and repair. He felt like he'd stepped back in time to the week he'd spent in the company of Baron Roenne. Well out of his depth. "I don't have a card, and I can't wait. I need to see Nadia—*Lady* Roenne. Is she here? Or does the earl know where I can find her?"

"Lady Roenne is not on the premises." The butler moved to close the door.

David shoved his foot in the crack. "You don't understand. I just arrived in London. I need to find Lady Roenne and the children with her. Someone here must know where they went after arriving in England." Maybe he should have started with the *Times*, but she had planned to come here, to live here until other arrangements could be made. "When will the earl be home?"

"Wait here." The man walked away, not bothering to force the door closed.

David followed inside, closed the door, and stared up the grand foyer, if it could be called that. He was pretty sure the place took up more footage than the whole of his parents' house. A woman appeared at the end of the hall and started in his direction over the marbled floor. Her nose wrinkled as she approached, and her gaze held just as much distaste as the butler's—maybe more. Either that or she was simply more expressive.

"I am told you are looking for Lady Roenne."

"Yes, ma'am." David removed his hat with an attempt at proper manners.

"She is not here."

"Your man said as much. But she would have spoken with Lord Wintour when she arrived in England. He would know where she is now." David gritted his teeth, impatience threatening to edge his voice.

The woman's chin tipped upward. "While I do not know what concern she is of yours, I know from my husband that Lady Roenne remained in Poland. Now, if you do not mind, please remove yourself from my home."

She continued talking while waving the butler over, something about expected callers. David's brain froze on *Poland*. "How. . .? Why? They were in the right location. I saw the plane. What happened?"

A hand gripped his arm with a tug toward the door.

"I need to know what happened." David yanked away and faced the woman. "Do you know anything? She was supposed to be on the plane. She should be here."

"From what I understand, she chose to remain."

"She *chose*?" His voice broke at the image of her first refusal, insistence that Jakub and his son take her place. "Was there not enough room?" And the children? Had they arrived in England?

Two younger men in navy blue livery were suddenly at his side. They gripped his arms from either side. "You will please come with us."

Back into the street with no answers? "Wait. What of the children? Bieta and Krys and Arek? Where are they?"

"The Polish children?" The woman waved a dismissive hand, igniting a fire in David's gut. "I would not know. My husband saw to the arrangements."

David's shoes squeaked against the marble before hooking on the edge of a rug. He tried to extract his arms from the men, but they held fast. David's rib pinched in protest, and the parcel dropped to the floor. "Tell me where they are."

The woman was already turning away, her hand to her forehead as though he had distressed her to the point of a headache. David turned his attention to the men pushing him out of the house. Their expressions remained surprisingly neutral other than some annoyance. The butler thrust the parcel into David's chest.

David grabbed it and jammed himself in the doorway. "The earl is likely the only one who knows where those children are and what happened to Nadia—why she didn't get on the plane. I need to speak with him. I've got to."

Someone gave a shove, and he found himself on the front steps. "I won't leave. I'll stay here until he agrees to speak with me."

The door closed. A lock slid into place.

David sank onto a step, fighting the urge to chuck the parcel into the street. Instead, he dropped it and planted his face in his hands. Why would Nadia not leave Poland when she had the chance? Again. There had to be a mistake. The woman must not be properly informed. It was midday now. Maybe the earl was indeed away. Maybe it would be better to return in the evening and try again after finding Thomas Kent. He or someone at the *Times* would know what happened, even if David had to track down the pilot himself and demand answers. He couldn't reconcile that Nadia remained behind.

David eyed the street with its light traffic of mostly cars. Nice cars—another reminder of the upper-crust neighborhood. People with more money and titles than common courtesy. Even if he had the fee for a taxi, he wouldn't likely be able to afford the variety that drove through this district. Upon reaching England, David had traded his meager funds for pounds, but most was already spent. Having no idea where he would stay or where his next meal was coming from, he'd be best off walking across the city to the newspaper's offices. He glanced to his worn brown shoes that barely held together. The left one had started to lift off its sole. His feet burned with exhaustion, but that hardly mattered. Not until he found answers.

David made it as far as the street when the door opened behind him. The butler stood with stoic expression. "You are requested inside."

David bit back the desire to refuse, his pride chafing. Instead, he set his jaw and pushed past. A man in his early fifties stood only a few feet within, arms across his tub of a chest. A thick mustache hid his upper lip, and his eyes narrowed, but more in curiosity than anything else David could sense. "So, you *are* here."

"And you are decidedly American. That is for certain." The earl said it almost glibly as he turned and started away.

David followed. "I was told you were not at home."

" 'Not at home to visitors' is the proper wording. I was attending to some important business, which your ruckus interrupted."

"My apologies." David couldn't help but mimic the tone.

The earl said nothing more until he entered a large study reminiscent of Baron Roenne's but with a lighter wood that bore intricate carvings over every square foot. He lowered into a large leather chair and leaned forward. "How are you acquainted with Lady Roenne exactly?"

David remained standing. "I met the baron just before the invasion, and he introduced me to his daughter. He tasked me with seeing her safely from Poland."

"Which you have obviously failed to do."

"I did everything within my power to keep her safe until. . .we were separated." For some reason, David didn't care to expound on how. The earl probably would find fault with his reasoning anyway. "There was no reason she shouldn't have been on the plane."

The man harrumphed and reached into his desk for a single sheet of paper that resembled a loose page from a notebook and slid it across the glossy surface.

David's heart thudded at the sight of Nadia's writing. He sank into the nearby chair to read.

> *Lord Wintour,*
> *I am not able to leave Poland at this time, but my father asked that I look to you for help if I have need of it. And so, with hopes of your friendship being sufficient, I ask a favor. Please see to the care of these children and the women accompanying them. I will hopefully be able to join them soon, but there is something I must do here. I will be making my way to Lithuania, God willing.*
>
>

Nadezhda Roenne

David wiped a hand down his face, a dozen questions ringing in his brain. Why did she remain behind? Why wasn't she here waiting for him? What was so important she couldn't leave it behind?

He looked at the paper again, his gaze dropping to a few scribbled words at the bottom.

> *A note for David Reid, if by God's grace he makes it to England. David, you are no longer responsible for me. This was my choice.*

"I assume you are the man she mentions."

"Yes."

"Why did you leave her? You admit that her father gave you charge of her safekeeping."

"You said you would keep him safe." His aunt's wails echoed across the years. He'd tried to apologize, tried to explain how they had warned Ben

away from the current, but he had chosen to swim deeper. In the end, the fault rested entirely on David's shoulders and excuses were pointless.

David found his feet and folded the note into his pocket.

You are no longer responsible for me. This was my choice.

No. He should have forced her onto the first plane the day the invasion had begun. Her life never should have been at risk.

"Where are you going?"

David looked back, forcing his mind back to the present. "I need to see Bieta and Krys. And the baby. Where are they?"

Another grunt of displeasure. "I have placed them in an apartment together with the others who arrived." The earl snatched up his pen and jotted down what appeared to be an address.

David took it and gripped it tight. While he longed to see the girls and make sure everyone else was well, Nadia's absence ate at him. "Will you send someone to Lithuania?"

"What?"

"Lithuania. Nadia said she would head there. I'll go. I'll find her and bring her back to London."

"You? Haven't you already failed? And where in Lithuania do you hope to find her? If she makes it that far. If she contacts us, we will be better able to plan."

David shook his head through the speech. "I'll figure it out myself if I have to, but I have to try." He strode from the room. First, he would check on the girls and then figure out how to find Nadia and bring her to safety. He refused to give up this time, no matter how strong the current.

≡ CHAPTER 31 ≡

David felt some of the weight he'd carried the past couple of weeks lift from his shoulders as two pairs of arms gripped his neck, holding so tightly that gaining another breath became a momentary concern. He hugged his girls back, soaking in the soapy smell of their shiny hair and the giggles when he planted kisses on their ears.

"I. . ." Bieta looked into his face, her smaller one only inches away. "I pray for you."

"And I felt those prayers," he whispered back. "Dziękuję."

"Thank you?" Krys said.

"Tak. Thank you." They had spoken a few English words to him in the past, but it was obvious Zoita had taken adjusting them to their new home seriously. Who could say how long before they could return to Poland, if ever? It was easier to picture them in America with him, where they could have the food, protection, and love they needed.

He tried to picture Nadia coming too. The thought might have made him smile if he knew she was safe.

When he moved to stand, Krys held on tighter, and he lifted her with him, a motion that sent a spasm of pain through his still-healing ribs.

Bieta's eyes widened. "You hurt?"

"Just some aches and pains."

Zoita raised a brow while Polish rolled from her tongue, her first comments directed at him, before turning her attention to the girls. A curse upon the Germans and instructions to be more careful. She offered him tea, and he pulled a chair to the table. Despite the warning, both girls had climbed onto his knees by the time she placed a steaming cup in front of him. He didn't mind the ache since it meant having the girls in his arms.

"Gdzie Arek?" David glanced around the humble room, barely large enough to hold the table, a stove, sink, and set of cabinets. A line with laundry hung over their heads, adding humidity to the already stuffy space.

"Sleep." Zoita motioned to a closed doorway. "Both boys sleep." She switched to Polish with the addition of a few English words to explain that the older girl, Mira, sat in with the napping boys, still hesitant to be away from her brother. The earl's man of business had found Aleksy work in a shop nearby.

David sipped the bitter tea, exhaustion creeping over him and pulling his eyes closed for lengthening moments. He finally set his cup aside and rested his chin on Bieta's head as she snuggled against him. He felt himself sag, then caught himself. He had no time to sleep, not yet. Not until he knew that something was being done to find Nadia. He gulped down the last of his tea but craved something stronger, something that might help him wake up a little. He planted a kiss on each of the girls' heads, wishing he could stay with them longer. They slid off his lap, their eyes searching his, pleading that he wouldn't disappear again.

"I'll be back in a couple of hours." He squeezed Bieta's hand. "*Zaraz wracam.*"

She gave a solemn nod. He pulled away and snatched the parcel from where he had left it on the table. He'd grown so used to its presence, he hardly thought of it anymore, but he had promised to mail it from England. For an officer of the Gestapo. He dropped it back on the table to deal with later. Right now his focus needed to be on Nadia.

Despite his short reprieve, David felt surprisingly rested as he started across London toward the *Times* building. Easy enough to get directions, and an hour or so later he climbed the steps to the second story and the office of Thomas Kent. The name greeted him from a windowed door in bold black lettering, and David pushed inside.

Stacks of papers and newsprint buried a desk and partially hid the man behind it, phone pressed to his ear as he spewed orders. The voice David recognized, though the man did not seem to match it. Short and stocky with a ring of gray hair around the back of his head and round spectacles perched on his rather large nose. Kent cast a thin glance at David but otherwise ignored him until he clicked the receiver back into place.

"What do you want?"

A way into Lithuania. But that was probably not the place to start. "I want to make sure you received my photographs."

His thin brows rose above his glasses. "You're American." His next take was one David would expect of a journalist, very thorough. "And you didn't have the easiest time of it by the look of things. I wondered if we'd ever have the pleasure. Reid, I presume?"

David provided a nod.

"What did happen to you? We received your film and a plane full of Poles, but no Lady Roenne and little by the way of explanation."

"I took a detour through Germany. Unfortunately, without my camera."

"More the pity." Kent stood and pulled a familiar satchel off a nearby shelf.

"Not as much as the fact that Lady Roenne is still in Poland somewhere."

The man handed David the satchel before settling back into his chair. "Though of her own choice. Not much we can do about that."

"I refuse to accept that." He glanced inside the flap at his camera and other belongings, all as he had left them in Nadia's care.

Kent's lips pursed, almost as if something amused him. "I must admit your photos are impressive. You have talent."

"That isn't why I'm here." Though he couldn't deny the sensation of pleasure he felt at hearing the praise he had worked so long for. Recognition. Acceptance. Somehow it felt hollow now.

"This is one of my favorites." Kent produced a medium-sized print of a photograph and laid it on top of a stack of newspapers. David glanced down at the smooth tones of gray depicting Nadia cradling Arek, her eyes narrowed in a playful glare. His heart hammered and he swallowed at the memories of that day. Of holding her one last time, kissing her, trying to keep her safe from forces he had no control over.

"I thought as much when I looked over your film. You're in love with her."

David took the photo between two fingers, the truth of the words no longer something he could deny. "I need to get to Lithuania. That's where she was headed."

"Unfortunately, our agreement was your photos for a plane out of Poland, and that has been met. Yes, I was acquainted with Baron Roenne and would hate to see anything happen to his daughter, but it's not as though I have personal say over the paper's resources."

David studied the photo, his mind working. "What if I were to get you more photos? A three-month contract to go wherever you want me to once Nadia is safe in London."

Kent leaned back in his chair while his gray brows rose. "Even if that were to take you back into Germany?"

David clenched his teeth, an all too familiar fear slithering through him. "Yes. Anywhere."

"A six-month contract, and we cover travel and living expenses here and abroad."

Six months seemed an eternity compared with the last month. But he would be making a living and a name for himself, and Nadia would be safe. He nodded.

Kent cracked a smile and motioned to the photo. "Take that with you. I'll see what we can put together, and we'll be in touch. Where do I reach you?"

David gave the address of Zoita's apartment, though there wasn't room for him to stay there. He would spend time with the girls while he waited and make sure Zoita could find him. He shook the man's hand and walked stiffly from the office. He tried not to think about what his agreement might mean for him or any future with Nadia.

He made it a few steps out of the office when he remembered his lack of funds for even basic needs while arrangements were being made. He turned back inside, catching Kent with his hand on the telephone. He looked up. "Change your mind already?"

"No. But my family hasn't heard from me since the Germans invaded Poland. I should let them know I'm all right." And ask them to forward what little savings were left in his accounts.

"Very well." Kent grabbed his pen and scribbled something on a notepad, his signature at the bottom. He ripped the paper free and held it out. "There is a telephone on the main floor that will grant you more privacy. Give this to Mable at reception, and she'll set you up and see that the company covers the expense."

"Thank you." David took the paper and turned to leave.

"Reid."

He glanced back.

"Transatlantic calls don't come cheap, so keep it short."

"Of course." He made his way back down the stairs, a new trepidation growing inside him. It had been a while since he'd spoken to his family, let alone asked for anything.

☰CHAPTER 32☰

"You have caused enough trouble."

David trudged back to the apartment, satchel over his shoulder, hat low on his brow, the short conversation he'd had with his father sloshing around in his head.

"Just come home. Your mother has been worried sick."

More rhetoric. More guilt. More failure on David's part.

A burst of feminine laughter slowed him in front of a large window that allowed him view of almost a dozen tables. Couples and small groups crowded around them, drinks in hand. David's own thirst ached in his throat. He turned inside the pub and found a dark spot against a wall. Alone. He dropped his hat on the table and raked his fingers through his thick, shaggy locks. He'd grown a beard over the past month too. And he still desperately needed a bath. The only thing he really wanted to drown in, though, was alcohol. He hardly cared what kind.

"Stop thinking only of yourself."

David hadn't been. He'd tried to explain about the girls and Nadia, of being needed here, but his father probably hadn't heard him. Had he ever really listened?

A woman appeared over David's table, and he mumbled that anything would do. She raised a fine brow and slipped away, returning a moment later with a pint of dark liquid. Beer. Something stronger would have suited his mood better, but this was safer. He downed it before she had turned away. She gave a nod and took the glass with her. The residual burn in the back of his throat served as a momentary distraction. But not for long before his thoughts returned to the conversation. Why did his parents even care what happened to him? So what if he hadn't made it out of Poland alive?

No, Mother had a kind heart. She loved him and worried about him. But Father? His concern was only for Mother's sake. That's why he lost his temper. Every time it was because David had been a burden upon Mother, made her worry, been thoughtless. He had to think a lot further back to remember any affection from the man, never mind acceptance.

This time the woman returned with a shorter glass and a bottle. The lighter liquid swirled inside. Whiskey—or scotch, according to the label. David nodded his thanks, hoping she mistook the moisture in his eyes for exhaustion or the premature effects of drink. He tipped the second glass back and then closed his eyes before a tear could escape. Exhaustion made him weak and raw. He needed to make his way back to Zoita's apartment and see if she'd allow him to sleep on the floor in the kitchen. There wasn't a lot of room there, but what choice did he have?

He wouldn't be in England long anyway. Soon he'd be on his way to Lithuania and then Poland if Nadia hadn't made it that far. He'd not stop looking. He couldn't stop.

Even if his family refused to accept that.

He didn't bother filling up his glass again. A waste of energy he didn't have. Deep down he had always been hunting for some way to make his family proud of him, to make them want him again. Maybe if his photos became famous, he'd get a clap on the back.

A laugh jammed itself into his throat. He had told his old man about his photos being published, being praised, that the *Times* wanted more.

"What they want is someone fool enough to risk his life for them. Any idiot can figure out how to use a camera."

David might have to ask for something stronger after all. His father was probably right. Maybe his photos weren't worth anything. Maybe *he* wasn't worth anything. He'd failed Nadia over and over again. He'd failed the girls. Everyone. Over and over. Even now. They'd all be better off without him. It was he who was needy. He who inserted himself into their lives whether they wanted him or not.

Just come home.

Why? So his mother could stop worrying? If he got himself killed over here, she could do the same.

He took another swig of whiskey. He'd do whatever was necessary to get Nadia to England, and then the *Times* could do whatever they liked with him. The girls were fine without him now. They didn't need him messing up their lives too.

———— ≈ ————

October 2, 1939

David woke to prodding with something hard. He forced his eyes open to the glare of the morning sun—and the darker glare of a policeman in black.

"Go home, or you'll find yourself sleeping it off in a cell."

Go home. Go home. Go home. The chant continued in time with his throbbing head. David dragged himself onto unsteady legs and searched the area for his hat. Nothing. His satchel with his camera hung around his neck, but his hat was gone. David raked his fingers through his greasy hair and started down the path leading to the street. He'd have to figure out where he was before he could figure out where to go. *Home* was not an option, though everyone kept insisting it. No one seemed to realize he didn't have one.

A horn blared, keeping him from crossing the street just then. He paused a moment, then plowed forward. He never had liked cities. Too noisy. Too pushy. Too many people judging. It took a while to reorient himself, but within an hour or so, his vision was a little clearer and he managed to find his way back to Zoita's. He raised his fist to knock, but the door swung open before he made contact.

"*Ojej!*" Zoita jerked back in surprise, then narrowed her eyes at him.

David waved the impending questions aside and glanced from the baby she carried to the two girls almost jumping in place—no, they were definitely jumping—with huge grins on their faces. They chattered in Polish, but his mind was still too sluggish to keep up as well as he usually could.

"What?"

"Lady Nadia has come!" Zoita actually smiled, something he had never seen on her face. "She send for *dzieci*."

David's thoughts sped along with his heart. What if he misunderstood?

How was it possible? "Nadia is in London?"

"Tak. Send *samochód*. She ask see dzieci."

The children, but not him? The sting dug deep before he found reason. She might not expect him in England, might not know he'd made it out alive. "I'll come."

"Nie, nie, nie," Zoita shooed him into the apartment. "You wash."

David wanted to protest that there was no time. But Zoita's stance detoured any argument, and she was right. He stepped to the sink and poured water over his hands. He washed his face, swished the bitterness out of his mouth, and combed his wet fingers through his hair. The few minutes of activity left much to be desired, but he couldn't do much more with Zoita standing by, and he didn't have a change of clothes or a razor.

He pulled Krys up and started down the stairwell. Nadia was safe. That was all that mattered right now. He would see her again. He couldn't quite believe it—wouldn't allow himself to until he saw her, held her, kissed her thoroughly.

Instead of walking, as he'd mentally prepared himself to do, a sleek burgundy Rolls-Royce waited out front. He held Krys on his knee for the ride across the city, then released her to climb out first, sudden nervousness making him less than steady. What if Nadia wasn't really in London? What if she'd been injured? What if she felt that he had failed her too?

David took Krys back into his arms to scale the grand steps leading to the earl's home. It felt longer than a day since he'd been there last. Again, hope sped him.

When the door opened, the butler eyed him, obviously aware David had not been on the guest list. Thankfully, the man said nothing and led them down the hallway to a parlor or sitting room or whatever the British called it. David allowed Zoita and Bieta to go ahead and let Krys down from his arms before stepping inside.

To nothing. An empty room decorated in lavender tones. He'd call it light purple, but sprigs of the plant ornamented the wallpaper and stood in arrangements in large vases.

"Lady Roenne will join you in a moment." The butler closed the door behind him.

Zoita glanced at him and then at the room before ordering the children to touch nothing. She hovered over them like a mother hen, a role she played well to everyone in her care.

They all spun as the door opened again and Nadia stepped into the room flanked by Lord and Lady Wintour. She was alive. And here. But her left arm wore a sling, and her face held little color. The smile she gave the children did not reach her blue eyes, but then she raised her gaze to his and took a sharp breath. "David." Hardly a whisper. "You survived."

So, they hadn't told her he'd already been here looking for her.

"How did you. . ." She started across the room toward him.

"A long story and journey." Though he surprisingly felt less weary from it than only minutes ago.

She took in every inch of him, as though checking to make sure he'd arrived in one piece. He did the same with her, the relief of seeing her finally safe giving way to questions about where she had been and why. He reached for her.

"How good that you were able to join us, Mr. Reid." The earl appeared beside them, his expression as hard as his voice. He seemed to take David's measure as well, and his nose wrinkled. "I sense you have been busy since your arrival."

Heat seared David's spine, a strange marriage between anger and shame. Of course he smelled of whiskey and sweat from walking back and forth across the city. His clothes were dirty, and his hair messed without even a hat to hide it under. The earl didn't hide his contempt, but how long before Nadia realized that she shared it?

ЕCHAPTER 33Е

Nadia wanted to weep from both relief and sorrow at the sight of David standing before her looking so worn and. . .broken. She could not help but feel at fault. The yellowing of bruising curved along one eye and up across his temple. A small scar tagged the side of his mouth. She ached to reach out and smooth her fingers over his face or to throw her good arm around his neck and hold on until the aching in her soul eased.

But the earl had already taken her arm and was leading her away, deeper into the gathering in the middle of the room. She glanced back at David and his tight jaw. She could not read his eyes; it was a look she had never seen before. A dark look. What had the Germans done to him?

The girls were back at her side, and Zoita brought Arek to her. Nadia would speak with David soon. At least she knew he was here. That was enough for now. She lowered onto a sofa and asked for Arek. The girls climbed up beside her while their gazes scanned the large room, wonder in their eyes. She wrapped the baby with her right arm, away from the pinching pain in her left shoulder. She would not be separated from him again if she could help it, from any of them.

"Why didn't you leave with everyone else?" David's voice rasped.

Nadia looked up from the children. "Frajda and her family. I could not leave them." But how to explain the intensity of her feelings on the matter—that they would not have survived if they remained in Poland. And now the questioning whether she had done the right thing. Yes, Binjamin was mending well in a hospital, but if things had ended differently, she would never be able to forgive herself.

"Where are they now?"

"They remained in Lithuania for now. Though I have spoken with Lord Wintour, and he has agreed to help make arrangements to bring them here."

"Of course. Lord Wintour is all goodness." David smiled tightly, his hands shoving deep in his pockets. If not for the tightness in his shoulders and the intensity of the gaze that he shifted away from her, he would look like a lost boy. "What happened to your arm?"

"A mishap along the way." Now was not the time to recount what had happened, not with the current audience. When they were alone, she would tell David everything, every dark secret that had torn her identity from her, every painful moment that had broken her heart.

His lips thinned and he nodded. "Well, I'm glad you made it to England in one piece."

Without my help—she could hear it in his tone and the way he withdrew.

"I hope to see you again soon." The last words had softened with a plea.

"Soon," she promised, craving time with him.

David nodded, then turned on his heel and strode out of the room.

"Good riddance," the earl mumbled from a chair opposite her.

Nadia wanted to argue, to chastise the man for his ill opinion of David, but her throat tightened and her eyes burned with the warning that words would open the floodgates that she had so carefully maintained since her arrival last night. She had been trained how to control her emotions, but she was so tired. All she wanted right now was to settle the children into the nursery where Lord Wintour had agreed to let them stay for a time.

The room lapsed into heavy silence. Nadia looked to Zoita. Speaking Polish in the presence of the lord and lady of the house would be considered rude, but the woman deserved the courtesy. "Thank you for caring for the girls and Arek in my place. I will be able to see to their care now, but you also have the young woman and her brother?"

"Mira and Amiel." Zoita's expression softened. "I will watch over them."

"Thank you." Nadia forced a smile for the woman though she did not feel it. Not as she should. Zoita had left more behind in Poland than Nadia had, including a husband who, as a soldier, may have been taken as a prisoner of war or killed. In the past couple of weeks, Nadia had learned how cruel a tormenter the unknown could be. She wished she had more to offer the woman who gave so selflessly to others. "I will see you have the funds needed to support them." What little Nadia could offer for now. Though she was not sure of her financial position, Lord Wintour had already mentioned investments and accounts Tata had moved to England over the past two years as German aggression had grown.

"Shall I ring for the nurse to come for the children?" Lady Wintour asked, rising from the chair she had occupied quietly. She was all grace but showed little compassion for those she believed so far beneath her. Nadia saw too much of her mother, and even herself, in the woman's proud gaze.

"Thank you, but I will take the children to the nursery and see them settled." She took another moment to thank Zoita again and promised to visit her soon, and then told the girls to follow. Bieta popped to her feet and gripped Krys' hand. As Nadia led them from the room, she explained that they would be staying here with her. They would have new dresses and shoes and toys.

"What of Tata? Will he live with us too?" Krys asked.

Words clogged Nadia's throat. Krys knew her father had been killed. How did she not remember?

"He looked so sad when he left," the child continued, her voice small. "But he will come back, won't he?"

Nadia's heart spasmed. "He did look sad. But we will see him again soon, I am sure."

"But won't he live here with us?"

Nadia paused and met the girl's pleading gaze. "I am afraid not. Not yet." Her own desires grew clearer with her final statement. What would it be like to have a home of their own with David? What if they could become a family? Was it even possible? She had never considered such a future, but now the thought left her head spinning and chest yearning.

"Good day, m'lady," a woman greeted as they stepped into the nursery. She was older than Nadia had imagined but appeared kind with gentle eyes as she turned toward the children. "Lady Wintour told me to be ready for the children."

"Yes. Thank you." Nadia's only regret was that the woman spoke no Polish, and communicating with the girls might be a problem at the start. "This is Bieta and Krys." She used their shortened names to make it easier for the woman. "And Arek."

"What are the names in English, if I may ask?"

"Elisabeth, Christina, and Aaron."

"Thank you, m'lady." She extended her arms to the baby. "May I?"

"Soon. I need a few more minutes with him." Though her left shoulder throbbed, she was not ready to leave him or the girls, who had already started exploring the shelves of books and toys. Lord and Lady Wintour's two children were closer to Nadia's age, and both were married if she remembered correctly. They likely had, or soon would have, grandchildren to visit their lovely nursery.

"Lady Wintour told me to encourage you to rest, m'lady. The children will be well enough here with me."

"I will rest here." Where she was needed.

In the larger of the attached bedrooms, Nadia set Arek in the middle of the double bed and stretched out beside him. His tiny hands patted her face, and she kissed his nose. Bieta slipped onto the bed behind Nadia and wrapped an arm around her waist. Her wound pinched at the pressure of the child's head from behind, but Nadia refused to pull away. Krys scampered around and climbed on with Arek, forming a crescent behind him.

Nadia tipped her head to rest against Krys', then allowed her eyes to close. Maybe now she would find sleep. It had eluded her last night in the large room with a four-post bed of mahogany. Matching furniture created a beautiful contrast to the soft blues and creams of the curtains and bedding. Beautiful but lonely. With no distractions to keep her from reliving the weeks of travel, endless nights steering a military truck north, the lives of everyone in the back heavy on her shoulders, always wondering if the next turn in the road would bring them face-to-face with more Nazis.

Watching Binjamin fall.

The feel of the trigger under her finger.

Death.

Her father, the German officer.

The lies that formed the tapestry of her life giving way, unraveling everything she knew.

The bite of a bullet ripping into her shoulder.

Having no option but to give all control over to God. . .

Nadia finally fell asleep with David filling her thoughts. . .and hope in her heart.

ᴇCHAPTER 34ᴇ

October 2, 1939

Twenty-four hours after their first meeting, David stepped into Thomas Kent's office. The man looked up from behind his stacks of papers and offered a nod. "Not quite done making arrangements yet."

David grabbed a chair from the wall and pulled it closer before dropping into it. It was even less comfortable than it looked. "No arrangements are needed. Lady Roenne arrived in London last night."

Kent's eyes widened, and he took the glasses from his nose to clean them with a hanky. "That's good news for you."

"Yeah." And it was. He was glad she was here, glad she was safe. He had no reason to feel how he did.

Kent pushed his glasses back on and eyed him. "Why are you here? Just wanted to let me know you have no plans for Lithuania now?"

"I guess. Thought you should know."

Silence made David want to squirm, but in reality he wasn't sure why he was still there. What was he waiting for?

"That bad?" Kent opened a drawer of his desk and pulled out a flask before offering it across the desk.

David shook his head. He'd already made that mistake and still paid the consequences.

Kent settled back into his seat. "So where does that leave us?"

"I need funds. Enough to rent an apartment. Living expenses."

"Ah." Again, he said it like he knew too much.

221

"I'm not asking for charity."

"No, you're asking for a job. And the one I have for you isn't in London."

"Where exactly do you want to send me?"

"You're American and not at war with Germany like we are. No reason we can't send you in for a couple of weeks with a journalist who knows the language. A descriptive article is great, but photographs really sell the story."

David filled his lungs, forcing past the stiffness and ache that remained. He'd been willing to do anything for Nadia. But was this for her? In a way, yes. He needed money to remain in London. He needed to be in London to see if he had any chance with her. Even if he convinced her to come back to the States with him, it would take time and money to make arrangements for her and the children. He couldn't leave them behind.

Yet, at the moment, all of that was slipping away. He'd felt more in control a few weeks ago dodging bombs than on the streets of London trying to figure out what came next.

"Here."

David refocused on the man and the twenty pound note he extended. "Get cleaned up and have a good night's sleep. You can give me your answer later."

"But if I don't take the job, I won't have the means to pay you back."

Kent shrugged. "Your last photos were a lot better than I thought they'd be. You don't owe me anything."

David sat a moment longer before finding his feet and accepting the offering. "Thanks."

"Good luck" was the only reply.

He'd need it.

David walked out of the office with a little more purpose than the last time. He asked at the building Zoita lived in, but although they had no available rooms, the building across the street offered him a one-room apartment with its own water closet. He cleaned up as best he could and then allowed himself a couple hours of sleep. It was still light outside when he awoke, so he went in search of a change of clothes and a hat. By dinnertime he felt like a new man. One determined to have a conversation with Nadia that lasted more than two minutes.

October 3, 1939

Nadia sat across from Lord Wintour and his solicitor, trying to fully grasp what he told her. All of Baron Roenne's holdings and properties in Poland were lost for the time being due to the Nazis, but Tata had been watching the turn of political tides and knew Poland's frailties. He had moved a large amount of his wealth to England for safekeeping. Other amounts had been placed in investments that fared well with Britain declaring themselves at war. Investments in steel alone were paying handsomely.

But what did that mean for her if she was not even his daughter?

"My mother. Would she not have rights to most now that my father is deceased?" She had not provided a proper heir—one the baron could truly claim, but she was his wife and had brought some wealth into their marriage.

"Your father made the necessary adjustments before his passing. Most of the accounts were amended to reflect you as the lone beneficiary," the solicitor supplied.

"Me?" But she was not even his—

"Needless to say, you will have every comfort while in England." Lord Wintour sounded as pleased as though he were responsible.

"Thank you." She rose, and the gentlemen hurried to do likewise. Yes, she had more questions, but they could be answered another day when she did not feel so overwhelmed. She had not seen the children since breakfast and was anxious to check in on them. Krys had awakened half the house with her screams in the night. A nightmare she had been too frightened by to speak of. She had cuddled against Nadia until they both fell back asleep.

"I believe my wife is waiting for you in the yellow drawing room, if you would be kind enough to join her. She has friends wishing to meet you."

"Of course." Nadia made her way in that direction instead of the nursery. She owed the Wintours for their kindness and hated to offend them. She knew very well what her mother would think of a woman who would rather spend hours in the nursery instead of seeing to her social duties.

Nadia paused outside the drawing room. Was her mother happy now back in Germany? She had never loved her life in Poland. . .or perhaps she had spent her life pining for the man she could never have. Even now a war separated them.

"Ah, here she is now," Lady Wintour crooned upon her entry.

The other two ladies smiled, albeit tightly, as they greeted Nadia and introductions were made. She was hardly of the frame of mind to listen to their niceties, but she was very capable of smiling prettily and speaking of meaningless things.

"Your English is beautiful, Lady Nadezhda," the younger of the pair complimented.

"You are so kind." *And so naive of anything beyond this drawing room and city.* The young woman was close to Nadia in age, but Nadia's soul felt old, as though the past month had aged her fifty years. She took the dainty cup handed her and managed a sip, all the while images of Warsaw and what her people endured wrung her stomach. With Germans on one hand, Soviets on the other, and the Polish government in hiding, hope was gone.

"What are your thoughts, Lady Nadezhda?"

"Nadia, please," she said to keep them from stumbling over her name yet again. "If it is easier for you, you may call me Nadia."

A blush rose to the younger woman's face, but she managed to hide her shock with a smile. "It is somewhat foreign to my tongue. Whatever does your name mean?"

At least they had changed topics and she was not caught with her wandering thoughts. "Hope. Nadezhda means hope. I was named for my grandmother who was born a Russian royal. Before the current Soviet regime, obviously." Except even that was a lie now. Why had Tata given her that name? Had he not known her paternity at the time? So much she ached to know, but any answers were buried under three stories of rubble halfway across Europe.

"Yes, it was quite horrid what became of the royal family when the Russians had their revolt." Lady Wintour shook her head as though it mattered to her.

"The world is changing quickly." As was her understanding of it. Nadia set her tea aside, no longer able to sit so calmly. All her life had been so focused on her role in society, continuing traditions and knowing her place. The daughter of a baron. Now the proud Roenne line had come to an end because she was the illegitimate daughter of a German farmer.

Despite the thick walls of the grand house, raised voices at the front door drew Nadia to her feet.

"What on earth?" Lady Wintour also rose and excused herself from her guests. Nadia followed her into the hall just as the large door clicked closed. The butler looked back at them and dipped his head.

"My apologies, m'lady. There shan't be any more disruptions."

"Very well." She turned and motioned Nadia to return with her, but Nadia had no interest in more pleasant chatter over too-sweet tea. She wanted to see the children and make plans on how to best move forward.

"I do not feel up to it at the moment. Please make my apologies to your guests."

The woman stiffened. "Go and rest, then. Though I do hope you feel better by the dinner we will be hosting in your honor this Friday. We would very much like to introduce you into London society."

A dinner party was the last thing of interest to Nadia, but she smiled her thanks and excused herself. She knew her place and what was expected of her. Had lived with it her whole life. Smile pleasantly and try to convince the world you are happy. . .when you have never felt more miserable and lost.

October 4, 1939

David tapped his fist against the door, grateful when a smile greeted him on the other side. A very different greeting than the last door he'd knocked on. If only Nadia had come to live with Zoita instead of some earl who evidently didn't want David anywhere near her. The butler said he would inform Nadia of his request to see her, but she would have come to him already if she had wanted to see him.

Wouldn't she have?

Zoita waved him toward the table and set a piece of cake or bread in front of him. He wasn't sure which until he took a bite. Definitely bread. Not sweet but quite savory, so he chewed it down and thanked her. He wasn't sure why he came here every day since learning Nadia had kept the girls with her. He fought a surge of resentment. Not toward Nadia—it was good she wanted to care for the girls. But it meant they were out of his reach now.

Zoita shoved an envelope into his hands, and his resentment met confusion. An expensive card stock with the earl's crest. He ripped the side to find an invitation within. To a dinner. At the very house that had refused him entrance the past two days.

He hadn't much time to consider what it meant when a parcel was shoved at him. He looked to Zoita, who raised a brow at him, to the parcel he had brought with him from Germany. He had quite happily forgotten about it, but his conscience pricked him now. The man had asked one thing of him, and David owed him his life. Even if the man was a Nazi.

David eyed the package. He couldn't in good conscience forward the package without knowing he was not forwarding harmful information or propaganda. If it contained a copy of *Mein Kampf*, David would burn it without regret.

He slid his plate aside and untied the string that bound the parcel. His confidence wavered as he began folding back the brown paper. An old book with a worn leather cover lay within.

Die Bibel.

The Bible? The book was probably more than a hundred years old by the look of it. He gently turned the page to lists of names, generations of births, marriages, and deaths. The following page bore the title again as well as a scattering of other words he couldn't quite understand. Until the name *D. Martin Luthers*. At least he thought the last letter was a fancy *s*. A date had been printed on the last line: *1787*.

David closed the book, a reverence settling over him. He sat a moment before opening the letter that accompanied it. Written in German.

Another reason to see Nadia.

He wrapped the book back in the paper but placed the letter in his pocket. He thanked Zoita and slid the Bible into his satchel beside his camera. He would mail it as directed, but first he wanted to know the contents of the letter—to know why this was what a Gestapo officer wanted safely out of his country and to the United States.

His fingers brushed the envelope Baron Roenne had given him a month earlier and froze. This wasn't the only letter Nadia needed to read.

⊰CHAPTER 35⊱

October 6, 1939

Poland had fallen. Lost. Sliced in half between the Nazis and Soviets. The news had arrived not more than an hour ago. Nadia stood in the foyer, smile pasted on her face as though she were unaffected by her country's pain, while her hosts welcomed their friends and introduced her to a long line of elegant strangers. This was her first evening without her sling in place to stave off the insincere and awkward questions she had no desire to answer. How had this been her life only a month ago? How was it possible to have changed so fully in such a short time?

"You are very beautiful," one woman commented. "No doubt you will steal many young gentlemen's hearts during your stay."

"And a few of the older ones' hearts as well," another woman stated with less kindness. "Men are fascinated by accents."

Nadia smiled demurely, not allowing the barbs to meet their target. "I hope they will guard their hearts, for that is not my intent while in London."

Lady Wintour glanced at her out of the corner of her eye, and Nadia sensed her hostess's displeasure. Perhaps the woman hoped for a gentleman to remove her from their care. Nadia would be careful not to overstay her welcome. She had endured enough of her mother's matchmaking over the years, and her heart was already taken, whether or not there was a future with him.

A terse whisper pulled her attention to the open door where the butler stood with a scowl. He looked from the invitation in his hand to the earl. David met her gaze before returning his focus to the butler who blocked his way.

"What is that man doing here?" Lord Wintour mumbled under his breath as he stepped forward.

Nadia matched his stride. "I invited him."

He stalled. "Now is not the time for entertaining such. . ." It seemed that the right word, or at least a polite variation, was not to be found.

"I assure you, Mr. Reid is able to navigate such an evening. He was my father's guest on several occasions." Though only one dinner party.

The earl motioned to the butler before returning to his wife. Nadia remained in place, grateful her greeting need not be under full scrutiny. She turned her entire focus on David—or was it him drawing it? Clean-shaven, with hair trimmed and combed, he reminded her of the first evening they had met, him in a plain tweed jacket and no tie. He had done better tonight, his coat still brown, but the color suited him. She smiled as he stepped near, and she brushed her fingers down his blue tie. "Impressive," she said in Polish.

"Dobry wieczór, Dama Nadezhda."

She did not like his stiff posture or the grim look in his eyes. "Hi."

"You never came." He shot a glance to their hosts, while keeping his voice low.

"Every day. I came every day. You were not there, and Zoita was uncertain where you are staying."

"An apartment across the street." His gaze bore into her, and she wet her lips. How could they stand here so properly after all they had been through together? She wanted his arms around her as he assured her that he wanted her.

"I need to talk to you."

"Tak, after dinner. We will slip away." She refused to repeat her mother's mistakes.

"Ah, Mr. Reid." Lord Wintour came alongside them. "So glad you could join us." Even if his voice betrayed the lie. "We must ask you not to monopolize Lady Nadezhda's time tonight. She has more guests to greet. Important men."

Nadia held her cringe. David would not understand the reference.

Lord Wintour had suggested this evening with a twofold purpose. The first was to bring Poland's plight to men who had the ear of the prime minister. The second was for her to gain a footing in English society—a purpose she was no longer certain she wished to pursue.

"Of course." David tipped his head and strode past. Instead of intermingling with the other guests, he stood stoically near a wall. So out of place. What had she been thinking, inviting him here? She should have focused her efforts tonight on Poland's behalf.

David Reid had already done what he could.

———≋———

David stabbed the potato with his fork but didn't bother raising it to his mouth. His appetite had fled as soon as he'd seen Nadia that evening, a stranger again. He'd become so used to seeing her in her worn skirt and simple blouse, he'd forgotten about *Lady Nadezhda*, daughter of a baron and a world above him. Even now she sat at the far end of the table in easy conversation with an earl and who knew who else. The only pleasure David found was that the smile frozen on her face was not real.

"You are an American?" the woman seated beside him questioned.

"Yes," he said shortly, not eager to engage in conversation.

"We visited New York several years ago. A fascinating city."

"I haven't been."

An older man across from them chuckled. "Where exactly do you hail from, Mr. Reid? We were told you were acquainted with Lady Roenne."

"I met her in Poland. I'm from Idaho."

That seemed to stump everyone for a few moments, no doubt unsure of where Idaho was.

"The far west?" the gentlemen ventured. "Are you a cowboy?"

"A photographer. For the *Times* here in London." Though he hadn't accepted the assignment, he wanted something to make him feel less like a. . .nobody.

The conversation continued around him, and he kept any replies to one-word answers. Finally, the ladies were invited to retire to the drawing room to visit while the men remained in place. A glass of port was placed in front of David, tempting him with something to take the edge off his discomfort. He lifted the glass and swirled the crimson liquid within.

Then he set it down and excused himself.

He couldn't very well track Nadia down and pull her away from a room full of women, but his girls were somewhere in this house. He needed to know that they were happy here.

Why wouldn't they be?

Every need was provided. They had Nadia nearby. The only thing they lacked was him, but most people got along just fine without him.

He asked a servant on the second floor where he would find the children. Thankfully, the young man was in too much of a hurry to question David and pointed him in the direction of the "nursery." His first thought was why the older girls were in a room meant for babies, but understanding grew when he walked through the doorway into what may as well have been a small house inside a large one. A small dining area with a half-sized table. A parlor with a sofa, and a tea set on a small side table. The library and toy area took up most of the space, with doors open to bedrooms.

The lights were low and no one was in sight, so David made his way to the bedrooms. The first held a crib and a sleeping Arek. David took a moment to watch the rise and fall of the baby's chest. The tension that had built during the meal finally found release in the child's peaceful slumber. David's own breathing deepened.

After a while, he turned into the second bedroom. The light was off, but a streetlamp outside the window glowed through lace curtains and lit his way. One fair-sized bed sat in the middle of the room holding two sleeping girls. Blond braids lay on the pillow they shared despite the two pillows provided. Krys cuddled against her sister so their heads nearly touched.

His girls.

But not really his. He had no claim on them, nothing to link them other than memories and how deeply they'd burrowed into his heart. Could a real father love them more? He didn't know. Probably never would.

David leaned into the footboard, reality ripping deeper with each breath. He needed to walk away, let them get on with their lives. Same with Nadia. She didn't need him hanging around and complicating her life. The feelings they had for each other had been born of a deep dependency on each other as they'd faced death. So what that he'd stolen a couple of kisses? They didn't mean he and Nadia were meant for something more.

If he was smart, he'd do like he always did, lock his feelings deep and walk away. The *Times* would provide distractions enough. Sooner or later he'd forget how much it hurt.

Resolve flickered like a new flame at the tip of a candle, but it was enough to pull him to the side of the bed where he laid a kiss on each precious head.

"*Do widzenia*, my little *myszy*." He stood upright and drew a hand across his face, catching what moisture had somehow escaped. He needed to get out of this house before he fell apart. Either that or he needed to get a grip on himself. He wasn't a little boy anymore. A man. One who knew pain and loneliness. Tears only made a man weak and sappy. They never fixed anything.

David swallowed hard and turned away, then froze as a shadow moved in the doorway.

"Why are you saying goodbye?" Nadia whispered.

David slipped past into the common area, or whatever they called it over here. He didn't trust his voice not to give him away.

She followed. "You were only saying good night, no? I thought I would bring the children to a park and meet you tomorrow. You will have time with them. And we can talk."

He shook his head. He wasn't strong enough to play that game, to pretend, to hope. "I don't think that's a good idea." He turned to face her, to say his farewell properly.

Her brows pushed together over her wide eyes. "Is it because of tonight? I am sorry, David. I should not have put you through that."

"Guess you forgot how horribly I fit into your world." He stood toe to toe with her, yet so much separated them.

"This is not my world. Not anymore."

"Fooled me." He looked away, not liking how closely she watched him or the moisture again building in his eyes. If only he could hold on to his frustration instead. Anger had served him well in the past.

"I fooled myself. I am a very skilled actress."

He nodded, feeling the sting. "Makes sense." He turned, not trusting her nearness. Not trusting himself.

"Stop! David, please stop walking away, stop turning away. Stop looking away every time I feel you are finally allowing me to really see you."

His eyes slid closed, and he dropped his head forward. She wouldn't like what she saw.

Nadia's hand slipped around his torso. She leaned into his back. "I need you, David."

He gritted his teeth against the sudden need, yet hopelessness. A tear slipped free. Still, he couldn't pull away. "No, you don't. You never did need me. And I don't know what's worse—knowing I failed or understanding that you did it on your own anyway."

≣CHAPTER 36≣

Nadia tightened her grip around him, her palm flat against his chest. "I did not do it without you, David. I could not have. You saved me so many times. What about the car you pulled me from? Or the river? I would be dead if not for you. Bieta and Krys might be dead." She shook her head against his shoulder. "You left me alone for a couple of days, and I got myself shot."

His hand moved over hers, holding it in place.

"You are the reason I had the courage to go back. I am not that brave." Her voice trembled, and she tried to clear it. "Not without you and your faith. You gave me that. And I cannot go forward—I do not want to try and figure out who I am and what I want without you." She pressed her eyes closed, and tears rolled down her cheeks and into the coarse fabric of his jacket. "Everything is so complicated now."

She was suddenly glad he faced away.

"My real father is not Baron Roenne. His name is Ludwig Jäger. That is as much as I learned before he returned to his men."

David's chest expanded under her hand. "A German?"

"The officer who came for my mother." She continued rambling, explaining how he had recognized her at the check stop and everything else that had unfolded. All the while, David slowly turned and reached into his jacket. He withdrew a letter. "What is this?"

"It's from your father—Baron Roenne. To you."

She sucked in a breath, not certain if she dared read it after everything she now knew. Yet there were still so many questions. She took the letter

235

and slid her finger to break the seal, then moved to the sofa and pulled the cord on the nearest lamp. The light glowed down on her tata's script.

> *Nadezhda,*
> *As war approaches, I find myself considering what I am most afraid to lose. Our lands, our home, wealth, the things I have come to place value on, like a fine car or well-bred horse? My life? My family?*
>   *The answer is you. I cannot risk anything happening to you. I am not one to show affection. It is not how I was raised. But I do not want to die with you uncertain of my love for you. I have made the necessary arrangements for you and your mother in London. You will want for nothing.*
>   *Your life is yours to chart. Choose well.*
>   *Your father*

Nadia stared at the page, wishing there was more. More explanation. She knew she was not his daughter—she shared too many features with the German. Why would he claim her? Did he not know? Had Matka never told him the truth?

"Nie." He had to have known that he had never fathered a child with her mother. And yet somehow he still loved her? The great Roenne line and everything his fathers had preserved were at risk, and the thing that concerned him the most was *her*?

She choked on a sob but found her gaze rising to David who stood silent in the middle of the room. He still looked far too torn, as though unsure of whether to offer comfort or flee the room. In his hands, he held another paper.

She sniffled and cleared her throat. "What is that?" If David had written her a goodbye letter too, she would toss it in a fire. If there was one. She would rip it and tear it and tell him she refused to let him leave.

"Another letter."

She braced herself, not sure she could take much more. "From whom?"

"An officer of the Gestapo."

"Co?" Even her real father was not that.

"Now is not the time." He motioned to the letter in her hand. "You have enough to deal with."

A laugh broke from her, though it sounded quite pitiful and tangled with her tears. "Tak, but you wave a letter from a Gestapo officer in my face and leave it at that? Why? How did you come by it?"

Hesitation gave way, and he handed her the folded sheet. "It's a long story. We probably shouldn't pry further, but part of me needs to know why it was so important for him to send a Bible halfway across Europe before mailing it to the United States."

Nadia laid her tata's letter on her lap and opened the German's.

"Dearest Renate," Nadia translated into English. She paused to clear the crackle from her voice. "I have failed. I thought I could be a tempering influence, but instead my hands are stained, and I find myself trapped. I cannot pretend any longer, so I send this to you. I am now glad you have gone from here." The words blurred, but Nadia blinked away tears. She did not understand the emotion or why a particular officer of the *Wehrmacht* came to mind. This letter was not from *him*. "I pray this does not bring trouble upon you. I have done everything I can to ensure you will not bear my shame." She glanced at David, suddenly understanding his role as a buffer between this woman in America and her connection to the increasingly infamous Gestapo. Already Nadia had witnessed the consequences of people learning of her own father's role in the war. She focused back on the heavy script and pressed forward. "May God watch over you and your family. I wish I could have known your children, and that they had known their grandfather, but am glad you have found happiness."

The letter was not signed, but it was too easy to imagine the father she would never truly know, who she should not *want* to know.

She felt the paper slip from her fingers and glanced at David, who folded it back into his pocket.

"I'm sorry. I shouldn't have asked you to read it."

She sniffed and wiped at her cheeks. "I do not remember you asking."

From another pocket, he withdrew a plain, cream-colored handkerchief and set it in her hands. "I never do seem to win arguments against you."

"Obviously because I am always right." She tried for a smile and tucked Tata's note away. Enough tears for one night. Her head already hurt.

David gave a stiff nod and backed away a step.

Why did he look at her as though she had just trampled his soul? Except, no, he would not look at her anymore. "You know better than anyone how often I am wrong, David." He was pulling away again, tucking himself behind the wall he so easily placed between them.

Just as Tata had done. And Matka. And everyone else. . .

What if she was who built the walls?

Or at least helped fortify them. . .

What if she was the one afraid of. . .of what? Being loved? Being wanted? Being seen?

She sank into the sofa, her heart quaking within. Her breath came short and jagged, her lungs refusing to be filled. She pressed her hands over her mouth so no one could hear the wail seeking release. Yes, her parents had been busy and often felt distanced from her, but she had done nothing to draw them closer. Instead, she had rewarded them with more distance, burying her own heart just as deep to protect it. . .for the little good it did. Her heart still ached while she hid behind books, wishing her life could closer resemble what was written on the pages.

Beyond the veil of tears, a blurred figure moved nearer. His hand brushed her leg as he knelt in front of her. Her pride screamed at her to hide her face and force him away. Tell him she needed to be alone—the biggest lie yet.

No more lies. Not to herself. Not to him.

"David. . ." Nadia wrapped her arms around his neck and held on as though nothing else could save her. Because she still needed saving. He drew her up with him, and his strong arms held tight while she cried harder than ever before.

She cried for Tata, wishing she could have heard him say the words in his letter. For Matka—both the miserable woman she had known and the girl who had been forced away from the man she loved into a life she never wanted. She cried for the German boy who had spent his life with a broken heart, never knowing about his daughter, and now entangled in a war that would not allow him to reclaim anything he had lost. She cried for the two little girls whose family had been stolen. For the baby boy who would never know his parents or country. For all the people of Poland who had already endured so much in one month and now had little hope of rescue.

And she cried for the boy who bore the weight of so many disappointments and expectations on his shoulders—the boy who had grown into a man who wanted very much what she did. Just to be seen. To be needed. To be loved.

☰CHAPTER 37☰

October 9, 1939

David lengthened his stride, nervousness battling against renewed purpose. Habit dictated he not hold too tightly to the hope that had been ignited in him over the past couple of days. So much could go wrong in the next few hours, snatching everything away again. Despite the lack of sleep the past couple of nights as they had waited for Monday to arrive, he had risen with the sun and started plowing through his list of things to do before two o'clock.

Parcel—mailed.

New apartment—no luck on that account yet, but they had made do in more cramped conditions than his apartment, and it would only need to house them for a short while. Nadia didn't want to keep the children in the city, so a home outside of London was what they really needed to find.

Flowers—hopefully the single rose with several sprigs of late heather would be acceptable. He had less than a pound remaining after finding a very simple ring.

Ring—he also hoped Nadia was more sentimental than most women.

Telephone his family—while it had seemed like a good idea in the wee hours of the morning as he'd walked back to his apartment after hours of talking with Nadia in the nursery, the light of day had changed his mind. They would likely only point out everything wrong with his plan, and he was quite capable of doing that himself. And yet no argument could shake his resolve.

Paperwork—what resided in his breast pocket should cover what was required.

Meet with Thomas Kent—David pushed through the door into the *Times* building and wound past and around the busy reporters and editors rushing between offices. No one seemed to notice him, and he took two steps at a time up the flight of stairs. He twisted the handle on Kent's door, but it didn't budge. The window was dim.

"Are those for me?"

David twisted and then shuffled aside so Kent could access the lock on his office door. "I had planned to give them to someone else, but if they're your color. . ."

The man barked a laugh and pushed into his office, switching on the light and moving to the other side of his desk. "I wouldn't want to disappoint the young woman, whoever she might be." He lowered into his chair and shoved a stack of papers aside. "Should I venture a guess?"

"I'll save you the strain. The soon-to-be Mrs. Reid."

Kent's eyes widened. "You're marrying Lady Roenne? You haven't been around long enough to take up with anyone else."

"Correct on both accounts." David lowered into his chair. "That's why I'm here. She wouldn't have me unless I agreed not to return to Germany."

Kent slumped and took his glasses off to clean. "While I understand, I'm disappointed to hear it. I do like your eye and looked forward to seeing more of your work."

"And you will, if you want it."

The man's head came up.

"Now that Poland has fallen, Nadia figures it won't be long before some sort of resistance and underground forms. She doesn't expect her people to lie down and submit—not all of them." David leaned forward in his chair, laying the flowers across his lap. The weight of his camera pulled on his shoulder. "I don't know when or where I will be going exactly, but both of us agree we can't sit this war out." Though Britain and France seemed content to do just that for now, David withheld the comment. "Also, looking at the pattern the Germans have started, anyone would be a fool to think Poland is the last country they will invade."

"So, you plan on what? Returning to Poland and anywhere else the Nazis go, trying to stay one step ahead of them while you take your photographs?"

"In essence. We hope to help get people out. Those who need our help." A sense of purpose and rightness settled into David's chest, just as it had when Nadia and he had discussed it. "And yes, I will be taking photographs, and you are welcome to buy the ones you want. Maybe the world will take a good hard look and realize the Nazis need to be stopped." David swallowed hard against a sudden swell of emotion. He knew exactly what he would be walking into, the risks he'd be taking, and he'd be lying to himself if he didn't admit the fear of never returning to Nadia and the kids—his family. But it was because of his family he had to go. There were children like his who were losing everything. Even their lives.

"I guess we will be in touch, then." Kent stood and extended his hand. "I look forward to working with you. Let me know what you need."

"I will." David took his leave, more subdued than an hour later. He opted to take a taxi to the church where Nadia had arranged for them to meet. While he rode, he combed his hair with his fingers and replaced his hat. Then straightened his blue tie.

A soft drizzle had begun by the time the car pulled to the curb outside the church. For the first time today, David was ahead of schedule. He jogged up the steps of the old stone building and pushed through the large doors, past the foyer, and into the large chapel. Stained glass windows added hues of red and blue to the already gold lighting. Silence, other than his shoes on the hardwood floor. No sign of the priest or rector or whoever would be performing the ceremony. For a moment, it was just him and God. David lowered onto one of the middle pews and set the flowers and his satchel down on the seat.

In the quiet, he could hear his heartbeat and feel the tension between his temples. Probably due to lack of sleep or the understanding of what lay before him. Not just the wedding, but the new path, so very different than anything he had allowed himself to consider before.

Now he would not only have a wife but children who depended on him.

"Tata!" A pounding of little feet accompanied the call.

He stood from the pew and turned into the embrace of small arms.

Krys was soon joined by Bieta, both in beautiful pale yellow dresses with matching ribbons in their hair. Nadia slowly followed, Zoita at her side, beaming like a proud mother. The older woman already held the baby and whispered to the girls to accompany her to the front to find the "best" seats, making it sound like a fun game.

Nadia waited several steps back until the girls had dutifully followed. While he loved his girls, he was grateful for the time to appreciate his soon-to-be bride. Despite the simplicity of her blue dress, she looked every bit the lady he had met in Poland, but this time the smile on her face twinkled in her blue eyes.

"You're happy?"

Her red lips stretched wider while she held his gaze. "Tak. And you?"

He fought the urge to glance away, to not let her see doubts that still lingered—on her behalf. David managed a nod, not trusting his voice. He moved to look to where the girls had gone, but Nadia gripped his hand, keeping his attention fixed. She peered deeper into his eyes, and he felt a tremor move through him. She would see everything if he didn't pull away, his very soul naked and bleeding before her. There were so many dark crevasses, so much he still disliked about himself. How long before she realized she was a fool to tie herself to someone as flawed as he?

But didn't he owe her the truth?

He gritted his teeth and remained in place.

Her blue eyes glistened. A tear trickled down her cheek, while her hold on his hand tightened. "I love *you*, David Reid."

Enough soul gazing. He drew her into a kiss, his mouth hopefully explaining exactly what those words meant to him. Her lips moved with equal resolve, deepening her meaning. She saw him, knew his flaws, and loved him all the same.

The tapping of a cane up the aisle was accompanied by the throaty voice of an aged man. "There will be time for that after the ceremony."

David and Nadia pulled apart to meet the censoring stare of the wiry rector who looked to be in his eighties at least.

The old man slanted a look at them. "Unless you are not Mr. Reid and Miss Roenne. If that be the case, I suggest you arrange for your own wedding as quickly as possible." He clucked like a hen while continuing to the front.

David smiled at his bride and her red face hidden behind a hand. He kept his hold on the other. "I guess that's our cue, *Dama* Roenne. Shall we?"

She rolled her eyes at him but kept her smile. "I am not one to argue." Nadia took his handkerchief and wiped a smudge of lipstick from his mouth.

He smoothed his thumb over the curve of her lip, removing a hint of errant red. "Of course not."

⬛ EPILOGUE ⬛

Idaho
September 1948

"Hurry! Or the train will be at the station before we are." Nadia turned the oven low so the roast would not cook too quickly while they were away. With her luck, it would still be half alive. She wished she'd taken her mother-in-law's offer to make dinner. She had employed a housekeeper in England, and a couple of years of attempting to become an American homemaker had not made a cook out of Nadia—though at least she could find her way around a kitchen now. "Arek? Ben? Did you hear me?"

"I think they're already outside, Mama," Krys sang on her way to the door. The fifteen-year-old stopped short and jumped out of the way as the door swung wide and Bieta burst inside.

"Why are you not in class?" Nadia questioned, tossing her apron over the back of a chair. Bieta had started her first semester at the local college a week earlier.

"And miss Tata's homecoming?" Bieta stooped to pick up her two-year-old sister from where she played on the floor with Nadia's measuring cups and several colorful bowls. "We are excited to see Tata, aren't we, Giesela?" She caught Nadia's stern gaze and shrugged. "A friend is taking notes. I promise I'll study tomorrow. The others skipped school today too."

Nadia sighed and waved the girls toward the door. "College is a little more complex than grade school. And Zosia is at school." The

247

eleven-year-old had been so stressed at the thought of missing a full day of school, Nadia had finally told her to go and they would pick her up on the way home. She would have plenty of time to see Tata. Nadia made her way to the boy's bedroom where Henryk lay on his stomach in his bed reading *The Hobbit*. The siblings were orphans David had helped rescue out of Lithuania in '41. The three- and six-year-olds had quickly found their places in David and Nadia's growing family.

"Time to go, Henryk." Nadia took the book from his hands, placed a bookmark in the page, and set it aside, knowing nothing else would pull the boy from his imagination. "We do not want Tata waiting too long. He might think we have forgotten about him."

"He'll know to blame one of the girls. They always slow us down."

Nadia tousled his dark blond hair that was already in need of a trim. "Only on Sundays."

They left the room together, but Nadia slipped into her bedroom to collect her purse. And straightened the rug with her foot. Then the photograph of their family on the edge of her vanity. Seven grinning children. She had never imagined such a joy. Yes, busy and messy and noisy, but oh so very worth all of that for the cuddles before bed and kisses on the nose. She needed David back, though. She was not meant to do this on her own.

"Mama!"

Nadia hurried to the front of the small house she and David had bought when he was released from the army. The American draft had finally found him in '42, pausing their rescue efforts. Things had become so dangerous by that point, it was just as well. He trained briefly in England before the US Army put his photographic skills to use in reconnaissance.

She had become very good at praying.

"Look at them!" Krys cried, flinging her hand toward nine-year-old Arek and seven-year-old Benjamin, whose pant legs dripped muddy water.

Nadia took a deep breath, hands on hips. "Thankfully, Tata loves you anyway. Into the car with you both. We do not have time for you to change." She tipped her seat forward and shooed the younger children into the back of the light brown Packard coupe. The three boys and Krys squeezed in tight, while Bieta held the toddler on her lap in the front. The automobile was merely a business model and not nearly as fancy as her tata's Packard sedan had been, but Nadia had smiled at her husband's enthusiasm for the car. It was becoming easier to think of Tata as years separated the pain of loss and regret. There were good memories, moments he had shown affection, that she had not been so good at recognizing in the past.

Nadia's heart raced as they neared the station—by some miracle, they arrived before the train. Almost five months had passed. Far too long since David had kissed her goodbye on this platform and headed to Europe on an assignment to photograph the growing tensions and the blockade between East and West Berlin. She had tried not to worry too much, knowing he would be on the American side and there was not any active warfare between the Soviet Union and America, but she had years of practice.

A distant whistle announced the train's soon arrival as Nadia pulled into the parking lot. They had not quite made it to the platform when the train appeared around the bend, slowing as it approached. Another whistle rang out, adding to the excitement surrounding her. Thankfully, Bieta kept a hold on Giesela, and Krys held Arek and Benjamin's hands. Henryk stood with hands in pockets, the intensity of his gaze the only indicator of his anticipation. A strange nervousness turned Nadia's stomach and weakened her knees. Oh, how had she survived months and years of this during the war?

She took a breath. Every family. Every man, woman, and child they had worked with underground networks to smuggle out of Poland or Lithuania, Holland, or Denmark had made the pain worth it. Every life saved from the horrors of the Nazis had been worth the sacrifice and fear. She could not look at her adopted children—Bieta, Krys, Arek, Zosia, and Henryk—without emotions welling within her to the brink of tears.

The only regret was not being able to do more.

Zoita had not learned of her husband's death during the German invasion until the end of the war. She remained in England with her son.

Frajda and her family had immigrated to the United States, but not before learning that her in-laws and most of the Jewish community in that area had been murdered by the Nazis, whether in ghettos or extermination camps, or simply executed for existing.

If Nadia had had any idea what death and terror the Nazis would bring, she would not have been able to leave *any*one behind. Especially since liberation from the Nazis at the end of the war did not bring real freedom to Poland.

Nadia blinked to clear moisture from her vision and compelled her thoughts back to the train that carried her husband. Minutes separated them, and anticipation tingled through her limbs.

Bieta groaned from beside her, holding Giesela at arm's length. "Her diaper is leaking."

Nie! Of all horrible timing!

Nadia took her daughter—at arm's length—and hurried to the parking lot and spare diaper. She changed the diaper on the seat of the Packard and almost ran back to the platform. The train was fully stopped, and passengers stepped from the cars by the time she had returned. As she drew near, the top of David's head became visible, his favorite brown fedora in place. He swept Bieta and then Krys into hugs while the boys attached themselves to his sides, used to fitting themselves around his ever-present camera bag.

Nadia could not suppress a grin as she rushed forward, making it up the steps of the platform before David saw her. His face split into an equally huge smile, and he started toward her, giving her a view of a couple standing nearby. A woman tall and thin—too thin—but still beautiful, with blond hair swept under a plain blue cap with a demi-veil.

Nadia's feet faltered.

Beside the woman, a man leaned heavily on a cane. The side of his face was scarred, but his blue eyes met hers as his lips raised in a hesitant smile.

David's arms slipped around Nadia, holding her up while taking Giesela from her weakening hold. She leaned against him, not trusting her ability to stand on her own legs. "How? You never said anything."

"I didn't want to disappoint you if I wasn't successful," he whispered in her ear.

She shook her head. He had never failed her, and she wished he would stop fearing he would. "That is why it took so long?" Two months had been the estimate when he left—not more than double that.

He squeezed her hand and offered a nod. "I wasn't offered the assignment, Nadia. I asked for it. We've been working on this for more than a year. She had kept her Polish papers, and they were easy enough to process and obtain an immigration visa with, but it took some time to figure out his, even with the marriage certificate."

"Oh, David." She looked into his open gaze and pressed her mouth to his, the only thanks she had to offer in the moment. "But how did you get them out of East Germany?"

His lips curved at the corners.

"Oh, you crazy, wonderful man." Oh, how she loved him for it. "But not again. I cannot do this life without you. Not with eight children."

The smile slipped from his face. He searched her eyes, then dropped his gaze to what even her loose dress could not fully hide.

"Thoughts?" The tension was agonizing.

"It's perfect." He kissed her slower this time. Then smiled against her lips. "It really is."

Nadia smiled her agreement. After all the death the world had known, it was time to embrace life. She looked back to her parents.

"Go on. I'll be here," David whispered, giving her a push. Tears blurred her vision before she even made it two steps.

Matka had tears on her cheeks too as she opened her arms. Nadia held tight, like she had never held—or been held by—her before. Soaking in her mother's whispers of apology and love, Nadia's tears turned to sobs. Why had it taken a war and almost a decade of separation to see and understand her mother's heart?

Nadia's eyes felt swollen when she finally turned to her *father*. He watched patiently, his gaze soft but fear buried in their blue depths. He looked as though he had aged twenty instead of the nine years since they had stood in Poland, he in his uniform, informing her of his mistakes, of his love for her mother, of who he was to her. Nadia had thrown her arms around his neck to save his life—to return the favor. Now she embraced him as his daughter.

And heard the click of a shutter, capturing this moment of perfect joy.

HISTORICAL NOTE

When I first decided to set a story during the invasion of Poland, I was woefully unprepared for the pain and horror I found there. I wasn't new to World War II and had just finished writing *A Rose for the Resistance*, which is set in France during the war and deals with the resistance and the Normandy invasion. The atrocities and genocide in Poland cut so much deeper.

In the early hours of September 1, 1939, the small town of Wielun, Poland, woke to a shower of bombs on their community. They did not house an army or warehouses, only homes and civilian businesses. Wielun was not the only town or village targeted—demonstrating the Nazi goal to spread fear and death. Six months earlier, Hitler had promised that if Poland did not bow to his wishes, he would wipe them off the map. Over the next month, and more so in the following six years, he came very close to succeeding.

For the full month of September 1939, while German armies rolled across the country, the city of Warsaw endured daily bombardment. Homes, workplaces, churches on Sunday morning, the Warsaw maternity hospital—nowhere was safe. On the tenth of September, someone recorded seventeen separate air raids over the city. I was moved to tears while viewing photographs of women and children who had been shot in the streets and fields by the bombers after they had dropped their payloads over the city.

No one came to the rescue.

Despite Britain and France's allegiance with Poland and declaration of war against Germany, they remained watching from a distance. In mid-September a surge of hope rose in the hearts of the Poles as the Soviets rolled across their eastern border. But their neighbors had not come to the rescue either, but to take their slice out of Poland, working in conjunction with the Germans. The Polish government fled, never officially surrendering, even as the country faltered and fell into the hands of their enemies on October 6.

During the thirty-six-day invasion, it is estimated that close to two hundred thousand Poles were killed, with many more injured or captured and thousands left homeless.

The invasion of Poland was unlike that of many other countries where the goal had been to gain power over the government and people. In Poland the goal seemed to be to hurt and destroy. Especially the Jews. Even in the earliest days of the invasion, Jews were targeted. Over the following six years, the robust population of around 3.3 million Polish Jews was reduced to only about three hundred thousand, most of whom were able to escape Poland.

Of the three million Jews who remained in Poland, only approximately fifty thousand survived.

These aren't just numbers; they represent husbands, wives, brothers, and sisters. Fathers who would give anything to protect their families. Mothers powerless to save their babies.

Lest we forget what hate brings. . .

To keep from freezing in the great white North, **Angela K. Couch** cuddles under quilts with her laptop. Winning short story contests, being a semifinalist in ACFW's Genesis Contest and a finalist in the 2016 International Digital Awards also helped warm her up. As a passionate believer in Christ, her faith permeates the stories she tells. Her martial arts training, experience with horses, and appreciation for good romance sneak in as well. When not writing, she stays fit (and toasty warm) by chasing after four munchkins.

HEROINES OF WWII

They went above the call of duty and expectations to aid the Allies' war efforts and save the oppressed. Full of intrigue, adventure, and romance, this new series celebrates the unsung heroes—the heroines of WWII.

Beneath a Peaceful Moon

By Debby Lee

Determined to end the war by any means necessary, Mary Wishram is willing to use her language skills as a Yakama tribe member to become a spy and face any danger in the Philippines in order to bring all her loved ones home safe. John Painted Horse volunteers as a Navajo code breaker, desperate to bring long-overdue recognition and honor to his people no matter the cost. Can they both heal from their past traumas and find peace, love, and a deeper relationship with God on the battlefront of the Pacific?

Paperback / 978-1-63609-571-4

The Starlet Spy

by Rachel Scott McDaniel

In 1943 movie director Henrik Zoltan approaches Amelie Blake under the guise of offering the Hollywood star a leading part in his upcoming film. But he actually has a more meaningful role in mind. Amelie's homeland of Sweden declared neutrality in the war. But with rumors swirling about their quiet partiality to Germany, the US government needs someone unexpected to spy on the Swedish elite. Who better than an "all beauty, no brains" blond starlet who speaks three languages and is subtle enough to fool even Finn Ristaffason—a millionaire entrepreneur and shipping magnate suspected of funneling funds and products to the Nazis.

Paperback / 978-1-63609-613-1